where are you going, you monkeys?

where are you going, you monkeys?

folktales from tamil nadu

collected and retold by
Ki. Rajanarayanan

translated from the Tamil by
Pritham K. Chakravarthy

with illustrations by
Trotsky Marudu

PUBLICATIONS
PRIVATE LIMITED

Chennai

Nattupura Kadhai Kalanjiyam published 2007 by Annam, Thanjavur

English translation copyright © 2008 Blaft Publications

Illustrations © 2008 Trotsky Marudu

First printing January 2009
Second printing November 2009

Blaft Publications Pvt. Ltd.
#27 Lingam Complex
Dhandeeswaram Main Road
Velachery
Chennai 600042
email: blaft@blaft.com
website: www.blaft.com

Printed at Sudarsan Graphics, Chennai

I would like to thank Ki. Rajanarayanan for answering my endless queries; both him and his wife Ganavathiammal for their cooperation and hospitality; Rakesh Khanna for his editing of the manuscript; Kaveri Lalchand and Anushka Meenakshi for their valuable comments and suggestions; Malavika.PC for her cover design; Trotsky Marudu for his illustrations; Sundar Kali and Charu Nivedita for clearing various doubts; and finally Chaks, for trusting that I could do it.

– Pritham K. Chakravarthy

table of contents

husbands & wives

friends & family

naughty & dirty

glossary

about these tales

It always seems to me that neither the writers nor the publishers of Tamil Nadu are very keen on bringing the folktales of our native soil into print. Even this effort of mine comes pretty late.*

Most of the tales recorded here are tales that have been told and retold among the people of the karisal kaadu, the dry red-earth country down south, where I was born. I have forgotten so many of the tales I had heard as a child—and there is no one left who can recall them for me. If such neglect continues, then even the few tales I've managed to gather will disappear into thin air.

There are many types of tales:
1. Stories that are narrated on a stage for an audience.
2. Stories shared by friends in private.
3. Stories shared by a man and a woman during their intimate moments.
4. Stories that children tell amongst themselves.
5. Stories that are told *to* children by adults.

...and many, many more types. There are also some that will never find their way into print, for they are so "obscene".

If a person masters a hundred folktales, his knowledge about the world in general increases. As we grow up, there are certain things taught to us at school and at home—but isn't there a whole other world of

---

* *Nattupura Kadhai Kalanjiyam*, from which this introduction is taken and the stories in this book selected, is a 944-page compilation of folktales published in 2007, some of which Ki. Rajanarayanan had previously published in magazines like *Anandha Vikatan* and in smaller book collections. In consultation with Ki. Ra., the publishers and I decided to limit this book to a sample—roughly one-third of the stories in the *Kalanjiyam*—which we hope will appeal not only to hardcore folklorists but also to the more casual reader. Our selection here omits many repetitions of certain stories with small variations; many stories on the theme of karrpu, female honour or chastity, which are very old-fashioned and moralistic (although we have included a few like this); and many stories which did not lend themselves to translation because they are based on complex cultural templates. – Pritham K. Chakravarthy

knowledge that is not spoken of? Perhaps that's the purpose of these tales: to act as our friendly tutor on these other matters.

Many educated people may scorn some of these tales for being dirty and offensive. But to me they do not seem very different from the explicit sculptures on our temple gopurams. If these tales are vulgar, then so are those sculptures!

In my native village, there was a frequent visitor called "Paangyam" Veerabaagu. He had a sharp nose, bright eyes and a neatly trimmed moustache, and wore a small naamam on his forehead. He had a paunch, and his teeth were stained by betel juice. *Paangyam* was the name of the brass instrument Veerabaagu held tucked under his armpit. At one end, it had a thin hide drumhead, and the other end was open. Attached to the centre of the hide was a thin string, which came out the other end and was tied to a slim stick. Veerabaagu would tuck the paangyam under his left armpit, hold the stick with his left hand, strum on the string with his right, and sing.

He would visit only a few specific homes. He'd begin by singing the Perandulu, a lamentation song praising the women of those homes who had sacrificed themselves on their husbands' funeral pyres as satis. This would be followed by a few other songs. Then, once the sun went down, he'd start telling stories.

The people of the neighbourhood, after returning from their fieldwork, having their bath, and eating their dinner, would gather around Paangyam Veerabaagu to listen to his stories. And what stories! Adeyappa!

The audience would be mesmerized, listening with their mouths agape, not noticing as the mosquitoes flew in and out. As a child it would seem to me that Veerabaagu had just begun the story, and almost immediately the cock would crow to announce the dawn. Very reluctantly, the women next to me would get up to wash their front yards and draw their kolams.

Veerabaagu would draw out a single story for seven long nights, sprinkling it with humourous anecdotes about the goings-on in the rest of the region.

My people have been telling stories like this for ages.

❖

Though I used to tell and listen to such tales all through my childhood, the idea of recording them came to me only after I read Boccaccio's *Decamaron*. So many of those stories resembled the ones from my own soil; the Italian had seen fit to write down what people here considered too vulgar to be published.

Once, when I was invited by Kerala University to deliver a talk on folktales, I was asked by one of the students: "Will new folktales still be created, in these modern times?"

A very good question! "Why do you doubt it?" I asked. "If all the jokes that were told about our last Defense Minister, Baldev Singh, are not a part of folklore, then what are they?"

The hall erupted in laughter.

"I'd classify them with the 'Singh Stories'," I said. "The Namboodri and Komuti Chettiyar stories are similar.*"

Those who have not made it big in life have always spun stories about those who have. There are plenty of tales told by the eggheads about the illiterates, and also by the illiterates about the eggheads.

In Tamil Nadu, it is common to hear stories about one caste told by members of another. Not a single group has escaped this; there are stories about each of the eighteen castes. Besides these, there are tales poking fun at zamindars, landlords, the poor, the rich, beggars, ascetics, mendicants… not even the omnipotent god Iswaran has been spared.

But these are times when the rigid structures of the caste system are slowly disintegrating. If I were to go about collecting all the various caste-related stories that exist, I would invite a lot of misunderstanding and anger. I can't afford that, can I? In this context, what provokes the anger? Only the perception that I'm trying to denigrate some specific caste group. But this is not my intention. I am only concerned with

---

* Baldev Singh was a Sardar; "Singh stories" here refer to the Sardar jokes that are very famous in India. I suppose in every culture there is a minority group who is the butt of racial humour, like Jew jokes or Polish jokes in the West. The Namboodri Brahmins and Komuti Chettiyars are the frequent butt of jokes in Kerala and Tamil Nadu respectively. – P.K.C.

the narrative: the mind that invented the tale, the style in which it is woven, and the expansive scope of human imagination itself!

There are three people on a thinnai outside a traveller's inn. The one who arrived first is fast asleep. It is nighttime; all is dark. The two that arrived later, not yet feeling sleepy, sit up chatting about this and that; after a while, they lie down, but keep on talking. Irritated by their constant patter, the first man thinks of asking them to shut up; but the subject matter is very interesting, so he stays silent and listens. The other two men are busy discussing how women of all castes have affairs with men outside their own caste, without their husbands' knowledge. No caste is left unmentioned... except their own!

"It is only in our caste that such things never happen," one of them finishes.

The first one, listening, now becomes restless. He rolls over, pretending to wake up just then. The other two wait for him to sit up, then start enquiring where he is from and where he is off to. Finally, as was normal in those days, they ask to which varnam he belongs.

Having heard their gossip earlier, the man does not want to commit himself. So he hems and haws for a while, and in the end he says, "Hmm; my mother is from caste A, and my father is from caste B. So you tell me, which caste do I call myself?"

Saying this, he walks off, pretending he has to take a leak. He hides in the darkness to see their reaction.

The two men on the thinnai look at one another, then sigh. One of them sadly shakes his head and says, "Chuck it! Our caste has gone to the dogs too. Let's sleep."

Every caste group has stories meant to make their own caste look the best. Nevertheless, these racial stories are primarily meant to be funny, not malicious; and it's the humour that gets us first, not the venom. It's only later that we might understand the meanness in them. This is common to every culture. What we think of today as jokes have grown from our native, organic folk language.

There was a forward-caste man who was having fun with his wife, and the night extended longer and longer. Then a stench touched his nose. The room was dark, and though he couldn't see anything except his wife, he could make out that someone else had come into the room.

"Adiye, there is a thief hiding in this room!" he exclaimed. "I've found him out!"

"How?" asked the wife.

"Our own farts will only have the fragrance of asafoetida spice," he said. "But this is a different fart smell, a cheap liquor stink!"

Rumours, gossip, and folktales are distinctly different from each other. Rumours are usually vicious. Gossip is always episodic. But a folktale has a clear beginning, middle and end.

The inventors of these stories range from intellectuals to common men. When we look carefully at the epics, we realize that it is impossible to trace them back to a single region or point of origin. Take the *Ramayanam*, for example: the story of the heirless raja comes from one place, the story of the raja conducting a yaagam to have a child comes from another, the story of the prince banished to the forest from yet another, and the story of the abducted wife from still another.... Valmiki's accomplishment was compiling all this into one coherent text. It is normal for the harikatha performers, while retelling the epic, to extend or reduce the text, depending on the audience's interest or time factors.

I remember a storyteller in Udukudi giving me a totally new and different interpretation for Dhraupadi's public disrobing by Dhuryodhanan in the *Mahabharatham*.

"It's common for a wife who doesn't want to have sex with her husband to blatantly lie that she is menstruating," he said. "Now, Dhuryodhanan was a very big raja. Imagine how many women like Dhraupadi he would have seen! Naturally, he doubted her claim. So he demanded that she actually prove that she had her period. He merely wanted to clear his doubt!"

Just see how far away this is from the standard epic!

Once there was a puppet show in our village of the episode from the *Ramayanam* about the burning of Lanka. It was a hot, sweltering summer; we spent the nights sleeping outside on the thinnai, on cots on the lanes, or under a tree. So when the show started, all the village folk gathered around to watch. I went too; not for the story of Raman and Sita, but for the three puppets Dhabedhar, Komaalli and Mottaiyan. They came on during the interludes to crack jokes, share local news and gossip, and sing extempore songs about the main characters. No matter how many times, or for how many hours I watched, they would never repeat themselves even once.

❖

Again, don't assume that all folktales were invented by commoners. Here is an example:

Once upon a time there was a raja and his minister. One day, the minister said, "Raja, cerebral bookish people are useless at everyday, regular jobs. They are only suited for their specific scholarly fields."

"I don't think you're right," contended the raja. "I say a genius is a genius! I challenge you to prove me wrong."

Accordingly, a logician, an astrologer, a physician, and a rhythmatist were brought to the palace. They were given a room, along with grain, rice, and spending money, and told to cook for themselves. The raja and the minister waited to watch what followed.

The four specialists had no clue about cooking. But what could they do? It was the raja's command. The rhythmatist, after some effort, managed to light the stove and put the rice in the pot to cook. The physician set out to buy vegetables, the astrologer to cut banana leaves, and the logician to buy ghee.

The physician reached the vegetable market. There were heaps of different vegetables, but he rejected every one of them: brinjal, because it ruins an ayurvedic diet; raw banana, because it causes gas; pumpkin, because it increases bile; and drumstick, because it increases body heat. Finally, he asked for beans. But it was not the season for beans.

"Do you have bitter gourd?"

No, was the reply.

"What kind of a vegetable market is this?" he demanded. "Don't you have a single healthy vegetable? Give me pea aubergine!"

No, not even that was available. *Oh forget it,* he thought. *Let me get home and we'll have lunch with rasam, appalam and curd.* And so he returned, empty-handed.

The astrologer who had gone to get leaves for plates found a bad omen in every direction he turned. As he stepped out, a Vanniya Chettiyar came by with a pot of oil. That was the first bad omen; so he turned and walked in the opposite direction. But then he realized he was walking westward. "Oh no," he said, "today is Friday, and that means west is the direction of my death!" So he turned back around, and walked and walked and walked, but there was no banana tree anywhere to be seen; only a lone banyan tree. "Not too bad," he thought, "we can eat off the banyan leaves." So he tucked in his dhoti, and started to climb the tree.

"Tk-tk!" said a gecko in the tree. "Don't go up!"

So he waited for a long time, until he heard another gecko behind him say "Okay, you can climb up now." Though not much of a tree-climber, he managed somehow to get up and pluck a few leaves. But where should he put them? He could not drop them at the base of the tree, because some members of the general voting public had fouled the area. So he tucked the leaves into his dhoti at his waist. As he started climbing down, his thighs started trembling with fear. "Why did I even climb up this tree?" he thought. Just then he heard another gecko call: "Don't climb down!" So our astrologer stayed in the tree until sundown.

The logician bought his ghee in a leaf cup. The ghee was set hard. On his way back, the logician tipped over the cup to check if the ghee would fall out. It did not. At once, his logical mind set to work. Was the ghee holding the cup together or the cup holding the ghee? Which was supporting which? He argued for a while in support of the ghee, then switched positions to argue for the cup. At the end of the debate, he tipped over the cup to recheck. By now, the ghee had melted to liquid and it immediately drained out on the ground.

"And therefore, it was the cup that was holding the ghee!" he declared and came back with just the cup.

By this time, back in the room, the rice was almost boiling in the pot. The rhythmatist sat watching it. As the heat was constant, the water was bubbling rhythmically, rising and falling in time. He counted the beats; they were steady. With a smile on his face, he started a konakol, speaking every syllable in rhythm with the bubbles. He clapped along, as if to encourage the water. Then, without warning, the water switched to a slower beat.

It irked the rhythmatist. He could not tolerate bad tempo; it irritated him terribly! He tried giving the pot a hard look. It did not change. Getting angrier, he added some wood to the fire. The bubbling started to pick up speed, but then suddenly died out completely, without a proper korvai coda. Furious, the expert rhythmatist took a burning piece of firewood and whacked the pot off the stove.

The watching minister gave the raja a triumphant grin.

Though what we normally define as folktales are the stories prevalent among the common folk—tales invented by the commoner, for the commoner—these stories travel to other regions and other tellers. As they travel, they gather more embellishments, more imagination, and more life, depending on the teller's skill.

Even educated people need stories: philosophical stories, moral stories, religious propaganda stories, political propaganda stories, hagiographic stories of leaders and heroes, etc. etc.

Political propaganda stories first arrived in our nation during the anti-colonial struggle. Sixty years back, when I was a young lad, leaders of the Congress Satyagraha Movement used to visit our village. They would erect a stage, gather a crowd and tell us anti-British stories about the imperial ignorance of Indian sensibilities. This is one such story:

In London, the capital of the British Empire, a Member of Parliament once asked an Indian minister, "Tell me, kind sir: What tree does rice grow on?" Of course, this question came from a white man. He knew nothing about rice, had never seen a rice plant in his life. The Indian minister had never been to India himself. Though a rice-eater, he had never seen a rice plant either.

So, requesting a little time to find the answer, he sent the query to the viceroy in India. But what could the viceroy know about rice? After all he was a white man too! So he passed the question down to the governor. The poor governor, also being white, had no answer. So he asked the collector. The collector was as white as the rest of them, so he passed the question down to the deputy collector, who was an Anglo-Indian*.

Now, a full-blooded white man might at least try his hand at a Tamil word or two, but an Anglo-Indian would never let even a word of an Indian language near his ear. He would touch nothing but bread. So, when he saw the query, he could not control his rage. He took the file and wrote on it: "Chee, what kind of rubbish question is this?" and threw it on his deputy's desk.

The question finally reached the desk of the revenue official. He was a Tamil, who ate rice every day; he even had a small paddy field in his home town where he grew some. But the file was marked *Very Important: What tree does rice grow on?* As a true Indian clerk, he said to himself, "Perhaps there is a variety of rice that *does* grow on a tree!

---

* Someone of mixed British (and/or other European) and Indian descent. The Anglo-Indian community is predominantly Christian and English-speaking. – P.K.C.

After all, this question has come from a White Man. He cannot be wrong! We must investigate this question thoroughly. We cannot afford to make a mistake." With that, he assigned responsibility for the investigation to the revenue inspector.

This revenue inspector was no fool either. He put the job in the hands of the judge of the subordinate court, who, not wanting to risk his own neck, made the village official responsible. "Dey, go into the fields and find out what tree rice grows on. Hurry!"

Now this village official was a man who was always fully boozed. As soon as he was given the order, he went straight to the toddy shop. Once he was sufficiently drunk, he swayed back towards the office. In his drunken stupor, he kept falling down and getting back up; finally he banged into a tree. He felt the tree, and realized that it was a palm tree. *It must be my Goddess Maariyaatha who has put the tree in my path*, he thought gratefully. He stumbled on, mumbling "Palm tree, palm tree..." over and over to himself, till he reached the office, where he exultantly declared, "Yejamaan, I've got it! Rice grows on the palm tree!"

"Are you sure?"

"Have I ever lied to you, Yejamaan? Trust me. Rice does grow on the palm tree!"

Since this was a state matter, the judge made the drunk village official leave his thumbprint in ink on the report. Then he sent the message to the revenue inspector, who in turn informed the revenue official. He translated it into grandiloquent English and sent it off to the deputy collector, who informed the collector, who informed the governor, who, totally relieved, informed the viceroy. When the Indian minister heard from the viceroy, he was overjoyed and waited eagerly for question hour in Parliament. There he announced to the British Parliament, "The rice grain grows on the palm tree!"

Hagiographic tales are another sort. The subjects range from epic heroes to today's politicians.

I've heard several oral folktales about Veerapandiya Kattabomman, the 16th century South Indian rebel chieftain. Here is one such story:

Once, Kattabomman, his brother Ummaitthurai and their favorite sister were escaping on horseback from the British troops. The horses sped like the wind.

Now, Kattabomman's sister had hair that was sixteen feet long. As her horse galloped, her locks came undone and became tangled in the horse's rear legs. The brothers knew how important it was to leave the place without being caught. But they knew not what to do. Then the sister said, "Do not waste any more time, dear brothers. Hurry, chop down both the horse and me, and run." Kattabomman looked to Ummaitthurai. Immediately, Ummaitthurai, who had never disobeyed his elder brother in his life, pulled out his sword and with one stroke cut both the horse and the sister in half. The two brothers sped away again.*

When I repeated this tale to historians, most of them denied that this was a real part of Kattabomman's life. A hagiographic tale may be invented out of ardent love for the hero. Even a modern icon like the first Prime Minister of our independent nation, Jawaharlal Nehru, has not escaped this.

When Nehru was a student in London, Prince Edward, the son of King George the Fifth, was his classmate. Nehru had a car with him then. It was the costliest car in the world, plated all over with gold and encrusted with pearls and nine kinds of precious gems. One day, Nehru gave a ride to the prince in his car. It was only after that ride that the prince realized what decrepit automobiles his family had in their royal garages. After school, the prince went back and demanded a similar car from his father. King George the Fifth said, "You idiot's son, you think we can afford to buy such cars? Nehru is the son of the crorepathi of all crorepathis! You and I don't match up to him." He went on to tell about the Nehru family's wealth. "They do not launder their clothes in India; instead, they send them to Paris. Every day a ship leaves India with their dirty clothes, while another leaves Paris with the laundered ones. Now do you understand how rich they are? Do not even try to compete with him, my son!"

And then there are tales whose origin can only be guessed at.

---

* There is a saying in Tamil: *To save your family, one of their lives may be sacrificed; to save your village, a family may be sacrificed; and to save your nation, a whole village may be sacrificed.* The greatness of Kattabomman here is that he is willing to sacrifice his own sister to escape and fight to save his people. – P.K.C.

When I was very, very young, the woman who sold brooms to my grandmother used to tell one such tale.

> Once upon a time there was a woman who was a mother of grown-up sons. Her husband had died a long time ago. One day, when the mother and her sons were gathering wood in the forest, her sari pallu got caught in a thorny bush. Strangely, she didn't try to untangle it. Without turning around, she whispered in a shy, coy voice, "Let go machchan, let go. My sons are watching."
> When the sons saw this, they thought: *Aha! Our mother wants a man.* And so they got her married.

In an earlier period of human history, the concept of marriage did not exist. A woman was free to find unlimited pleasure with whichever men she desired. She was the more powerful. Gradually there was a shift, and she was disciplined and controlled by marriage. Perhaps the story above was one which appeared during the period of transition.

These are stories invented by our ancestors; they are our wealth. They reveal the tension caused by highly moralized sexuality. They also help us to appreciate story structure, story line, the scope of human imagination, the dexterity of language, the range of dialects and human psychology. Let us continue to gather these stories and tell them to the outside world.

I must admit, though, that when I first published some of these stories in popular weekly magazines, several editorial atrocities had to be committed. It was impossible to publish the exact words of the storyteller as recorded. This is, in a way, a loss to the Tamil language itself. Perhaps the best solution is to publish them in books.

A gatherer of tales needs certain necessary qualifications: the patience of a fisherman or a hunter, and the capacity to record a tale without making any additions or subtractions of his own. When you extract honey, you don't adulterate it. You must also record the physical expressions of the storyteller, and the input of the listeners, and their criticisms.

One day in Madurai, after watching a really bad film with some friends, we went to Prakash's room to sleep. But no one was sleepy. Vikramadhithyan asked me, "Naina, tell us a story. It should be an excellent story loaded with fabulously dirty words."

We had switched off the lights, ready to go to bed. I was the only elder person; the rest were young men.

I made a condition before beginning my story. "First, one of you tell me a dirty-word story. Just one. And it should be a story I haven't heard before. If you can do so, then I'm ready to tell you stories till dawn."

Koothu Ramasami, the shadow-puppeteer, was known as an expert in dirty-word stories. So he offered to tell one. But every time he began a tale, I would quickly finish it for him. Finally, before he began his brahmasthiram* tale, he said, "Switch on the lights."

"Why put the lights on?" I asked.

"I can't show this in the dark. I need light," he replied.

"Is it the tale of the dumb man giving witness?" I asked, triumphantly.

Everybody, including Ramasami, burst out laughing.

This tale, the story of the dumb man giving witness, can only be told with the fingers. Therefore, it can never be written down or recorded on tape. The only option is video.** There are several folktales like this. I recently heard that folktales have been classified into 300 different types. In which category would this story fit?

I began my career as a folktale gatherer more than fifty years ago. I've completed my golden jubilee in this field. But youngsters today are proving to me that everything I know is but a handful of earth!

Ki. Rajanarayanan

---

* In the *Mahabharatam*, the "ultimate weapon" used unsuccessfully by Karnan against Arjunan. – P.K.C.

** A video clip of Ki. Rajanarayanan performing this story is available on the Blaft Publications website (www.blaft.com/kira/).

birds & beasts

the hunter and the elephant

Once, a hunter went to hunt. He lost his way and wandered deep into the forest. There he met an elephant, who asked him, "Sir, why are you here alone in this jungle?"

The hunter told the elephant about having lost his way.

"Stay with me for a few days, as my guest. I shall then take you back to the town myself," offered the elephant. The hunter agreed, and went home with the elephant.

The elephant treated his guest very graciously. After a few days, he carried the hunter back to town on his back.

The hunter walked down into the market place, where there were a lot of shops. In one of them he saw some beautiful toys and dolls on display. He asked the shopkeeper what they were made of.

"They are made of a very rare and costly material called ivory — the tusk of an elephant. If you bring me some ivory, I will make you rich," replied the shopkeeper.

Avarice took over the cunning hunter's heart. *Why don't I return to the forest, kill that elephant, bring back the ivory, sell it and get rich quick?* he thought.

He returned to the elephant's cave at once. Taking out his bow and arrow, he announced, "Oh Elephant, your tusks seem to be worth a lot of money in the town. I am going to shoot you down and cut them off."

"You horrendous human! I was your only friend in this jungle. I showered you with so much love. You want me dead just so you can be wealthy, do you? Do I look like an idiot?" bellowed the elephant. It lifted the hunter high with its trunk, crashed him to the ground and trampled him to death. ❖

emperor goat

One day, when there was no one at home, the goat, which had been tied to the same spot since the day he was born, found that his tether had worn out and he was free to move. When he stepped out into the open, he was overwhelmed by the splendour of the world around.

Nearby was a big jungle. In the centre of the jungle was a huge hill. All around was a lush green. The hungry goat happily pranced and ate his way towards the hill. He had never experienced such joy in his short life. He sampled a hundred different flavours of leaves, until he could eat no more. He drank the clear, bubbling water from a cool stream, and then looked around for a comfortable spot to lie down and chew his cud. But there was no place in sight. As he searched for a cozy niche, warm like his own pen, he happened upon a cave. The bones strewn on the floor and the strange stench of death were a bit off-putting to the vegetarian goat, but he thought the place would do for a short stay. So the goat sat down, half-shut his eyes and began chewing his cud.

Now, this cave was the abode of the lion, the king of the jungle, who had stepped out for his daily hunt. On returning and seeing a strange pair of tracks near the cave, he was momentarily stunned. There were no goats in the jungle, so the lion did not recognize the tracks. Also, up until then no other animal had dared to approach the cave. They were too scared. *So what is this animal that has so bravely entered my cave?* he wondered. To tell the truth, the lion was slightly shaken. *Perhaps the animal that's inside there now is much larger and fiercer than me,* he thought and silently peeked in.

Remember that our lion had never seen a goat before! A glimpse of his face, with his pointed beard, half-shut eyes and patiently chewing jaw, terrified the king of the jungle. The goat had never seen a lion before, either... but then our goat was very brave.

The lion did not know what to do. Thinking it would not hurt to find out who was now occupying his lair, he asked hesitantly, "Excuse me please, who is inside my home?"

"Who's the cheeky chap who has the gall to speak to me?" demanded the goat in a stern voice.

4

Unnerved by the loudness of the goat's tone, the lion was now very sure the beast inside was really huge. Still, he thought it best to be civil to the guest, and introduced himself.

"I am Lion, King of the Jungle, and you are in my house. Welcome!"

It's true that the goat had never seen a lion. But he had heard many horrifying tales about lions and other predatory animals from his mother. *Oh, no! I'll be dead by tonight. Still, why should I die a coward? Let me face death like my brave forefathers,* he thought.

"Ah, you are that chap who calls himself the king, are you? King of the jungle indeed! Step inside, mister. I am Emperor of *All* Jungles. I am waiting to gobble you up. I knew you would return to your dark cave. Hurry and come in," he called out.

The lion did not wait a moment longer. With his tail tucked between his legs, he ran off, making the ground quake as he sped.

The wily fox saw the lion scampering away in fear. It was normal in the jungle for other animals to bolt this way on hearing the king's roar, but this was too strange! So the fox trotted alongside, calling out, "Oh King, oh King...!"

The lion, desperate for someone to listen to him, stopped and gasped. "Fox, am I happy to see you! Have you ever known an emperor?"

"An emperor? What is that?" asked the fox, scratching his forehead.

"The king of all kings, the greatest of us all..."

"Oh, those! Only humans have those. Why should we animals bother with stuff like that?" asked the puzzled fox.

" 'Stuff like that?' Are you crazy? I am running from one such emperor—in fact, the Emperor of All Jungles. Come along, let's run off together. We'll look for a forest that has no kings or emperors," begged the lion.

Wow, smirked the fox to himself. *Our king may be huge; he may have a loud roar; he may look majestic. But when it comes to brains, he's a nincompoop.*

"Oh King, why don't you sit for a while in the shade, under this tree. I have never seen an emperor. So I'll go take a quick look, and return soon..."

"Why would you want to do that, silly?" asked the lion. "The emperor will pick you up, fling you in the air like an appalam and crush you to bits. He wanted to eat me, and here I am running to escape. Do you think you are braver than me?"

No, there's no one braver than the king. The beast that can fling him in the air and crush him like an appalam is yet to be born. I must check out this new creature, thought the fox, and ran off to the cave.

The lion hid under a thick bush to wait for the stupid fox.

At the cave, the fox recognized the prints as goat's tracks. He knew because he had stolen several goats from the village himself. He peeked in to be sure, and then returned to the lion, laughing to himself.

"Oh King, that is no emperor. It's a mere billy goat! Perhaps you were scared of its tiny pointed beard. Some goats—the highly intelligent ones —do have nice, shiny beards. Now come with me. I'll show you how it trembles on seeing me," the fox said.

The lion was not ready to believe the fox. *That beast dared to challenge even me, the king. I'm supposed to believe that it will tremble with fear at the sight of this fox? Ha! Pure humbug!*

The fox could see that the lion was not yet convinced. "King, you stand behind me. Let the beast eat me first. While it's doing so, you will have time to run away," he said.

The lion almost burst out into a roar. *A lion, hide behind a fox? What a thought!* "This is sheer nonsense. Idiot, why would the beast want to eat you? It's waiting there to eat me. It will attack me and you'll immediately take to your heels. I know how wily you can be, mister.... So get lost!"

"So, now you're afraid that I will run away and leave you to be eaten, is that right?" said the fox. "Fine—then tie our tails together. Make the best knot you can. Then I won't be able to run away."

The lion thought this was the best suggestion so far. He tied their two tails together, and they both headed to the cave.

The fox poked his head into the cave and asked sarcastically, "Hello sir, when did you arrive?"

He had expected the goat to spring up in terror and race out of the cave. But this was no ordinary goat. This goat had made a lion scuttle off in fear. How could a mere fox outfox him? The goat remained seated with half-shut eyes, chewing on his cud.

"Dey, didn't you hear me? Are you deaf?" the fox challenged. "What gives you the guts to stay seated in front of the king? Don't you know how to respect authority?"

The goat turned his head reluctantly and softly said, "Go ask your king to come in!"

The fox winked at the lion and signaled him to step forward. The lion did so, trembling.

When the goat saw that their tails were knotted together, he could not control his delight. "Very smart, my friend! So you have brought the lion, as you promised. You are indeed the wiliest fox I have known. Thank you!" he congratulated the fox. "So what are we waiting for? Is the lion going to come in and offer himself, or do I have to come out to attack him?" he asked, and made a move to rise.

The lion squeaked loud enough to be heard all through the jungle and fled, dragging the poor fox all the way. Soon, of course, he was a dead fox.   ❖

amaravathi

Every full moon night, at the banks of the village pond near the edge of the forest, there was a festive gathering. That was the time when the ladles from all the homes would meet to discuss their kitchens and the people who worked in them. "Today, I served saambaar!" one ladle would yelp. "Oh, is that all? I served sweet payasam today," another would say. "Lucky you! I was made to serve kanji all through the day," another would grumble.

But there was one old, worn-out ladle listening to all this chatter who was sad and despondent. Because it was of no more use, it had been discarded in the loft. Disgusted with its life, it jumped into the pond and drowned itself. God, seeing this honourable suicide, decided to revive it and turn it into a beautiful golden lotus flower in the same pond.

The next day, after finishing his kingly duties, the raja of the land was taking a stroll when he happened upon the pond. He saw the beautiful golden shining lotus, plucked it out, and took it back to his palace, where he put it in a glass case. That night, he heard a weeping sound from the case and opened it to find a beautiful baby girl. The childless raja and his rani decided to bring the child up as their own. They named her Amaravathi.

The time came when Amaravathi was old enough to be married. Her father decided to give her hand to Indrakumaran, a prince.

One day after the marriage, she was giving Indrakumaran an oil bath. Thinking of something funny, she burst out laughing. Indrakumaran looked at her puzzled.

"Oh, it's nothing!" said Amaravathi. "I was thinking of my birthplace. There, snails would plough the land, crabs would pluck weeds, and the trees would bloom with pearls, with corals strewn below."

Indrakumaran knew the story of Amaravathi's birth from the lotus. So he was confused and angered by her statement. "If what you say is true, take me to your birthplace and prove it. If you're lying, then you should prepare to leave this palace forever," he ordered.

Amaravathi didn't know what had come over her to make such a tall claim. Perhaps she had been narrating a dream, something she had imagined. Not knowing what to do, she went out to walk around. If she couldn't prove her claim, she would be chased from the palace. *It would be better just to die right now*, she decided. She came upon a snake's burrow in a termite mound, and thrust her hand in to be bitten.

The snake that lived in the burrow had had a boil on its back for a long time, and was in great pain. When Amaravathi pushed her hand in, she struck the boil and broke it. The snake, finally relieved from its suffering, came out of its burrow to see whose hand it was, and saw Amaravathi.

"Amma, who are you?" asked the snake. "You have done me a great favour. Think of me as your brother and tell me your problems. I shall help you in return."

Totally surprised at the snake's pleasant nature, Amaravathi said, "Anna, this is what happened." She told him about her boast. "There's no home I can show off to my husband as my birthplace. That's why I had decided to die."

"Do not worry," said the snake. "Bring your husband here. I shall make all what you said come true."

She returned to the palace. After a week, she asked Indrakumaran to accompany her to her birthplace. She took him to the snake's burrow, and found that it had transformed into a beautiful palace. The snake had become a young man, who received them as her brother.

It was a full moon night. Amaravathi took her husband out into the garden. There were many snails slowly making their way across the ground. She pointed to their glistening tracks and asked, "Doesn't it look as if the snails have been ploughing the land?"

Then she pointed to a cactus bush on which crabs were crawling, opening and snapping their claws as they moved. "And there you can see the crabs plucking weeds," she said.

A little further on was a tall murunga tree, with white pearl-like flowers. Its tiny fallen leaves in the red dirt beneath the tree looked almost like hard corals. "Do you see the tree blooming with pearls and the corals strewn below?" Amaravathi asked Indrakumaran. The prince had to agree that she had indeed told the truth.

Amaravathi thanked the snake-brother and begged to do something in return.

"Nothing much, just give me your first-born," said the snake. Without thinking, Amaravathi promised to do so.

The days passed into years. Amaravathi gave birth to a handsome son. On hearing the news, the snake came to the palace demanding the boy.

"Snake-brother, the child is still very young. I shall slowly wean him and then hand him over to you," pleaded Amaravathi. The snake agreed and went back.

The boy grew into a young lad, and the snake came back.

"Please do not be angry with me, Snake-brother. I just want to see him going to school. After that I shall hand him over." Once more, the snake agreed and left.

The boy began his schooling. Not wanting to delay any further, the snake came and took its seat on the windowsill in the boy's bedroom. The boy, seeing it, rushed to his mother and said, "Amma, your brother, with his round ruby eyes and his pointed snout—your brother who saved you that day, my maternal uncle—he's here to see you!"

Fearing the snake's anger, Amaravathi came running into the bedroom. But the snake had tears in its eyes.

"Don't worry, Sister," said the snake. "I was only testing you. Your son has called me his maternal uncle. He will be blessed."

Promising to always look out for his nephew, the snake returned to its burrow. Indrakumaran and Amaravathi lived happily ever after with their son. ❖

garden lizard shastri

Once upon a time in a village there lived a mother and a son. The son was an idle simpleton. One day, the mother came to him with their cow.

"Listen son, this cow is all we have. Take it to the market, sell it and bring me the money," she said.

The son drove the cow to the market. On the way, he saw a garden lizard, which stared at him with unblinking eyes.

"Garden Lizard Shastri, do you want this cow?" asked the son.

The garden lizard bobbed its head up and down.

"Okay. I shall tie it to your tree trunk before I leave, so that it doesn't stray. Give me my money, Garden Lizard Shastri," demanded the son. The garden lizard just ran into its burrow without a word.

"Are you trying to get out of paying me?" exclaimed the boy, and put his hand into the burrow to catch the lizard.

What a surprise! His hand brushed against something. He pulled it. It was a pot. of gold that someone had hidden there.

"What a nice Shastri, he paid me in gold!" cried the son, and took the pot to his mother.

The mother knew how stupid and naïve her son was. She did not want him to blabber about the gold to anyone.

So, that night, when the son was asleep on the thinnai outside, she came with a pot of cold water and sprinkled it on his face.

"Dey, dey! Get up. It is raining," she said. "Come and sleep inside."

The next day the son went into the village, excited to meet his friends.

"Yesterday Garden Lizard Shastri paid me a pot of gold for my cow!" he told them.

"Really? When did it give you the gold?" they asked mockingly.

"Yesterday," said the son.

"Are you sure you didn't imagine it?" they asked.

"Of course I'm sure—just as sure as I am that there was a heavy rain last night," the son said.

"Get off, it hasn't rained here for months!" said the friends, and left laughing.   ❖

the bulls' appeal

—

Long, long ago, all the bulls of the world were having a very tough time. Humans tied them to ploughs to till their fields all through the day. The bulls were beaten up to hasten the work. Some were made to draw wooden carts for miles carrying very heavy loads. Holes were bored in their noses, and thick ropes drawn through them. The blood and the pain were unbearable.

Cows, on the other hand, enjoyed a royal treatment. Not one was so much as smacked. On auspicious days, they were bathed, smeared with sandal and turmeric, and worshipped. Whenever hungry, they were served fresh grass and hay.

The bulls, naturally, were unhappy about this. They assembled to discuss their common agenda: *Why should the cows alone be worshipped? What are we, idiots? After all, we are the ones who slog for the humans and bear their burdens!*

Finally, they decided to appeal to Lord Shiva and Parvathi, his consort. The bulls arrived at Kailasam, the snowy abode of Shiva. The Lord listened to them, but his only response was, "I am very busy now. You may all leave. I will get back to this issue when I have more time."

The bulls, pleased that Shiva had at least listened to their case, returned to Earth to wait for him. They waited and waited. But Shiva, with his busy schedule, did not seem to have time for the bulls at all. Every time they appealed, he would send back word that he would be with them very soon. But it never happened.

The season arrived for the Pongal harvest festival. People were cleaning up their homes and cooking pongal with rice from the fresh crop. The following day was the one day of the year when people would gather all their bulls together, bathe them, smear turmeric and sandalwood paste all over them, garland them with flowers, decorate their horns and celebrate them, and the bulls were allowed to graze wherever they wanted to.

It was on that day that Shiva finally found the time to come down to Earth to investigate the plight of the bulls. He looked around at the festivities and became very angry. "You lied to me. You told me you were oppressed and overworked, but here you are having a great

11

time. How dare you lie to the Almighty!" he roared, and returned to Kailasam.

And so the bulls of this world continue to have a tough time. ❖

Ki. Ra.: Doesn't the Shiva who appears in this story remind you of one of our local politicians, who never have time for us?

Of all of our domesticated animals, the bull's job is the hardest. Clearly, the person who came up with this tale was someone who felt sympathetic towards the bull. The story touches the heart.

Note that it's common to say "I've been slogging like a bull," but nobody says "I've been slogging like a donkey." It's also common to say to an employer, "I've been working like one of your leather shoes."

the tiger and the dhobi

There was once a raja who was very kind to his people. In the forest nearby was a tiger. It had eaten up all the animals in the forest and had now turned to the town. It started by killing a goat, then a cow, then finally started to go after humans.

The people did not know how to contend with this man-eater. They ran to the raja and cried, "Oh Raja, you should save us from this terrible tiger. Or else we will all soon be dead!"

The raja made an announcement in all the surrounding towns: "To whomsoever kills this man-eating tiger, I shall give half my kingdom!"

Hearing this, several brave men ran off to kill the tiger. But they were killed themselves.

In the same town, there lived a dhobi, whose donkey had gone missing a few days earlier. He had searched high and low for it, but could not find it.

That night, the dhobi, fretting about missing donkey, was unable to fall asleep. At midnight, he walked to his backyard to take a leak. At the edge of the garden was the tiger, lurking behind a bush. But the dhobi was thinking about his donkey, and in the semi-darkness, he mistook the lurking tiger for it.

When the tiger saw the dhobi walk towards it confidently, it was shaken. *What is this man going to do? Even the bravest of men piss in their dhotis when they see me! Why isn't he scared?*

Just then, the dhobi called out to his wife, "Adiye! Adiye! Bring me a thick rope. Here we've been running around looking everywhere for this stupid donkey, when all the time he's been hiding behind the bush. Here, let me tie it to the tree."

By now, the tiger had lost all its bravado and stood timidly, while the dhobi tied it to the thick tree trunk.

It wasn't until the next morning that the people of the town discovered that what was tied to the tree was not a donkey, but a trembling tiger.

The raja kept his promise. He gave the dhobi half his kingdom, and the dhobi finally stopped worrying about his missing donkey. ❖

the tiger and the thief's wife

Once there was a thief. Each night, he would steal one fat goat from the village, bring it home and ask his wife to make a tasty curry out of it the next day.

One night as usual he set off to steal. He came to a pen and stuck his hand into it, trying to catch hold of a goat. It so happened that in this same pen, there was a tiger hiding; it too was after a goat. The thief felt the tiger's thick muscles and thought to himself, *Now this is one well-fed goat!* So he slung it over his shoulder and went home. It was only as he was setting it down on his doorstep that he discovered it was not a goat but a tiger. He swung it by the tail and threw it far away, then ran into the house and shut the door. The tiger scampered away, resolved that it would return the next night and eat the thief who wrecked its hunt.

Now the thief's wife, unlike her husband, was very sharp. When she heard about the incident, she was sure that tiger would come back to seek vengeance. The next night, she peeked out the door and caught a glimpse of the tiger lurking behind the bushes. *I must use my brains to get rid of this beast,* she thought to herself as she shut the door.

Through the window, she watched the tiger climb onto the thinnai and crouch in wait. Immediately she gave her child a stinging slap. The baby began to cry aloud.

"Why did you have to hit the poor child?" asked the thief.

"Please, don't even ask me!" said the clever wife. "You brought a fat tiger from the forest this evening, didn't you? Didn't I make a nice curry with it? And wasn't it so tasty that we ate it all up for dinner? Now your son wants some more tiger curry. He's insisting that you go to the forest again and bring back a tiger. I can't handle him anymore. There must be another tiger roaming around the forest—please go fetch it. I can't stand your son's tantrums."

The tiger outside heard this. *This woman sounds quite capable of finishing me off herself,* it thought, and fled back to its cave. Once there, it realized that as long as the woman was alive, it would never be safe. It decided it would kill the entire family the next day.

The wife was certain that the tiger would return the next night too. This time she wanted to make sure to finish it off forever. So that night, she tied palm fronds around her husband's waist, back and chest, gave him a heavy wooden pestle, and told him to climb up the tree outside.

The tiger arrived and stood under the same tree waiting for the thief. The wife, spying through the keyhole, began yodeling loud. At her signal, the husband leapt down from the tree onto the tiger's back.

The tiger jumped high in the air. "Oh no, this must be a demon! That horrible noise! The thick, spiny skin! This ghost is going to kill me! No, let me go! Let me go!" squealed the tiger, and he took to heels, never to return.   ❖

the tiger and the appams

Once there were a brother and sister who gathered firewood from a forest for their livelihood.

One day, when they were walking through the forest, they met a tiger. They were terrified.

"Oh no, son," said the tiger, "you have nothing to fear. Your sister is very beautiful. If you will let me marry her, I won't harm you. What do you say?"

Fearing that there was no other way out, the girl agreed to marry the tiger. The tiger presented the brother with a pile of gold and jewels in exchange for his new bride. Before leaving his sister behind, the boy whispered something in her ear.

The tiger took the girl to his cave, where he lived with his cub. All the girl had to do throughout the day was to bathe and feed the cub and clean the cave. As the days went by, the tiger began to trust his human-wife. He left his cub in her care when he went out on his prowl.

The girl was waiting for this moment. One day, when she was alone with the cub, she killed it. She hung it from the roof of the cave and below it she placed a hot frying pan. Then she shut the cave entrance and left for good.

After a while, the tiger returned. Seeing the entrance shut, he called out to his human-wife to open it. Inside the cave, drops of blood from the cub's body were dropping on the hot pan. The tiger heard the loud sizzles—*soi, soi*—and thought she must be busy making aapams. *Oh, so once I am out, you make aapams and eat them all yourself, is it? Wait! I shall make you answer for this*, growled the tiger, circling the cave.

By then, the girl had reached her brother's home. After this, they never ventured into the forest. The gold and jewels that the tiger had given them were enough for them to launch a new business.   ❖

Ki. Ra.: Money and intimidation can never buy love; it is probably the moral of this story that such bondage will erase the buyer's entire lineage. There are several such stories, in which the fear in a human heart is represented by a terrifying creature like a tiger or a pey.

To think that the tiger could hear the sound of the blood dropping on the pan—*soi, soi*—through the thick rock wall of the cave requires a huge stretch of imagination. It makes us wonder where such imagination springs from!

tchu tchu!

There was once a mouse. One day, it ran out of its mousehole into the village. On its way it saw a garbage dump. The mouse searched and searched the dump till it found a piece of cloth. It ran with the cloth to a tailor.

"Tchu, tchu, make me a shirt with this cloth, make me a shirt with this cloth," it asked the tailor. The tailor made him a shirt. The mouse took it, and ran to a woman selling aapams.

"Tchu, tchu, I am hungry, give me an aapam, I am hungry, give me an aapam," it said. The woman served it an aapam. It began to eat.

"Tchu, tchu, this is too spicy, this is too spicy!" exclaimed the mouse. The woman gave it a mug of water, which it drank.

"Tchu, tchu, I am sleepy, I am sleepy," said the mouse. The woman gave it a mat. The mouse lay down.

"Tchu, tchu, I am cold, I am cold," said the mouse. The woman gave it a blanket.

"Tchu, tchu, I am scared, I am scared!" cried the mouse. An old man sat beside it.

"Tchu, tchu, I don't like this, I don't like this," wept the mouse. An old woman sat beside it.

"Tchu, tchu, I don't like this, I don't like this," sobbed the mouse. A young man sat beside it.

"Tchu, tchu, I don't like this, I don't like this," wailed the mouse. A young woman sat beside it.

"Tchu, tchu, I love this, I love this!" cried the mouse gleefully.

The young woman dropped a stone on its head and the mouse died on the spot. ❖

Ki. Ra.: The natural urge for sex cannot be avoided, either by a man or a mouse. All the elders will agree on this point. A man first of all requires food. Once that need is satisfied, he must have work. Once that need is satisfied, he will want to have sex with a beautiful woman.

Then why does the woman drop a stone on the mouse's head, you ask?

Oh, that was just a small whack for the stupid mouse's impropriety. That's all!

the sixth wife and the crow

There once lived a raja who had six wives. One day, he called each one separately, gave each a measure of sesame seeds, and asked them to make sesame oil. The six wives went to the mill to press the seeds. Just then, a white crow flew up to the wives and begged, "Amma, Amma, please give me some sesame seeds. I am hungry." Five of the wives shooed the crow away, but the sixth wife gave it a few seeds. After making the oil, they returned to the palace.

The raja measured each portion of oil and found that the sixth wife's portion was less than the others'. So he chased her out of the kingdom.

The sixth wife walked and walked and walked till she reached a forest. She appealed to the forest: "Oh forest, oh forest, tell me where the white crow lives!"

"Walk around me three times, and I shall tell you where the white crow lives," said the forest. So the sixth wife went around the forest three times, and the forest told her, "Amma, Amma, do you see that Pillayar temple over there? Go there, and you'll find out where the white crow lives."

And so the sixth wife walked and walked and walked till she came to the Pillayar temple, where she once again asked for the white crow's house. Pillayar said, "Go round my temple three times, bathe me with three pots of water, light three lamps, and pray. Then I shall tell you where you can find the white crow's house." So, the sixth wife went round the temple three times, bathed Pillayar with three pots of water, and lit three lamps. Then Pillayar said, "Amma, Amma, do you see that portia tree over there? Ask that tree, and you'll find out where the white crow lives."

And so the sixth wife walked and walked and walked till she came to the portia tree where she asked for the white crow's house again. The tree said, "Go round me three times and bite me three times. Then I shall tell where you can find the white crow's house." So the sixth wife went round the tree three times and bit it three times. Then the tree said, "Amma, Amma, do you see that cowherd over there? Go ask him, and you'll find out where the white crow lives."

And so the sixth wife walked and walked and walked till she came to the cowherd and again asked where she could find the white crow's house. "If you herd these cows all day, bring them back and secure them in their pen, then I shall tell you where to find the white crow's house." So the sixth wife herded the cows, took them back and secured them in the pen. Then the cowherd said, "Amma, Amma, do you see the dhobi's house over there? Go ask him and you'll find out where the white crow lives."

And so, the sixth wife walked and walked and walked till she came to the dhobi's house, where she again asked for the white crow's house. "If you can make a solution of cow-dung and water, soak these dirty clothes in it, rinse them and then steam them on a mud pot, then I shall tell you where to find the white crow's house," said the dhobi. So, the sixth wife soaked the dirty clothes in the cow-dung solution, rinsed them, and steamed them on a mud pot. Then the dhobi said, "Amma, Amma, do you see that big tree over there? On the left side is the white crow's house."

And so, the sixth wife walked and walked and walked till she came to the house. There she said, "Oh white crow, oh white crow, are you in?" The crow came out and asked her what the matter was. She told the crow everything that had happened. "Amma, Amma, don't worry," said the crow. "Do you want a box that rattles or a box that's soft?" it asked. She asked for a box that rattled.

Immediately the crow gave a box full of gold coins, arranged for a cart and sent her off.

The sixth wife went on and on and on till she came to the dhobi's house.

"Aiya, Aiya, I am going back to my husband's house," she said. The dhobi gave her a cartful of new clothes.

She went on and on and on till she came to the cowherd's house.

"Aiya, Aiya, I am going back to my husband's house," she said. The cowherd gave her a herd of cattle.

She went on and on and on till she reached the portia tree.

"Tree, tree, I am going back to my husband's house," she said. The tree asked her to dig into the ground near its roots, where she found ten sacks full of jewels. The tree let her keep the treasure as a gift.

She went on and on and on till she came to the Pillayar temple.

"Pillayar, Pillayar, I am going back to my husband's house," she said. Pillayar gave her his jewels.

She went on and on and on till she came to the edge of the forest. "Forest, forest, I am going back to my husband's house," she said. The forest gave her ten sacks full of money.

The sixth wife took all her gifts and returned to her husband's palace, where he ran out to welcome her. The raja then chased off his other five wives and lived happily ever after with the sixth wife. ❖

Ki. Ra.: This story may bore the adult storyteller, but it remains an all-time favorite of small children.

There is a tradition in India that sesame seed should never be given as alms. It is only offered to the dead forefathers. On the other hand, it is also believed that the forefathers visit the living in the form of crows.

The crow's albinism is added just to keep you interested.

Since the story is the invention of ordinary people, the raja is also portrayed without all the regal trappings.

Perhaps this story dates from a time when the number of wives was not an issue!

P.K.C.: There are many other Indian superstitions involving the sesame seed. It is said that if the first person who comes to a newly-opened shop buys sesame seed, then the shop is doomed to go out of business.

the pious sparrow

Once upon a time there was a sparrow, a very devout bird. The sparrow would religiously visit the Kali temple three times a day to pray. Every day, she would cross seven countries and seven seas to bring back exotic flowers as an offering. In the same town was a male sparrow. The two birds built a cozy nest and lived happily as a couple. They had just hatched their first batch of eggs.

In the same town there also lived a merchant, who travelled to far-off places on business. Though he was a smart businessman, he had no belief in god. His ancestors were very pious and had done a lot for the Kali temple over the generations. But this man refused to spend even a pie for this cause.

Once, during his travels, he came down with a terrible stomach pain. He consulted several medical experts, but found no relief. Finally, one medicine man told him to make an electuary from sparrow chicks and eat it immediately to relieve him from his pain.

The merchant went in search of hatchlings. This was just after our devout sparrow's eggs had hatched, and she had left the nest to hunt for worms for the chicks. The merchant found them, and stole away with the tiny baby birds.

The devout sparrow returned to the empty nest. She searched for her babies in a panic, but could find them nowhere. Steeped in sorrow, she flew to the Kali temple. Standing in front of the goddess, she wept,

> Oh the pain, the pain I went through to lay my eggs
> And now I've lost them to those cursed humans...

She threw dust in the air and sobbed her heart out. Unable to bear seeing a true devotee in such despair, the goddess appeared in her cosmic form and promised: "He who caused you such distress shall be born in his next life as a sparrow, and lose every chick of his own."

Satisfied, the sparrow laid her head at the goddess's feet and gave up her life. ❖

the lost needle

"This hen is messing up my house," grumbled Paatti.

Thatha saw the hen scratching at the empty ground and grinned behind his moustache. However, the children gathered there for their stories were curious. "Thatha, why does the hen keep scratching the ground like it's searching for something?"

"Hens always do that," piped one of the children. "And not just the ground; they scratch at garbage dumps too. When you scatter their feed, they almost bury it in the dust with all that scratching."

"Don't you know?" asked Thatha. "The hen is looking for the needle that it lost!"

"No, we don't know," cried the children, hurriedly shutting their school-books. "Tell us! Tell us!"

God had created birds and sent them down to earth, but he had not given them wings to fly yet. So all the birds walked around like us humans. Back in those days, there used to be constant traffic between heaven and earth. Devas used to fly down all the time. The birds, seeing this, wanted to fly as well. But they did not know how.

One of the birds, the brahminy kite, gathered up his courage and asked God, "I want to fly too. Can I have a pair of wings please?" God was very fond of the brahminy kite. He gave it a tiny needle and said, "Pluck out some of your down, stitch it into a pair of wings, and sew them onto your sides. Be careful with the needle, though. You have to return it to me when I ask for it."

The kite followed God's instructions and made a tiny pair of wings. As soon as it sewed them on, to its great surprise, they grew large in seconds, and the kite was able to soar very high into the sky.

God, with his busy schedule, forgot to ask for the needle back.

When the other birds saw the kite flying about the sky, they also wanted wings. So the kite ran a regular business hiring out the needle, on the promise that it would be returned safely. Almost all the birds were now equipped with wings; only the crow and the hen were left.

Now it was the crow's turn to borrow the needle. As it plucked out the fine down to make the wings, the hen stood by watching closely. Once the crow had stitched its wings on, it left the needle with the hen and went off to try them out.

The hen hurriedly plucked out some of her down, made a pair of wings, and stitched them haphazardly to her sides. In her haste to finish before the crow came back, she let the needle fall out of her grip. Scared of the crow's anger, she began scratching the ground to search for the needle.

The crow returned. It saw the hen busily scratching the ground, and guessed the reason. "What happened?" it demanded. "Quick, give me back the needle. What am I to tell the kite?"

Hearing the crow's loud cawing, the kite flew in too. The hen was too scared to do anything but keep scratching the ground.

The enraged kite screamed, "I don't care how long you have to look for it—you must return that needle! If you don't, then I, all my cousins, and this crow will prey on you and your children and your children's children, for generations to come."

The hen never found the needle. That is why, even today, kites, vultures, eagles and crows fly away with newly hatched chicks.

"The poor hen, though she has wings, never had the time to practice flying. Ever since, she and her chicks have had to take refuge at the feet of humans for safety. She is still scratching the ground for that needle. If only she could find it and give it back to the kite, she could put an end to her humiliation," said Thatha, finishing his tale.

The children felt a wee bit sorry for the silly hen. ❖

the sparrow and the payasam

Once, in a forest, there lived two sparrow sisters. One day, the younger sparrow sister, after hunting for worms for a very long time, knocked on the door of her elder sister's nest. "Akka, please open the door," she said. "It's windy out, and the dust is getting in my eyes."

The elder sparrow sister called from inside, "Please wait. I'm giving my baby sparrow a bath."

The younger sparrow sister waited for some time and then knocked on the nest door again. "Akka, please open the door," she said. "It's windy out, and the dust is getting in my eyes."

The elder sparrow sister called from inside, "Please wait. I'm just getting my baby sparrow dressed."

The younger sparrow sister waited for some more time and then knocked on the nest door again. "Akka, please open the door," she said. "It's windy out, and the dust is getting in my eyes."

The elder sparrow sister called from inside, "Please wait. I'm just giving my baby sparrow its milk."

The younger sparrow sister waited for some more time and then knocked on the nest door again. "Akka, please open the door," she said. "It's windy out, and the dust is getting in my eyes."

The elder sparrow sister called from inside, "Please wait. I'm just singing a lullaby to my baby sparrow."

Finally, the elder sparrow sister opened the door. By now, the younger sparrow sister was unbearably hungry. "Akka, if you have some jaggery and toor dhal, please make me some sweet payasam to eat."

The elder sister sparrow quickly made her some payasam. It smelled so appetizing that the younger sister sparrow could not wait till it cooled down. She picked up the piping hot payasam and poured a gulp of it into her mouth. Her tongue was badly singed.

"Chee! I don't want this payasam," she said, and went and threw it into the temple tank.

After a long while, she licked up one tiny bit of the payasam that had spilled on the floor of the nest. It was so sweet and tasty! *Aiyyoyo,* she lamented, *I poured all the payasam into the temple tank!* So she quickly flew down to the temple tank and drank up all the water in it.

She flew back to the nest with a huge, distended stomach, but could not fit in the door. She was waiting outside when a cow, who had been standing beneath the tree swishing its tail, gave an extra hard swish. The end of the tail hit the younger sparrow sister's swollen stomach, all the water and payasam gushed out of her, and all she could do was watch as the nest was swept away in the flood. ❖

P.K.C.: When my grandmother used to tell me this story, there was a slight variation. After drinking up all the water in the temple tank, the younger sparrow sister, not wanting to lose even a drop of the tasty payasam in her belly, corks her rear end with a ball of straw. Then the cow's tail, instead of hitting the stomach, knocks the ball of straw so that it pops out, and the ending is the same.

the hen and the fox

Once there was a woman who owned a hen that disappeared one day, just as it was ready to lay eggs.

The woman searched for it high and low. She cursed everyone she could think of who might have stolen it. But she could not find out where it had vanished to.

A month later, the hen returned to her backyard with ten of its newly hatched chicks. It had been hiding under a bush behind her house the whole time. She was overjoyed at seeing the hen and chickens, and fed them grains.

Just then, a fox peeped over the wall.

"Hey woman," called out the fox. "It was I who protected your hen and its eggs from ants and snakes all these days. What about my fee?"

"Please wait for few days," said the woman. "Once the chicks are fully grown, I shall give you the fattest one."

"I don't want the fattest chick. I want the mother hen," demanded the fox.

"All right, but you have to wait till she has reared her chicks a bit."

The fox agreed and went away.

The hen, which had been listening to this exchange, cried aloud, "Is it really my fate to wind up in that fox's stomach?"

Her chicks gathered around her and asked, "Aatha, Aatha, why do you weep? What makes you so sad?"

"I am weeping because once you are grown, I will be eaten by that fox," replied the mother hen. "I don't mind if the human woman eats me; after all, it is she who fed me for so long. But a fox, which came from nowhere, eating me for free?"

"Don't worry Aatha. The fox is going to wait until we are grown up," said the chicks. "Stop crying. When the fox comes for you, we will surround you so that you will not be seen."

Days passed. The chicks were now all majestic roosters. The fox returned to the pen, but could only see the roosters, not the mother hen. *Aha, those roosters think they are so clever, don't they? I have been very fair, waiting all these days for them to grow up. Now these upstarts think they can outfox me. Ha!* thought the fox. "You idiots, give me your Aatha, or else I shall eat you up too," he roared.

"Our Aatha left yesterday. She has not come back. We are huddled here, worrying about what's become of her," cried the roosters.

The fox leapt on them and tore with its front paws. The roosters' feathers flew all over the pen. "*Wayyaaa...!*" they wailed aloud.

The mother hen was pained by their cries. *This fox is hurting my babies, even while I am still alive. What will it do to them once I am gone?*

She sprang into the open and pecked at the fox's eyes. Soon the roosters joined in the battle. They pecked at the fox so hard that it was bleeding all over. Unable to bear the pain, the fox scampered from the pen, its tail tucked between its hind legs, never to return.   ❖

the ascetic and the snakes

There were two snakes in a huge forest, copulating whenever they felt like it, living in peace. Just a little way beyond the termite mound in which they had made their burrow was a huge banyan tree, and past that, a perennial river. This naturally made the snakes' lives even more pleasant.

One day, an ascetic came upon that idyllic place. He saw the cool shady tree and the overflowing river, and wanted to live there forever. So he began to build a hut. When they saw this, the snakes rushed out of their burrow and slithered past him.

The ascetic stopped them. "Why are you leaving?"

"We cannot live alongside with humans, or one day they will kill us. So please, let us go," cried the snakes.

"I agree that is a danger, for sure, with ordinary humans. However, I am not ordinary. I am an ascetic, free from all earthly desires. So fear not. I will never kill you. Go back to your burrow."

"What is the difference between you and other humans? You are a man too," said the snakes.

"Ordinary humans have to do away with every other creature to find a place for them to be happy. It is an ascetic's duty to protect all living things. So please don't go away," pleaded the ascetic. The snakes were convinced, and continued to live there.

After some days, the raja of that land came for a hunt to the forest. On his way, he decided to call on the ascetic, who was then washing his clothes in the river. The raja waited as the ascetic dried the wet clothes, cleaned the hut, and made a simple dish for his lunch.

The surprised raja said, "Oh Guru, you are living here in this forest, meditating for the well-being of all in this world. Shouldn't you have someone to help you with your chores?"

"I am all alone in this vast forest. Shouldn't I do my own work?" laughed the ascetic.

"I understand," said the raja. "But that was before. I am going to leave one of my maids behind to do your work for you, so you can go ahead and meditate as long as you want." He called one of the maids and told her that her duty was now to serve the ascetic, and that every day, the king would personally send whatever provisions were needed. Both the ascetic and the maid agreed to this plan, and the raja left.

When the snakes saw that there was a woman now staying with the ascetic, they once again rushed out of their burrow. "The ascetic is not an ascetic anymore. He has set himself up with a woman permanently. So let us get out. Fast!" they whispered. Once again, the ascetic stopped them, saying the woman was only a maid, not his mate. He also called the woman and told her to leave the snakes alone.

But the silly woman, on seeing them, began screaming loudly. "Aiyyo, aiyyo! I have always been told by astrologers that I am going to die from a snake bite. And just look at these two! They are huge! They are as thick as an ogre's thigh. No, please either kill them or let them go." She went on and on, until the ascetic had to remind her that it was on the raja's orders that she was here in the first place. Seeing the ascetic's rage, she calmed down, but decided that she would get rid of the snakes, one way or another.

One midnight, not long afterwards, there was a massive hurricane with continuous thunder and lightning. The skies rang with loud bangs that shook the ground with a deafening *Damaar, Damaar!* Lightning slashed the sky as if ready to slice off a man's head. The maid, scared out of her wits, leapt out of her bed and ran into the ascetic's arms.

That was it! Here was a man who had lived absolutely alone for years and years, never knowing the warmth of a woman's touch. He hugged her tighter and tighter and would not let go. Even after the storm had petered out and dawn had broken, he held on.

The snakes came out early that morning, and saw the ascetic and the maid coiled in pleasure. The maid spied the disappearing snakes, and wrenched herself out of the ascetic's arms. Frustrated, the ascetic went to bathe in the cold river water.

At the riverside, the snakes met the ascetic and said, "Oh Guru, it is definitely not wise for us to stay here anymore. Please let us go."

"Why?" asked the puzzled ascetic.

"An ascetic should be free from all human bonds. Desire for a woman is a definite no-no. We saw you writhing on the floor with that woman. How can we believe you are an ascetic any longer? We'll be off."

"Oh no, dear snakes! You are very wrong. I am indeed an ascetic. When a woman approaches me in distress, it is my duty to help her," said the ascetic soothingly. The snakes gave in once more.

That night, there was no thunder or lightning—not even a light shower. So the ascetic had to once again sleep on his cot outside the hut. The maid was peacefully sleeping in the hut. However, the ascetic was unable to fall asleep. His body was now thirsting for the same comfort of the previous night. He tossed this way and that, sat up, paced around restlessly for a while, and finally went for a dip in the ice-cold river. Even then, his nerves throbbed with desire. Unable to bear it any longer, he barged into the hut and grabbed at the maid. But the shrewd woman evaded him and ran into a corner. He stood there in front of her, begging pitifully, "Please, please, come and touch me. My body is on fire."

"Fine, I'll help put out the fire, but only on the condition that you go out right now and kill those two snakes," she demanded.

"Why bother with the snakes? It is your body I want," pleaded the ascetic.

"It will be yours only if you do away with the snakes," she insisted.

The ascetic ran out of the hut with a spear and knocked down the termite mound. As the snakes emerged terrified, he gave each snake a hard knock on its head.

The snakes gasped, "What are you doing, oh Guru? We offered to go away from here so many times. You insisted that we stay, and now you're trying to kill us?"

The ascetic snapped back, "I am not being allowed to be a true ascetic, or even a human. That woman came here and has changed me into an ordinary man. As an ordinary man, I cannot bear to see other creatures happy."

So saying, he gave two more whacks, and the snakes dropped dead. The woman rushed out of the hut and sprang into his arms.

"Oh God, oh God," he wept as he melted into her. ❖

gods & goddesses

the stone pillar son-in-law

Every time God created a human life, he would make her stand with her head facing him, while he wrote her destiny on her forehead. While doing this, he would never look at the person's face. Actually, even while he was writing, he would never know what he was going to write. For some, the scripted fate might be very good, while for others, it might be horrible. Whatever it was, he would never erase it or rewrite it.

That day, he was busy writing these destinies when his daughter's turn came up. *Now, this is my own child. While I write her destiny, I will look at her face,* he thought, and so he held on to her soft cheek while he wrote. It was only afterwards that he read what he had written. His daughter was fated to marry young, but her thali would not last long; she would be widowed soon afterwards!

God was greatly disturbed. He might be God, but even he was not allowed to change what he had already written. So he thought and thought and thought. Finally he decided: *My daughter can only become a widow if I get her married to a human. If I get her married to a stone pillar, then I can beat her destiny. After all, a stone pillar does not die! My daughter will be happily married all her life.*

The very same day, he ordered a tall stone pillar, had his daughter decorated in gold and finery, and got them both married. The daughter, in her new married life, fed herself three times a day, played with her mates and slept peacefully.

But still God was not happy with the situation; everyone laughed at the sham marriage. Then one night, there was a crashing storm with thunder rending the air and lightning setting the sky on fire. Terrified, God decided to stay safe indoors. The next morning, at dawn, when God stepped out of his house, all that was left of his stone-pillar son-in-law was a small pile of rubble.

It was then that God understood: not even *he* could change destiny! ❖

31

a life in his stead

Whenever God wanted to see the world, he would come down for a leisurely walk on it. During these visits, he would take on a disguise, and this time he came as a drifter.

There, he saw an old, old woman drying out soaked oats and guarding them from being picked by the crows and sparrows. The drifter approached the woman and asked, "So, what is new in this town?"

"Oh, please don't even ask!" exclaimed the woman. "The young son of the richest man of this town, just sixteen years old, died this morning. Is that any age to die? He died from a snake bite. There are so many old people in this town, waiting for death. Take me for instance, why didn't that death choose to come to me? Why him?"

The drifter gave a wry smile and went to the rich man's house.

There was a huge crowd gathered there. "Why wasn't it one of us?" some cried. "Why should such a young life end so soon?" wept others. Wails and sobs rent the air. The drifter pushed aside the people around the weeping father and said, "I can make this boy come back alive. But I need another life in his stead. Is any one of you ready?"

Very quietly, the crowd began to thin out. In a few minutes, the bawling relatives had all disappeared.

The drifter turned to the father, who was seated next to the dead son, steeped in sorrow. "Can I have your life instead?" he asked.

"I would gladly give it," said the father. "But I have lent money to several people, at different rates of interest. If I die, who will collect that money? My family will be reduced to poverty if no one can recover it. Also, I bought a piece of land only a few days back. I have to get it ready for my family…" He went on and on like this.

The drifter looked at the mother and asked, "What about you?"

"If I do not offer my life for my only son, who will?" asked the mother. "But my only daughter has come home for her first delivery. The moment her child is safely delivered, I will gladly give my life, sir."

Next, the drifter asked the sister the same question. "I never do anything without my husband's permission," she said. "Also, I am carrying another life inside me now. This is the first grandchild in my husband's family. I was even married to him as his second wife so that the family would have an heir. If I die now, my child will die with me! You wanted only one life!"

The drifter then hurried back to the old woman he had met on the road and asked for her life.

"Aiyyo!" she yelped. "Are you crazy? Why do you want me to die, you drifter?"

"But weren't you the one who was ready to give up your life?" inquired the drifter.

"Even now I am not refusing. But I want a death that is painless, like dying when I am fast asleep," said the woman. "My grandchildren have gone to the field to work. They will return for lunch. I have put out the wet oats to dry. Once they are dry, I must pound them to make the kanji. Also, I've had nothing to eat since I woke up. I'm starved. So hopefully, there will be enough kanji left for me too. And ..."

The drifter was not listening any more. He was roaring with laughter. First, he doubled over, and clutched tight at his stomach. Then he put his hands on his hips and looked up at the sky and laughed and laughed and laughed.   ❖

yaman and the woodcutter

There was once a poor woodcutter. Every day he would chop wood, gather it in a bundle and go the market to sell it to feed himself and his family. What he earned was just enough for one full meal. For that one meal, he slogged through the day. This hard labour took a toll on his health. He lost weight and became weak—so weak that he was now unable to carry his bundle of wood to market.

One day he had gathered enough wood to feed the family and also to earn a little extra. He tied it up into a big bundle. He had had nothing to eat since morning, and his limbs were aching. Thorns had ripped his body and scratched him all over. Hungry and tired, he was unable to lift the bundle onto his head. It was just too much! But there was no one around who could help him. He became disheartened. *What kind of a life is this?* he wondered dejectedly. He wanted to die.

"Dey, Yaman, where the hell are you?" he shouted aloud.

It just so happened that Yaman was coming down the same jungle path, astride his bull, when he heard the call. He hurried to the woodcutter, wondering why he had yelled for him.

"Why did you call for me, human? What do you want?" asked Yaman.

The woodcutter looked at Yaman, the tall, strong Lord of Death, with his huge paunch and massive shoulders. "Oh, good thing you came along," he said. "Come give me a hand so I can lift this bundle of wood onto my head. Hurry up!"

Yaman lifted the bundle as easily as if it were a light bouquet of flowers, and placed it on the man's head.

The woodcutter hurried off with his bundle without another look back!   ❖

ukum, ukum, ukum

As usual, as Shiva set off to work, he told Parvathi, "I am off to take care of the world. Keep my lunch ready."

Parvathi, feeling mischievous, caught hold of a tiny black ant, split open the pit of a mango, stuffed the ant inside it, and sealed the mango back up.

Shiva returned late in the afternoon, breathing a sigh of satisfaction at having fed the entire world. "Ah, husband dear!" said Parvathi. "There is one life that you are yet to feed."

"That's impossible. I counted every head," exclaimed Shiva.

Parvathi opened the mango pit to show him the ant, but the ant was sitting peacefully sucking on a strand of fiber from the pit.

Oh, Parvathi's face was a picture to watch! "I am sorry. I wanted to hide this ant to prove that your head count is not always correct, but I failed!" she said.

Shiva's only response was, "That's understandable. Tell me, which wife hasn't tried to find fault with her husband's work?"

"I feel bad," said Parvathi. "You work through the day to feed the world, while I sit at home, whiling away my time. From tonight, I want you to tell me, in detail, about every life you feed, how much you feed it, and all the difficulties you face in your work. I shall sit beside you on the bed, press your legs, and listen to the whole story."

Shiva agreed, and so from then on, every night after dinner, he would stretch out on the bed with Parvathi next to him pressing his legs, and narrate his work-tales. Parvathi listened patiently for a few nights, but the head count was endless, his accounts of rationing out the food were deathly boring, and his difficulties seemed trivial. But she could not tell her husband this. So one night, when he was very engrossed in his stories, she caught a dove, put it in a cage, placed it under the bed and went off to sleep alone.

So here was Shiva in his bed, with his eyes shut, telling his stories, while under the bed the caged pigeon would periodically coo, "*Ukum, ukum, ukum.*" One night, after a particularly long story, Shiva's throat was drying up. "Parvathi," he asked, "can you get me a glass of water?" But there was no Parvathi beside him, just a cooing dove. A little distance away in the same room, Parvathi was fast asleep and snoring.

Shiva could barely control his rage. He kept silent, fuming. *Right, let her sleep now. But she will have to pay for this.*

A few days later, Parvathi was flying over the jungle when she heard a child whimpering. She landed on the ground. There she saw a woman gathering firewood and her child next to her, sobbing, "Amma, I am very hungry. I am very hungry." The woman took the child to the stream, cupped both her hands, and dipped them into the water. The moment the woman took the water in her hands, it magically changed to milk. After a few mouthfuls, the child was no longer hungry.

Parvathi, though the Ruling Goddess of This Earth, could never have managed this feat. She was green with envy of this ordinary woods-woman. *Can this mortal be even more powerful than I am? I must test her tomorrow,* Parvathi thought to herself. The next day, just as the woman was lifting her bundle of firewood and placing it on her head, Parvathi made the stream flood.

There was water everywhere. But the woman did not seem to worry. She nonchalantly picked up her child and held it to her waist. Carrying both child and bundle, she stepped into the seething stream. Wonder of wonders! Every time she stepped on the surging water, it dried up under her foot.

Parvathi was astonished. Wild with anger, she marched up to Shiva and demanded, "This commonplace woods-woman is able to change stream water to milk, and to dry up the flood I created. Here I am, the Wife of the Lord Who Rules this Universe, and even I am unable to accomplish such things!"

"Stop making a scene and come along with me," said Shiva and took her to the woods-woman's house. As they entered, the woman put down her child and placed her bundle on the floor. Her husband was hollering from inside. She went to him and asked softly, "Yes husband, what do you want?" He yelled back, "I have been calling for hours. Where were you whoring around?"

"I was feeding the child. Please forgive me. I am sorry," the woman pleaded, and served him.

The husband's body was wasting away with sores and pus. The woman sold the firewood, used the money to buy grain, fed the man, bore his beatings without a whimper, and even fanned him while he slept in the night.

"Is she mad?" cried Parvathi. "Not enough that she's so dutifully serving his rotting body, she's putting up with his abuse every day. Why doesn't she throw him out?"

"But that is her greatness," said Shiva, with a smirk. "She loves her man even though he is a horrible person. Yet you snore away while I'm talking to you, and try to fool me with a cooing dove. Tell me, who will be able to command the stream? You or she?"

Parvathi replied meekly, "You may be right, dear. What I did was wrong. But tell me: if she is so powerful with her magic touch, why doesn't she heal her husband's sores?"

"Oh no! I can't allow that to happen, or I would lose my status as the Lord Who Rules this Universe," whispered Shiva with a sheepish grin.   ❖

lord shiva's rain

Once upon a time, Shiva and Parvathi created this world, and all the living things in it. They then commanded Brahma to write the fate of each living thing on its forehead: the kind of habitat it should choose, and the kind of food it should eat.

However, all the living things were extremely unhappy, for there had been no rains at all for a very, very long time. What little grass and greenery had survived had been eaten by the cattle. So now, the animals turned to one another for fodder.

When Shiva and Parvathi saw that their creations were so close to destruction, they became concerned.

Parvathi turned to Shiva and asked, "So, how do you plan to save the world?"

In answer, Shiva roared aloud with ringing laughter. His glistening teeth caused flashes of electric lightning. When his mouth opened, howling winds emerged, followed by booming thunderbolts. Then he decided to take a piss, which turned into typhoon storms at once. Only after that could all forms of life begin to live in peace on this Earth! ❖

Ki. Ra.: When this story is told to children, it's not advisable to use the word "piss". Instead, you can say that the rain was Shiva's sweat.

meenakshi vs. aiyanaar

The temple of Meenakshi, in Madurai, needed a flag pole. People searched everywhere, but could not find a suitable tree. Meenakshi was in tears. *What will I do now?* she thought. Her sons, Big Ottakaran and Small Ottakaran, seeing their mother worried, wanted to know the reason. She told them.

"Phoo! Is that all? We'll bring you your flag pole, even if we have to go to the farthest forests!" they swore and left immediately. They searched everywhere.

In Rajapalayam, in the thick jungle which grew around the Aiyanaar temple, they found a tree which was perfect for the flag pole. They could not contain their happiness. Big Ottakaran told the servants who had come along to chop the tree down. But when the first axe cut into the tree, blood streamed out. Terrified, the servants fell away.

Small Ottakaran snatched the axe impatiently and began to chop on his own. But the blood did not stop; now it was gushing from the tree.

Hearing the noise, Aiyanaar came down from his temple. Seeing the brothers standing there, with their men and axes, he was enraged. "How dare you come into *my* forest and cut down *my* trees!" he roared, and lifted his mighty weapons to strike.

At this, the brothers threw themselves at his feet and cried, "Oh, please forgive us. The only reason we are cutting down this tree is that our mother, Meenakshi, wanted it for a flag pole in her temple."

"Oh! If it's for Meenakshi, that's another matter. You may take the tree. But you still have to pay the price for coming into my forest and trying to chop it down without my permission. Take the tree to your mother, but you must come back in eight days and become the guards of my temple!" ordered Aiyanaar.

The brothers agreed. "But Aiya, we are not able to cut the tree down. It keeps bleeding. What do we do?" asked Big Ottakaran.

"Try now. It will no longer bleed. But remember, you only have eight days," Aiyanaar reminded them, and went back to his temple.

The brothers felled the tree and took it to their mother. Meenakshi was pleased. Elaborate pujas were organized in the temple for the inauguration of the flag pole. All through the rituals, the brothers looked very tense. The mother could see that her sons were troubled about something, but were not telling her what.

She beckoned them to her and asked gently, "What has happened, my sons? You are as strong as Bheeman and Vijayan. There is no one in the world who can stand against you. Why do you both look so down?"

After some hesitation, the brothers told her the whole story, and that they would have to leave her forever in just eight days.

"What? This is me, Meenakshi, who rules over the whole of Madurai!" she exclaimed. "How dare that Aiyanaar order my sons to become his temple guards? Who does he think he is? Let him come here, in front of me. I shall tear out his guts and drink his bile," she swore. Then she told her sons, "Let eight days pass, eight months or even eight years. You're not going anywhere. If he wants you, let him come here. We shall see to it then." The sons acquiesced.

Eight days passed.

Aiyanaar, who had been waiting impatiently, finally realized that the brothers were not going to turn up. His anger knew no bounds. It grew so large and destructive that it could have blown up the entire universe. He too swore an oath: "Those two had the guts to come into my territory and chop down a tree that belonged to me. I should have taken their lives on that day. It was my mistake to have let them go. They have no idea of my power. Now it won't just be their lives! Let them see what I do to every life within the boundary of their rule..." And he put a terrible curse on Madurai, that all the humans there would get raging fever, and vomit and purge ceaselessly until they died.

The entire city of Madurai, with no exception, was in bed, sick and dying. No one knew what to do. Those that could still move crawled to the Meenakshi temple and begged her to save them.

Meenakshi could not understand what was happening. Even in the worst epidemic, there would be a few survivors. But now it looked as if the entire town was going to perish. She called on a soothsayer and asked for his predictions.

Aiyanaar chose to take possession of the soothsayer's body. He told Meenakshi about his curse and demanded that her sons come to him within the next eight days. "If you fail this time, there will not be a life left in Madurai to even cry *whaa*," he said, and left.

Oh no! thought Meenakshi. *Here I was thinking I was the biggest god, but Aiyanaar seems to be even bigger than I am! I cannot afford to be obstinate any longer. I may as well give my sons to him.* She called them to her. "Sons, I could not win over Aiyanaar with my intelligence. Now it looks like I will lose not just you, but my whole town. Please go to him and save my people. I promise that I shall visit you every year without fail, bearing three garlands. Now go!" she bade them.

The sons went down to Aiyanaar. But as they neared Rajapalayam, every god in heaven ran away and hid, unable to bear the brightness that emanated from the brothers. Even Aiyanaar himself could not bear their radiance. He called on his assistant Thalai Malai Veerar and asked for his help.

The brave Thalai Malai Veerar offered to accept their intensity into himself.

After that, the curse was lifted, and the people of Madurai lived happily and free from illness.

Even today, in Aiyanaar temples, the Thalai Malai Veerar idol leans to one side because of that glow of light within him.

As promised, Meenakshi visits her sons with the three garlands, every year without fail, even to this day.   ❖

variations on the ramayanam

"When Sita is born, it will spell the ruin of Lanka!" bellowed a massive voice from the heavens.

And it was just at that moment that Sita was born, the daughter of Ravanan.

Thinking that keeping her with him could be fatal to his kingdom, Ravanan placed her in a golden basket. He also broke off a tiny bit of his powerful bow, Sivadhanusu, and tucked it under her blanket for her protection. Then, taking care that no one saw him, he set the basket afloat in the ocean.

Luckily for Ravanan, the divine bow Sivadhanusu immediately regenerated its broken end.

The basket gently floated in the sea towards the North.

Bhumadevi, the goddess Mother Earth, prayed to the Sea and the Air: "Please bring my baby safely back to me."

A huge storm rose up over the sea, and the rocking waves lifted the basket ashore. Bhumadevi gratefully accepted and embraced her child.

A few days later, in exactly the same spot, King Janaka was planting a garden. He himself was tilling the soil with a golden plough, when he came upon the golden basket buried in the earth. Inside was a chubby, cuddly, gurgling baby girl. She looked like a replica of Bhumadevi herself.

Now, King Janaka had no children. In fact, that was why he was planting the garden; he had been told by the elders that in this way, he could get a child. Now he had both a daughter and a tiny piece of Sivadhanusu, which had grown into a complete, though tiny, bow. It was King Janaka who named the girl Sita.

My grandmother used to tell me; "As Sita grew, the tiny bow grew larger too. If she grew one inch then it would grow nine inches. This was the bow that brought down Ravanan in the end."

At this point, just as you are now raising your eyebrows, I would raise mine and demand, "But didn't Raman break that bow? Wasn't that the challenge he had to meet in order to marry Sita?"

My grandmother would contradict me vehemently, "Certainly not! He did not break it, he bent it. The challenge Janaka set for his daughter's suitors at her Swayamvaram was that the bow should be lifted and bent. That was what Raman did."

These folk versions of the Ramayanam and Mahabaratham epics are so widely varied. Perhaps these are the original versions, which were later strung together into the ones that are standard today!

I will give you another example:

One day, another of Ravanan's daughters was sitting with King Nala's daughter under a tree, chatting. Ravanan's daughter said, "My father is the emperor of the world. He rules over the gods, humans, birds and beasts. They all obey his every command. Right now, if he ordered all the birds to line up single-file, they would do it. If he commanded them to line up in pairs, they would do that too."

Nala's daughter laughed off this boast, and said instead that *her* father was the emperor. She said that the birds would obey orders even from herself, the daughter of the emperor.

They decided to test to see who was right.

First, Ravanan's daughter ordered the birds to line up in pairs. But not even a single bird responded.

Then Nala's daughter looked at the birds and asked, "Oh birds, oh birds! Will you listen to me please?" All the birds bobbed their heads. "Please come and stand in front of me in pairs," she said. Birds of every species lined up in front of her on the ground, in pairs.

Ravanan's daughter was so jealous she nearly broke into sobs. She walked off without a word and went to her father and told him the whole story.

Ravanan was furious. *I thought I was the greatest emperor. I rule this world! Is there someone above even me? All right, let me go see for myself how great this King Nala is,* he thought, and left the next day to meet him.

When he reached Nala's home, Nala was not there.

"Please wait, he will be back soon," he was told.

"Where has he gone?" he asked.

"He has gone to milk the cows in the cowshed."

"Oh! Then I shall go to cowshed and meet him," said Ravanan, and went there.

As he entered the shed, Nala had just finished milking a full pot of milk.

Seeing him, Nala called out, "Come da, Ravanan!"

How does this King Nala know me, and how dare he refer to me so casually as "da"? thought Ravanan. *I refer to the Sun and the Moon like that! And I am perhaps the only one in the universe who can! The rest of the world can see the full moon only for a day, but in my fort, I see it full every night. How can he be so disrespectful to me?*

Nala took Ravanan back to his house. The path led through an open ground. It was high noon; the sun was scorching. Nala took off his top-cloth and flung it into the sky. It rose up and spread itself out as a canopy over their path.

On their way, they saw a crowd in front of a shop. Ravanan wanted to know what was going on. So both of them walked up.

Inside the shop, there was no attendant. Instead, people came in a queue, took what they wanted, put down their barter in exchange and went on their way. Ravanan wondered aloud, "Now, if I were to take what I wanted, but did not drop my barter items, how would the shop owner know?" Saying this, he took something and walked off. At once, from out of nowhere, a bladed disc came flying through the air towards his head. Scared, Ravanan dropped what he had picked up. The disc stopped in midair, turned around and flew away.

At his palace Nala said, "Can you wait for a second? I have to go deliver this milk to Devalokam. I will be back soon."

"I will come along," said Ravanan.

"Okay, catch hold of my right toe."

Ravanan took hold of it, and Nala launched into the air, with him hanging below.

Far beneath them, they saw a beautiful orchard with a few men working in it. Ravanan, of course, wanted to have a look. So they landed there.

"We have heard of a raja on this earth called Nala," the men said. "Apparently he is a very just and fair raja. We have grown this orchard so that in case he passes by here, he will be able to rest."

Some distance past the orchard, a few men were digging a huge, deep pit. Nala and Ravanan asked them what they were doing.

"We have heard of a raja on this earth called Ravanan," the men said. "Apparently he is a very cruel and unjust raja. We are digging this pit so that in case he passes by here, he will fall into it."

"Oh dear! It looks as if even my death will not peaceful, Nala. Please tell me a way out," begged Ravanan in tears.

"Very soon there will born on this earth a raja by name of Raman. If you die by his hand, then you will attain instant Nirvanam," said Nala.

"How will I manage to die by his hand?" asked Ravanan.

"You must to do something that will make him so angry, he will kill you," answered Nala.

And that was why, much later, Ravanan abducted Raman's wife Sita.   ❖

P.K.C.: In the standard epic, Sita is not said to be Ravanan's daughter, only Bhumadevi's. Ravanan abducts Sita out of lust and revenge, not for any desire to attain Nirvanam. The meeting here between Ravanan and Nala is also non-standard.

the sun, the moon, and the pearl

One fine day, the Sun and the Moon came down to visit the Earth. They brought along a human servant to do chores and run errands for them. While they were walking through the woods, they found a very beautiful pearl on the path. The Sun and the Moon were amazed to see such a beautiful gem. The Sun guessed that such a precious pearl must have been dropped there by an equally lovely woman; perhaps a rani or a princess had been walking in the forest. The Moon disagreed; he said that the pearl must have been dropped by a rich king, for only someone like that could afford it.

The servant kept quiet. The Sun turned to him and said, "Go on man! Tell us who you think is correct!"

The servant's only reply was, "Excuse me, but both of you are wrong."

The Sun and the Moon were furious. *The two of us are aware of all three worlds; the heavens, the earth, and the netherworld. This man is just a servant, assigned to do our bidding. How dare he call us wrong?* they wondered. "Go on, prove it then! How do you know we're wrong?" they challenged him.

"Does it matter? I just know," replied the servant.

The Moon was not satisfied with this. He suggested that they go into the town and find out more about the pearl. They agreed that if either of them turned out to be right, they would chop off the servant's head on the spot. On the other hand, if it turned out that the mortal was correct, they would obey whatever he commanded.

When they got to the town, they found the people there in a terrible fuss. Men were running back and forth in the palace, looking for something. No one paid any attention to the Sun and Moon, not even enough to stop and ask them, "Where are you going, you monkeys?"

The divine beings could not understand the reason. *What's going on here? Normally, they would be rushing forward with chariots and feasts to welcome us,* they thought to themselves as they entered the palace. *Today, not even an old hag on the verge of death is looking out for us.* Inside the palace, too, everyone—including the raja—was anxiously running helter-skelter. No one even spared them a glance.

The Sun was raging in anger. He strode up to the raja, grabbed his arm and hauled him to a stop. "What's happened? Why are you so disturbed?" he asked. The raja merely gazed at him with tearful eyes. He was too pained to speak.

When the Sun and the Moon saw that the raja's sorrow was real, they softened and asked for an explanation.

"I bought the rani, my wife, a beautiful pearl necklace," said the raja. "One of the pearls fell off somewhere. When the rani saw that a pearl was missing, she fell unconscious. The palace physician says he can revive her only if the pearl is found. We are looking for it now."

The Sun inquired where the pearl could have got lost and was told that it must be in the palace grounds. The Moon showed the pearl he had found to the raja, who immediately had the necklace brought over, checked it and confirmed that it was indeed the missing pearl. His rani was now safe, out of danger.

It was only later that the raja thought of asking the Moon where he had found the pearl. When he heard it was found in the woods, he thought and thought and thought; how could the pearl be lost in my palace grounds, but wind up in the forest? No one had an answer to this.

Just then, a saamiyaar came looking for the raja. On hearing their quandary, he solved the problem—the pearl must have been picked up in the palace and dropped in the forest by the pet peacock!

The Sun and The Moon turned to the servant and said, "You were right, after all. So, we will do as you wish. But tell us. How did you know we were wrong and it was neither the raja nor the rani who had dropped the pearl there?"

"Lords, there were no other footsteps on that path except ours. If the pearl had been dropped by a raja or a rani, there would have been at least traces of horse hooves, or a track of chariot wheels. But there were none. That was why I was sure I was right and you were wrong," replied the servant. With great humility, he continued: "I do not need any wealth from the two of you. My only wish is that all your human servants may take their place next to you in the sky."

The Sun and the Moon agreed to this condition, and at once, they made every human servant of theirs into twinkling stars.

That is why there are so many stars in the sky. They are still mortal, however. When they get old, they drop to earth and die. Only the Sun and Moon can occupy the sky forever.   ❖

the apsara in the lake

Long, long ago, there was a lake. Even in the scorching heat of the hottest summer, the lake would be full of water, with crow feathers gently floating on the surface.

There had been no rains for months and months. Every forest was parched; every pond and every well had dried up. But in this lake, the water still rippled ceaselessly: *gethik, gethik....*

One day, the raja of that land, who had come on a visit, happened upon the lake. He could not believe his eyes, and just went round and round the lake staring at it. Finally he stopped under a bael tree, wondering: *Every other water source in this town has already dried out. How is it that this lake has not lost even a drop of its water?*

At that moment, he heard two jungle crows on top of the tree, cawing to each other. "Did you see the look on the raja's face? Actually it's not just him; even I'm surprised that the lake is still full," said one crow.

"Every full moon night, an apsara comes down from the heavens to bathe in this lake. It is for her that the lake stays full," replied the other.

The raja, overhearing this, had to have a look at the apsara. He could hardly wait for the next full moon.

The full moon night arrived—and so did the raja. He had bathed himself in rose water, decked himself in silk, gold and jewels, and hid in the thick undergrowth, waiting for the demi-goddess.

It was already midnight. Not even a leaf rustled. Only the moon shone, white, as if it had been polished clean with a cloth. The raja stood there, determined to wait until dawn, no matter what happened.

All of a sudden, all the peacocks and cuckoos in the forest began to trill. The doves joined the chorus. A fragrance of screw pine, jasmine and pichi swelled around him. Every tree, bush and vine seemed to dance to the music of the cool breeze. The ripples in the lake grew larger and beat against the shores. Then a bright red shaft of light appeared, descending slowly from the sky towards the earth!

Something began to emerge from the column of light... a woman, with a body so perfect it must have been sculpted. Along with her came the aroma of sandalwood and turmeric. She removed her top-cloth, dropped it to the ground and stepped straight into the lake. The stunned raja had not batted an eyelid. He stared, unblinkingly, not believing that such boundless beauty was possible.

Silently scheming, he took her cloth and went back into the bush holding it behind his back. The apsara came out after a long swim and looked for her missing top-cloth. Not finding it, in the blink of an eye she rose into the air and disappeared.

The sad raja returned at dawn. Everyone in the town saw him slowly trudge towards the palace, with his head bent and a strange top cloth in his hand.

They murmured to themselves, "Why is the raja walking so miserably?"

The next day, there was not a drop of water to be seen in the lake.

People from all the nearby towns gathered to look at the dry lake, shocked.

"What is this? Only last evening I drank from this lake, enough to fill my stomach," said one man.

"Last night my cows were thirsty and mooing. Just before midnight, I came with my son and took four pots of water," said another.

They went on and on like this. Finally, one man from the town said that he had seen the raja come from the lake at dawn. "Then it must have been the raja! He must have done some magic and cursed the lake to dry up," they grumbled. "No ordinary man could possibly dry up a full lake overnight. That must be the answer to this riddle; it must be the raja's fault!"

And so, the people from that town and all the other towns around it paraded to the palace, stood at the gates and shouted: "Sinner! Traitor! What are we poor people to do now? That lake quenched the thirst of this entire region. If you don't give us a proper answer, we and our children will die right here on this spot!" The whole crowd sat at the gates, stubborn and waiting.

The worried raja did his best to pacify the angry crowd and send them home. Not knowing how to solve the puzzle, he returned to the lake. It was now just a huge pit of caked rugged mud. He went down the crusted slope of the lake to the bed. On his way down, he thought he saw something glinting at the bottom. Going closer, he found that it was a bangle. He picked it up and came back to the bael tree.

One of the jungle crows which lived in the tree said, "This raja's luck has still not run out completely."

"Hmm, why do you say that?" asked the other.

"He has been fortunate enough to find the bangle. He can use it to get the water back."

"And how will he do that?"

"He must go to the top of the hill over there, with the bangle. There is a magic mango tree up there. On top of the tree is a fruit that has not ripened for twelve years. If he places the bangle at the base of the tree and meditates for forty days, that mango will ripen. Then every apsara will rush down from heaven for that fruit. But none of them will be able to touch it except the one that came to the lake to bathe. She will then share it with the others. The raja must use that opportunity to meet her."

Overhearing this, the raja left at once. The trek was difficult; it was a very, very steep climb up the hill. But the raja scrambled up tirelessly to find the tall, magic mango tree almost brushing the sky. He sat under the tree, placed the bangle on the ground and began to meditate, without taking in a drop of water or a morsel of food, for forty days.

On the twentieth day, the fruit began to ripen, and on the fortieth day it shone red, fully mature. Its scent wafted up through the forest and banged on the gates of heaven. At once, all the apsaras streamed out, shoving each other aside to get to the fruit. But no one was able to touch it.

Finally the apsara he was waiting for arrived. The moment the raja saw her, he rushed forward and threw himself at her feet and held out the top-cloth. He confessed to having stolen it. He told her that since she had dried up the lake, the people of the region were threatening to fast to death at his palace gates. He pleaded with her that the common people should not suffer for his mistake.

"I forgive you for your stupid act. Your people should not suffer," said the apsara. "Go down to the bed of the lake and burn sandal-wood for a yagna. Call every person in the land and feed them. Then go fetch a pot of water from the Ganga. Find among your people a woman who has lived honourably with her thali, true to her husband, who has given birth to children and seen her grandchildren flourish. Make her pour the pot of holy water into the lake. It will immediately fill up, and never dry out again."

"I shall follow all your instructions. Will you come and bathe there again, once it is full?" begged the raja.

"That cannot happen. But I will ask the other apsaras to fill the lake with lotuses to beautify it forever," said the apsara.

The raja returned to his land and did everything the apsara had told him to do. The lake became full once again. All the peacocks and cuckoos in the forest began to trill once again. The doves joined the chorus. The fragrance of screw pine, jasmine and pichi swelled around him. Every tree, bush, and vine seemed to dance to the music of the cool breeze. The ripples in the lake grew larger and beat against the shores. Then a bright red shaft of light appeared, descending slowly from the sky towards the earth! The lake filled with lotuses in full bloom.

The people were happy once again. ❖

rajas & ranis

the first face of the day

There was once a raja who was a strong believer in omens. He was convinced that the first face he happened upon, on waking, would decide the course of the day for him. If the face were that of a good person, then the day would be pleasant. If it were the face of a bad person, then the day would not be worth experiencing at all.

On waking up, the raja would open the window next to his bed. His eyes would fall on whoever was there on the palace road below his window. The people of the town, unfortunately, were also believers. They thought that if the first face they glimpsed was a royal face, it would bring them luck. So the palace road was always full of people down on their luck.

One morning, the raja had woken up, but was too lazy to get out of bed. He tossed and he turned. For some strange reason, he was feeling low. Something was irritating him.

Finally, he sat up on the bed, swung open the window and peeked out. There was not a soul on the palace road except a leper dressed in dirty rags. *Chee, is this the face I have to look at, first thing in the morning?* thought the raja. At that moment, the leper too looked up and saw the raja.

The raja hated the sight of him, yes. And it irked him even more that the leper had dared to look at him. The raja pulled back his head and shut the window. In his haste, he banged the shutters on his fingers.

Ouch! I knew this would happen. It's all because of that wretch! This day can only get worse. So many of the townsfolk must have seen him; everyone's day will be ruined. Imagining more and more misfortunes, he called for his minister.

"Catch that filthy leper. Take him to the palace courtyard and have his head chopped off," he ordered.

At the palace courtyard, the leper was read out his punishment and asked about his last and final wish. (It was a general rule of most states to grant any last wish of a prisoner before execution.)

"Before I die, I want to see the raja once and ask one question," said the leper.

The raja was informed. *Poor soul! It is indeed my duty as a raja to satisfy his last wish,* he thought.

At the courtyard, he asked the leper, "What do you want?"

The leper's hands and feet were bound. So he bowed down his head in respect to the raja and said, "I, too, am convinced that the first face I glimpse upon waking will decide the course of the day for me. This morning, the first face I saw was yours. You, who saw me first, had your fingers banged by the window shutters. But I—a poor, meager leper—who saw you first, am going to die!

"If the face is that of a good person, then the day will be pleasant. If it is the face of a bad person, then the day will not be worth experiencing at all. All I want now is an opinion from you, oh Raja: which of the two of us is the bad one?"

The raja bent his head in shame and ordered the leper to be released.   ❖

the raja's relatives

Once there was a man whose family had come from North India. Due to his gallant heroism, he actually managed to become the raja of a kingdom in the South. After many months, he learned that some cousins of his were living in a remote village within the boundary of his kingdom. So he sent an emissary to the village to ask his cousins to come and meet him.

The cousins in the village assembled to discuss the invitation. After a long debate, they decided not to go. *Why should we go and meet him? After all, he is one of us.*

When the raja came to know that his cousins were acting strange and avoiding meeting him, he decided to go to the village himself.

His cousins heard that he was coming—riding atop an elephant! Frantically, they wondered what to do. *He's one of us, one of our own clan. If he's coming on an elephant, we can't welcome him from the ground. Hello, here's an idea: let's stand on our roofs and welcome him from there,* they decided.

So they brought out their ladders, climbed up on top of their roofs and stood there, arms akimbo, waiting.

When the raja arrived, he was surprised to see the men standing on top of their houses. He inquired as to who they were, and learned that they were the very cousins he had come all this way to see. Controlling his laughter, he jumped down from his elephant.

Look at him, showing off. As if only he can jump down from a great height! Does he think we are weaklings? scoffed the cousins, and promptly leapt down from their roofs. There were bruises, and even some serious wounds; still, they bit back their tears and stood strong and erect.

What kind of fools are these? thought the raja. *Can't they be proud that one of their clan has made it as king? They're so jealous that they're just standing there like stumps.*

Only after the raja took the first steps forward to greet them did the cousins relax their stance. After a short stay, the raja invited them to his palace. The cousins agreed and fixed a date for the visit, after which the raja left.

On the day the cousins came to the palace, the raja showed them around. They came to the kitchen, which had a very low doorway, and the raja entered first, bending his head. The cousins stood outside. Unwilling to bow down to the raja, they turned their backs to him and walked in backwards through the doorway.

At dinner, the raja had a royal feast served for the cousins on fresh banana leaves. Now, it is a sign of respect for a host to clean up his guests' leaf-plates after a meal. But the cousins weren't sure if the raja would be cleaning up himself, or if he would have a servant do it, which would be an insult to them. So after the meal, they ate up their leaves as well.

In a final bid to get his cousins to show some respect, the raja decided not to give them the soft beds he had ordered for earlier. Instead he gave them rolled straw mats. Not wanting to bend down before the raja to spread the mats on the floor, the silly cousins opened the mats out behind their backs and fell backwards onto the floor.

These fools are so proud that one day they'll die of it, thought the raja, and cut off all ties with them.   ❖

the chain of droplets

Once upon a time, there lived a raja who loved his daughter dearly.

Since walking on the ground could hurt her dainty feet, and walking on the floor could hurt her pretty toes, he carried her in his eyes and his heart! Whatever she wanted, he fetched. If it did not exist, then he had it created for her.

The princess was aware of the depth of her father's love, and made good use of it too. When she could not have a thing, she would fling herself on the ground, roll over, and throw a royal tantrum until the raja gathered his forces and got her what she wanted.

One day, she went with her friends to a hilltop temple. A huge army of soldiers went along to guard her. On the way, they passed a waterfall—a huge waterfall that cascaded from a shelf of rock, broke into five streams and fanned down, scattering pearls of water along the way.

The princess longed to bathe in the sparkling water. She sent the soldiers away and jumped in with her friends. While frolicking under the falls, she noticed the shower of water droplets strewn from above.

How beautiful it would be if these droplets could be strung into a long chain! she thought, amazed.

Once possessed by this idea, she forgot all about bathing. She gathered the soldiers and her friends and returned to the palace at once. As she entered, she announced to the raja, "Appa, I want a long chain of water droplets. Now!"

The raja panicked. *What foolish demand is this? Has anyone ever heard of a chain of water droplets? Still, my darling daughter wants it. How can I refuse her?*

He called for the goldsmith and asked for a long chain of water droplets, strung in gold. The goldsmith fell at the raja's feet.

"Oh Raja, you may as well go ahead and chop off my head right now. I can never do what you want. I have never even heard of such a chain. Please spare me...!" he begged.

The enraged raja snapped, "I don't care what you have to do. If you cannot make the chain, then find me a goldsmith who will.

My daughter has asked for one. I have never refused her anything until this day. If you make me this chain, then I shall give you half my kingdom. Otherwise, you will be thrown into a pot of boiling oil. That's it. You may go."

The goldsmith flung himself on the floor, flailed at his stomach and mouth, wailed aloud, returned home and cried to his wife, "Adiye, forget about making dinner. We are soon going to be stewed in boiling oil. Find me a rope. I'd rather hang myself than be cooked."

"Surely there are other goldsmiths in town who can do what you cannot," said the wife.

"Are you nuts, woman? Have you ever heard of a chain made out of water droplets? Even the best goldsmiths are going to die in the raja's oil pot. Why should I be responsible for so many deaths? I may as well die before all that. Hurry, fetch me a rope."

"What will I do once you are gone?" demanded the wife. "I'll get a rope for myself too, and die with you. But let's wait till our son returns tonight. We'll say goodbye to him, and then die."

They sat on the doorstep, with thick rope nooses looped around their necks and their heads in their palms. When the son saw them like this, he wanted to know what had happened. What he heard made him roll on the floor laughing.

"What is this, son? There is a sword hanging over my head, and you find that funny?" asked the dejected father.

"The sword will drop only if you cannot make the chain," said the son. "You go tell the raja that I shall come and make it for the princess tomorrow."

The next day, the son arrived at the palace. "Oh Raja, I shall make the chain with water droplets," he told the raja. "I need your daughter's help though." The princess eagerly agreed to help.

The son took her, along with the entire retinue of soldiers, back to the waterfall. There, he sat on a rock beside the cascade, took out a long string, and threaded a needle. "Princess, will you please gather the water droplets, and hand them to me one-by-one, so that I can string them?"

The royal entourage stood by silent, feeling silly.   ❖

garden flowers

The raja had come to the forest on a tiger hunt. He tied a calf to the trunk of a tall tree as bait, and climbed up the tree to wait for a tiger. He waited for a long time, but no tiger came.

A tribal woman with a bundle of firewood was passing under the tree, when she suddenly went into labour pains. She dropped her bundle and crawled into the bushes, writhing from the cramps. After a little while, she had her child. She bit off the umbilical cord and tied the end with a string from her sari. Then, she walked to a stream close by, cleaned herself and the baby, picked up the bundle and left, carrying both the firewood and the child.

The raja, hiding in the tree, watched the entire episode. *Is delivering a child such a simple matter? Then why do my ranis make such a fuss? It must be a lot of play-acting!* he decided.

Back at the palace, he dismissed the midwife who was to attend on his pregnant ranis. He also ordered that all the medication prescribed to them should be stopped.

The worried ranis appealed to the chief minister for help.

The chief minister was well aware of his raja's stubbornness. He knew he would need a sound argument to convince the raja of his folly.

Days passed. One day, on his evening stroll, the raja saw that the plants in his royal garden were dying. He called for the gardener.

"Why are the plants dying?"

"The chief minister's order, oh Raja," said the gardener. "The plants are not to be watered any more."

"What nonsense! Bring the chief minister here at once!"

When the chief minister came, he said casually, "Yes Raja, I gave that order."

"Why?" demanded the raja.

"Why should we keep watering these plants? There are millions of plants and trees in the forest and mountains. Does anyone specially water them? Don't they grow perfectly well on their own?"

"I agree with you, minister. However, the plants in the forest are wild plants. They depend only on rain and groundwater. My garden is not the same. It takes careful maintenance for these plants to survive. Just look at them!" said the raja.

"I am sure the raja is right," agreed the minister in a quiet voice. "But then, wouldn't you agree that that tribal woman you saw is like a wild plant or tree, while your ranis are like these garden flowers? Shouldn't your ranis be maintained in luxury for them to be happy?"

"Hmm, so that was your game plan, was it?" grinned the raja, with new clarity. ❖

the rani with the famous hair

There was a raja who sent ministers all over the world to find a woman for him to marry. But every woman that was referred to him, he found some vague reason to refuse. All those commissioned to find him a wife were convinced that he was never going to wed and they would never have a rani.

One day, a man arrived at the palace in a palanquin, wanting to meet the raja.

"I am a stranger in this town, oh Raja," he said. "I need a safe place to stay for two days."

"How many of you are here?" asked the raja.

"I am here with my daughter and four of her maids."

"You don't have a servant of your own and yet your daughter has four for herself?" asked the raja, surprised. "Do they do any work, or they're just for her to gossip with?"

"You should see them for yourself," said the man.

The raja lent them the royal guesthouse. The next morning, he went to see for himself what kept the four maids occupied. There, the woman had let her hair loose out of the third floor window. It rolled down like a dark waterfall to the ground below. The four maids removed the tangles in it and rolled it up one storey at a time. Finally, on the third floor, they styled it on top of her head and decorated it with flowers and jewels.

That hair needs more than four maids. Eight would be more like it, thought the raja. He fell hard for her beauty and wanted to marry her. The father agreed and left behind the maids as a part of the dowry.

After the wedding, the raja was very restless, for there always seemed to be a crowd of people around his wife. Not just the four maids, who were constantly cleaning and dressing her hair; people came from all over to admire it. There was an endless stream of traffic. He had no private time with his wife.

Everyone seems keen on admiring her hair. The maids are either combing it or drying it. I am the raja of this land, and I have only two servants. Why should she have four maids just to do her hair? If ever I am going to have a life with this woman, it can happen only if I chop off her hair. Then I can send those maids off, he decided.

The rani wept. The entire kingdom appealed against such a drastic move. But the raja's anger would not abate. Their imploration only made him more determined. Now he wanted to get rid of his wife completely!

So, when she was asleep, he gave her a sleeping powder and told his two servants to abandon her in the forest. Unbeknownst to him, she was forty days pregnant at the time.

In the forest, the rani sobbed, sighed, and bitterly cried. She wound her hair around her neck and the other end onto a branch of a tree and attempted to hang herself. But the crows, sparrows, deer, monkeys and peacocks all stopped her, saying, "You should not die. You are now carrying a child. Don't worry, we will help you raise it. Instead, why don't you spread your hair all over the branches of this tree. We will build our nests in it."

She agreed, and spread her hair around the thick branches. Birds of every colour built their nests in it. They vied with each other to bring her exotic, tasty fruits. She too became a part of the paradise of birds and beasts. After a while, she bore a son, as beautiful as the white moon in the sky. All the creatures of the forest lent a hand in raising the boy. They taught him to tussle, swim and climb trees.

Back in the kingdom, the people were angry with the raja for the mysterious disappearance of the rani. They began blaming him openly. "That sinner! What a woman his wife was! After one look at her hair, how could anyone think of chasing her off? He searched the whole world for a bride. When he finally found one, he could not keep her happy. God knows what he did to that beautiful woman! Today he claims she is lost. He must have done something really awful for her to have run off like that."

The raja was aware of all the hatred around him. He knew that neither the rajas of the neighbouring kingdoms nor his own people wanted anything to do with him. No one cared for him anymore. He became deeply depressed. He stopped dealing with state affairs, and would just stare vacantly at the ceiling all the time.

One of the raja's ministers thought this was an opportune moment to impeach the raja and become the ruler in his stead. So, he declared the raja insane, and had him imprisoned.

The birds brought this news to the rani in the forest. Her son wanted to leave immediately to free his father. However, he was just a young lad. So, the birds that nested in her hair and all the beasts of the forest offered to go along. The army of creatures set off towards the kingdom along with the son.

When he saw the strange army, the minister was terrified. *I can fight off any human. But how will I be able to wage war against wild beasts from the forest?* He fled the country overnight, without informing anyone.

The son and his army arrived, freed the father, and told him about the rani in the forest. The repentant raja rushed off to the woods to meet his wife. He fell at her feet and begged for her pardon. The rani, appeased, wanted to return to the palace with her son. But the birds in her hair pleaded, "It was the dense forest of your hair that protected us for so long. What do we do now?"

"Don't cry, please," said the rani. "This hair, which has caused me so much pain, has at least been of great service to you. I do not need it anymore. So I shall leave it behind." With that, she chopped off her hair and went back with her husband and son. ❖

the dream tree

The Raja of Azhagapuri had four sons, of which the youngest was a very good and intelligent boy. One night the raja had a dream in which he saw a strange tree. The roots of the tree were made of gold, the trunk of silver, and the leaves and flowers were made of pearls and corals. When he woke up, the raja called for his four sons and sent them out to find the dream tree.

The four sons travelled through many jungles. In one forest, at sunset, they decided to rest for the night. They climbed up a tree, and the three elder brothers fell asleep at once.

But the youngest brother was not sleepy. He began inspecting the area. Near the tree there was an old dry well. At midnight, he spied a cobra slithering out of the well. The snake spat out a bright ruby, and went foraging for food in the ruby's bright light. The youngest brother climbed down the tree, cut off the cobra's head, and tucked the ruby in his waistband. Then he woke up his elder brothers.

"Anna, I am going down this well. You tie a rope around my waist and slowly lower me down. When I want to come up, I shall tug the rope twice. Then the three of you haul me up."

The three elder brothers tied a thick rope around the youngest one's waist and lowered him down the old well. There at the bottom he saw a huge, long tunnel and walked into it. He passed through a silver door, a golden door, a pearl door, and a coral door. In each chamber were four princesses, sleeping on beds made of gold, silver, pearl and coral. He woke the four women.

"Dear ladies, fear not. I have slain the cobra who held you captive, and I shall now rescue the four of you."

"Why did you come here in the first place?" asked the princesses.

The prince told them about his father's dream and asked, "Do you know where I can find that tree?"

"We do. However, you have to perform a brave act to see it yourself. Lay the four of us on the ground, one on top of the other. Then, chop off our heads with a single stroke."

"Once I do so, how will I bring you back to life?" asked the prince.

"All you have to do is to rejoin our heads to our bodies, and shine the beam of the ruby's light on our necks. Then we will come back to life," replied the first princess.

The prince then piled the four women one on top of the other and chopped of their heads in one stroke. The heads flew far from the bodies. The bodies stood upright, climbed on top of one another, and changed into the strange tree that had appeared in the raja's dream.

It had roots of gold, a trunk of silver, and leaves and flowers made of pearls and corals. When the prince shone the beam of the ruby's light on the tree, it became the four women's bodies again. As instructed, he brought them back to life. Then he took them out to the dangling rope, tied them to it and tugged it twice.

The three brothers up above began pulling in the rope. Instead of their brother, what emerged from the well were four beautiful women! When the last one had climbed out, the eldest brother asked, "Is there anyone left?"

"Yes, your youngest brother," replied the fourth woman.

The eldest promptly threw a look at the other brothers, turned around and cut the rope.

If the youngest one comes out alive, he might marry all four women, thought the three brothers. They quickly took the princesses back to the palace.

The youngest one, stuck in the well, scanned the area with the help of the ruby's glow. He saw a flight of stairs going up the side. He climbed up those stairs and—again using the power of the magic ruby—flew back to the palace before the others. There he related the events to the Raja of Azhagapuri.

The three elder brothers reached the town limits. The raja's army was ready waiting to arrest them and they were put to death instantly. The youngest prince married all four women and they lived happily ever after.   ❖

the hen-pecked raja

"Oh all right, you may sit," the rani would say, and the raja would plonk down in his seat. "I don't want to hear a peep from you," she would say. The raja would twist himself up into an 8 and cover his mouth with his palm. After that, he'd open his mouth only to eat.

That raja had been wondering something for a very long time: *Is it only me, or is every man in my kingdom so hen-pecked? Do they too dance to every call of their woman?* He felt he had to solve this puzzle.

He called for his minister, who arrived very late.

"Why are you late?" asked the raja.

"I was going to come at once, oh Raja," replied the minister. "But my wife stopped me because of a bad omen."

"That's right! Never set off if the omens are not good. Your wife was right," said the raja. He followed this with an order. "Ask every married man to assemble in front of the palace tomorrow, early morning."

The minister had a messenger-drummer announce the raja's order throughout the kingdom.

Not wanting to disobey the raja, every married man, both young and old, assembled on the palace grounds the next morning. When the raja and the rani stepped onto the balcony, there was a loud, welcoming cheer. The crowd fell silent only when the raja raised his arm. His speech was loud and clear; they could hear every word.

"I have called you here to see how many of you obey your wives, and how many of you act on your own," said the raja. "Those of you who follow your wives' commands, step over to left. Those of you who think for yourselves, step to the right."

The entire pack scrambled to the left, except for one lone man.

The raja gaped at him with great respect. The rani, however, looked on smugly.

The raja, with a sigh, signaled the lone man to approach him, wishing he could give this brave, masculine lion half his kingdom. When the man came, the raja hugged him tight with pride and presented him with a bag of gold. The man stood, arms at his sides, not reaching out for the bag.

"Take the bag, man!"

"I am sorry, oh Raja," said the man, shaking his head. "I cannot. I will take it only if my wife tells me I can."

"What do you mean?" asked the puzzled raja. "Then why didn't you step over to the left?"

"Because my wife has told me never to follow the crowd!"

The rani lifted an eyebrow at the raja and gave a smirk. The raja could only grin sheepishly.   ❖

what's so funny?

A man was on his way to the woods one early morning to attend the call of nature, when he happened upon a golden pot. Hoping his run of bad luck was over, he picked it up and ran home. He hid the pot carefully. He did not say a word about this to anyone except his mother.

Once her son had left for work, the mother took out the pot and examined it carefully. *This ornate pot looks like it's from the palace. It must belong to none other than the raja. The smartest thing to do now is to return it to him. It's very wrong to covet the raja's property,* she decided. She took the pot over to the palace, told the raja how her son had found and hidden it, and gave it back.

The raja took the pot and sent her away. Then he ordered his guards to find the man, bury him in the ground up to his neck, and have him trampled by the court elephant.

So, the guards caught him, buried him up to his neck in the palace grounds, and brought out the court elephant. A huge crowd had gathered to witness the spectacle. Just as the elephant lifted its foot to stamp down on the man's head, the man spied a beautiful temple dancer in the crowd, and his organ hardened. The man burst out laughing.

The mahout atop the elephant was confused. "What's so funny?" he asked.

"I'm laughing at my stupid mind that revealed the secret to my mother, her stupid mind that returned the pot to the raja, his stupid mind that ordered me to be trampled to death, and finally at my mindless organ that is even now, at death's doorstep, throbbing with lust," said the man.

"There is no doubt, they are all the same," the mahout laughed, as the elephant smashed the man's head.   ❖

the brinjal

One day, the raja's brinjal fry was delicious. Even as the raja stuffed himself, he turned to his minister and said, "This is the tastiest dish I have ever had!"

"Of course, oh Raja," replied the minister. "The brinjal is indeed the best of all vegetables. That is why God has given it a crown on top of its head."

"Is that right?" asked the raja, amazed. "Then pass on this order to my kitchen. I must have brinjal served in every meal."

Consuming endless brinjal dishes three times a day eventually took its toll on the raja's taste buds and health—even though the food was prepared in the royal kitchen. Finally, one day at lunch, he snapped.

"Chee! I cannot stand one more brinjal. It's awful!" he cried.

"Of course, oh Raja," replied the same minister. "The brinjal is indeed the worst of all vegetables. That is why God has driven a nail into its head!"   ❖

idiot's canal and kandiya canal

Many, many years back, before the country became independent, in Nellai District, there was a plan to build a canal to bring the water from the Chithaaru River from Naagalkulam to Aalangkulam, via Pulangkulam, for irrigation. A group of well-educated engineers came from the city to do an initial survey. None of the village folk went near these men, who were dressed in neatly pressed, creased pants and spoke in loud *dhas-bhus* English. The locals stood far off in small groups and whispered amongst themselves about the new canal. Some of the village folk did not believe such a canal would work. "Why not?" demanded the young and the bold. "Who do you think those men are? It's not for nothing that they went to foreign countries and earned so many degrees. It's not for nothing that they come in their big loud jeeps, and sit in them with their legs crossed, surveying our land. You're just jealous."

One old man put his hand on his brow, gazed into the distance and said, "Do these idiots really expect the water to climb *upwards?*"

"Get lost, old man," laughed the villagers. "Wait and see the wonder."

The canal was completed. A huge celebration was arranged. Men from far-off cities travelled down for the occasion. Rose garlands were brought in. The applause tore into the air like tamarind fruits falling off a tree in a heavy gust of breeze. The canal locks were opened...

...and not a single drop of water came from Naagalkulam.

"That's alright, just wait until the first monsoon shower," said the engineers. Once the city folks left, the villagers sat waiting. The first shower came and went. The Southwest monsoon came and went. The Northeast monsoon came and went. The Southwest monsoon came again. This time the entire area was under water, except the canal, which was still bone dry. Several generations of villagers stood on the banks of the arid canal, threw off their clothes, and laughed their hearts out.

Now the pre-independence government had given this canal a name, but no one in the area remembers what it is. They only know the dry canal by the name *Idiots' Canal*. It's not for nothing that the proverb says "The common man's verdict is God's verdict!"

The following story, about how Kandiya Canal got its name, is in a similar vein.

The Raja of Kandiya had a daughter who was very beautiful—so beautiful that even a girl would instantly fall in love with her.

Since it was not easy to find a perfect match for her in the nearby lands, the raja brought in portraits of kings and princes from all the eight directions. He showed her all the pictures and asked her, "So, which of these do you want as your husband?" But she did not like any of them. The raja was worried.

One day, she saw a portrait of the Prince of Singampatti. She lost her heart at the first glance. *What a trim moustache! What eyes! They seem to be smiling into mine.* She could not take her eyes off the handsome face.

"If I am to marry, I will wed only a hero like him," she declared.

The Raja of Kandiya sent this message across to the Raja of Singampatti. That raja could not believe his ears. "How dare he?" he roared. "After all he is not a raja of the same status as me. He is much, much below me. How dare he want my son as his son-in-law?"

The messenger repeated every word to the Raja of Kandiya. The Kandiya Raja was enraged. "Is that what he said, that motherfucker?" said he. "To save my honour, I must crush his kingdom to dust!"

For all the raja's pride, Singampatti was but a small zamin. It had only a tiny army to protect its borders, unlike the Kandiya Empire, which was huge.

The Kandiya Raja called his general and ordered, "You take the army and demolish Singampatti, but see that no harm comes to the prince. Bring him back safely."

The Kandiya army was marching south with great fanfare. The Singampatti Raja had not expected such a huge assault. He got his meager force ready. He knew he was not going win over the Kandiya force, but at least he would face death with courage.

Nevertheless, losing the war was only a part of his worry. Once lost, the enemy's army would march into the land, capture every young virgin and despoil her. It was one thing to lose the war, or even die fighting. But one could not lose one's honour. That had to be prevented at all costs!

Therefore, before marching out into the battlefield, he arranged to protect his women. He asked every virgin in the zamin to gather in the palace, then climb up onto Papanasam Hill, and wait near Neelakanta Valley.

He then had a series of drums tied atop the trees, from the valley to the battlefield. If his army was losing in the war, the drums at the battlefield would be struck; the next drummer would hear them and start drumming. The chain of drumming would continue until the last drum sounded in the valley, and reached the ears of the virgins on the hilltop. Then the women were to leap off the cliff into the valley. If any of the virgins tried to escape this honour death, they were to be caught and thrown off the ledge.

The battle was raging at the foothills. It was not easy to say who was winning. Both sides displayed enormous courage and were fighting hard.

Then something strange happened. In one of the trees, a tiny monkey dropped a mango it was carrying onto one of the drums. *Dhoom* went the mango on the drum. Promptly the other drummers began to strike their drums, until the last drum in the valley beat very loud. "Oh, our raja has lost the war," wailed the virgins on the mountain. "We cannot wait a moment longer. We must protect our honour." One by one, they leapt off the mountain down into the valley below and died.

The news reached the Singampatti Raja in the battlefield. "Some great misfortune has befallen me. God is not by my side," cried the raja, and dropped dead. The moment the raja died, his army dropped their arms and surrendered.

Perhaps the gods were on the side of the Kandiya general. Whatever the case, the Prince of Singampatti was captured, locked and sealed in a carriage, and taken to Kandiya under heavy guard.

Locked inside the cage, the prince thought: *The virgins of my land died to save their honour, and here I am, a captive weakling! I do not want to live without honour, either.* He removed the diamond from his signet ring and swallowed it. His life departed from his body just as the carriage drew up at the Kandiya palace.

The general was saddened; just as the butter was foaming upwards, the milk pot had shattered! The women of Kandiya finally got to see only the corpse of the handsome prince. The beautiful princess came running out. She thought the same as the other women, *What beauty, what dignity! No one can say he is dead. He seems to be only in deep slumber.*

The Kandiya Raja took his daughter aside to find out what to do next.

"Appa, will you do what I ask for?" asked the princess. "Get me married to him, this very instant. I will not marry any other."

The people were shocked.

The dead prince was dressed up as a groom, and the princess as a radiant bride. An elderly man touched the garland to the prince's hand and then put it around the princess's neck. She, in turn, garlanded the dead prince. Then the elderly man touched the thali to the dead prince's hand, and tied it around the princess's neck.

The people watched the sight full of tears. *How can a woman willingly marry a dead man?* they wondered. The dead prince, still dressed as a groom, was placed on the funeral pyre. As the corpse caught fire and the flames rose to the sky, the princess jumped into it.

At this point, a rational listener might ask, "What kind of a woman is this? To get her wish, so many lives were sacrificed, and finally she kills herself. And then... what happens?"

The Raja of Kandiya thought long and hard. *So many warriors lost their lives in the battle, the Raja of Singampatti, his son, my daughter and all those virgins who jumped off the mountain... I have to do something to cleanse myself of all these unnecessary deaths.*

He consulted many elders. Finally, it was decided that a dam would be built over the river between the two lands. A canal would be dug from the valley and linked to every water source in the two kingdoms, so that no soul living there would ever suffer thirst again. The Raja of Kandiya had the plan executed immediately, and that is how Kandiya Canal came to be!   ❖

kodumpaavi raja

Kodumpaavi, the Raja of Kodumpavur, was a very brutal man. His tyrannical rule resulted in utter poverty throughout his kingdom. The people cursed their ruler; some even fled to other lands.

Seeing the weakness of the state, Patchi, the raja of the neighbouring land, marched towards Kodumpavur and defeated Kodumpaavi.

Frustrated at having lost the war, Kodumpaavi Raja withdrew to the forest with his wife. There in the woods was a lone Vanni tree, still lush and green in spite of the draught that had been plaguing the land. The secret behind this was a water-crow that gathered a few droplets of water from somewhere and sprinkled them on the tree every day.

One day, Shiva and Parvathi, during their celestial watch, happened to see the water-crow sprinkling water on the tree. Now, the Vanni tree is Shiva's favorite, so immediately Shiva and Parvathi appeared before the water-crow to grant it whatever boon it wished for. The water-crow wanted to be reborn as a human prince.

At exactly the same moment, the Kodumpaavi Raja was praying intensely to Lord Shiva for a son. As Shiva had to bless him as well, he granted a twin wish. He granted the water-crow's wish to be born as a prince, and a divine voice announced to the raja, "Your wife will be blessed with a special son. Name him Neermukam. In his tenth year, he will restore you to the throne."

A few months later, a son was born to Kodumpaavi's wife. They named him Neermukam.

When the son was ten years old, Patchi Raja came to the same forest for his annual hunt, along with his entourage.

Among Patchi Raja's provisions were sixteen pots of fresh cow's milk. While the entourage was asleep, Neermukam emptied the milk and stuffed the pots with poisonous snakes.

In the morning, Patchi Raja tried to pour some milk from one of the pots. Instead, a snake slithered out and bit him. The raja died, foaming at the mouth.

What happened next? What else! The Kodumpaavi Raja changed his name, but not his nature, and regained his throne. ❖

Ki. Ra.: This was told by Dhanamma, a sixty-three-year-old Yadava Naidu woman. Surprisingly, it lacks many of the usual characteristics of a folktale. In the first place, the characters in a folktale are rarely given names. A folktale would usually begin: "Once upon a time, there was a raja," not "Kodumpaavi, the Raja of Kodumpavur, was a very brutal man."

the kurathi rani

The Prince of Rajasimhamandram wanted to marry the most beautiful woman in the world. He travelled to several lands in search of his bride. Once, while journeying through a forest, he met an ascetic, to whom he told his wish.

"Rajasimha, fear not. Your wish will be granted," said the ascetic. "There is a lone mango tree in this forest which bears only a single fruit. Pluck that mango and hold it up to the sun. When the fruit is fully ripe, it will burst and out will come your bride. However, when you try to pluck the fruit, many voices will try to scare you off. You must remain brave."

The prince searched long for the mango tree, until he found it. There, he braved all those forces that tried to scare him with wails and moans and plucked the fruit. He held it up to the sun, the fruit burst open, and out came the most beautiful woman he had ever seen.

"Salutations, oh Prince! I am Maangani. I am here to marry you," said the woman.

The happy prince told Maangani to wait under the tree until he brought around his horse. After the prince left, a hill tribeswoman, a Kurathi, passed by. She saw Maangani and stopped to hear her story. The Kurathi became mad with envy, quickly strangled Maangani, threw her body into the pond and dressed herself in Maangani's clothes and jewels. When the prince returned, he mistook the Kurathi for Maangani and took her away on his horse.

As they passed the pond, the Kurathi saw that Maangani's body had changed into a beautiful lotus. She said to the prince, "Athaan, please get me that lotus."

The Kurathi began living in the palace as a princess. One day she had her hair done up. Then she put the lotus in her hair, and admired herself in the mirror. The lotus spoke in Maangani's voice: "Chee, chee, you Kurathi, how dare you wear me on your hair!" Recognizing the voice, the Kurathi snatched the lotus, crushed it and flung it out the window. On touching the ground, it instantly changed into a mango tree and bore a single fruit.

The gardener's wife, while watering the plants, saw the mango and took it home. At lunchtime, when she sat down to cut the mango, she heard Maangani's voice say, "Amma, please cut me gently."

The surprised woman did so and out came Maangani, with her long hair caressing the floor.

"Amma," she said, "if you bring me up as your daughter, I will grant your every wish." The gardener's wife agreed.

One day, when the gardener's wife was bragging about her daughter's long hair to a friend, the Kurathi rani overheard and wanted to know the daughter's secret.

"It's not difficult, Amma, for your rani to have long hair like mine," Maangani told her mother. "Ask her to tonsure her head and smear it with rice gruel. Then ask her to sleep with her head stuck inside a rat burrow. Every time the rat chomps her head, the hair will grow a foot."

The gardener's wife repeated this to the Kurathi who did exactly what she was told. But instead of her hair growing, the rats chomped on her head so hard that she died. Maangani told the prince what had happened. The happy prince married Maangani and they lived happily ever after.   ❖

P.K.C.: A Kurathi is a tribal person from the Western Ghats. In ancient Tamil epics like *Silapathikaaram* or *Kutraala Kuravanji*, Kurathis are not demonized as they are in this tale; women in the villages in the foothills eagerly wait for the Kurathi women to come down from the mountains to sell them exotic beaded necklaces and make predictions with cowry shells.

In colonial times, any group that could not be neatly classified into the five varnams was listed as a "Criminal Tribe" – Kurathis were one such group. It was not until 1952 that the tribe was denotified. As is apparent from this tale, vicious prejudice against these people continues.

the lost necklace

Once there was a rani, who removed her jewels, placed them on the banks, and was bathing in the pond. A monkey ran off with her necklace. The rani sent her servants to catch the monkey, but they could not. The necklace was an heirloom and she knew that the raja would be mad that she had lost it.

In the palace, she confessed the loss to the minister.

"Do not worry, oh Rani," said the minister. "All you have to do is tell a tiny lie and you will be spared. Tell the raja that the guard of your chamber stole the necklace. I'll even arrange a false witness."

The rani did as the minister advised. The raja threw the poor guard in the prison and had him tortured.

Months later, the raja was touring his kingdom in disguise, when he overheard two people talking.

"That poor guard," said one man. "That innocent man is being tortured on false charges. Meanwhile, the man who found the necklace is living in luxury."

The raja sent out his spies, who discovered the man who had actually found the necklace and sold it. When the raja heard that the man had got the necklace from a monkey, he called the minister and the rani and asked them once more, "How was the necklace lost?" But they both stuck to their story about the guard.

What happened next? What else! Turning a deaf ear to the rani's pleas of love, the raja chucked his lying wife into a pot of boiling oil, and threw the minister in prison for the rest of his life.   ❖

Ki. Ra.: Teaching the royalty the proper administration of justice is an age-old theme in Tamil culture. Beginning from the Sangam age, right up through the Colonial era, there are stories on the subject of justice. In spite of such moral tales, there have been several instances where kings fail to investigate a case completely and end up punishing the innocent, like King Pandian in the epic *Silapathikaaram*.

the minister and the barber

Once upon a time, there was a raja who had a very intelligent minister. The raja placed great trust in the minister and did whatever he advised. The raja also had a trusted barber who, as he shaved the raja every morning, passed on information on the happenings in town. The barber had a secret yearning to have the minister thrown out, and was ready to go to any lengths to accomplish this.

One day, while shaving the raja, the barber said, "Oh Raja, your ancestors have long been dead. But did you ever try to find out if they wanted anything? You know, a soul that has an unfulfilled want will never rest in peace."

"You're right," said the raja. "But how can I find out if they want anything?"

"Oh Raja, your ancestors were all great men," replied the barber. "Certainly they will all have gone to heaven. Why don't you send your minister to heaven to find out if there's anything they need up there?"

The raja was convinced. At once, he sent for the minister.

"Minister, leave to heaven at the earliest. Speak to all my forefathers and see if they need anything," he ordered.

The minister realized that this must be a plot by the barber to get rid of him. He asked for three days to prepare for the journey. Then he called his trusted mason and had him make a stone slab, under which he had a tunnel built to the woods nearby.

On the third day, the minister went into his tomb with great aplomb. He asked the raja to lay the grave slab and seal it. Then he took the tunnel and went deep into the woods. He stayed there for many days, until his face was covered with a rugged, wild beard.

After several months, he returned. The raja welcomed the strange bearded man, not recognizing him as the minister.

"Who are you, stranger?" asked the raja.

"Don't you recognize me, oh Raja?" asked the man. "I am your minister. You sent me to heaven to find out if your ancestors wanted anything. They are fine there, Raja. However, there is no barber in heaven. Just look at my face! Your forefathers, too, have not had their hair or beards trimmed for all these years. They need a barber at once."

"Is that right?" exclaimed the raja. "I shall send my royal barber there immediately."   ❖

the prince with thirty-five legs

"Do you know the story about the princess who insisted that she would only marry a man with thirty-five legs?" asked Thatha.

"Oh, please tell us!" we cried.

Once upon a time, there was a princess who refused to marry any man unless he arrived on thirty-five legs.

"What kind of a demand is that, thirty-five legs?"

"That's just what she said! And she said it had to be exactly thirty-five, not thirty-four or thirty-six."

Every nobleman in the kingdom, and in the fifty-six kingdoms around it, was flummoxed by this demand.

"What? Would anyone with thirty-five legs even resemble a human? He'd be more like a demon or bootham! Maybe she's a bootham herself. I definitely don't need her as my wife," they decided, and kept away from her.

The father, worried that his daughter would be left unmarried, made an announcement. "The suitor need not be from a royal family. The first man who arrives on thirty-five legs will be married to my daughter!"

What commoner doesn't dream of marrying a princess? But dreaming wasn't enough!

"This must be some kind of puzzle. She can't mean thirty-five literal human legs," the people mused. "Even if a man comes on a horse, his legs and the horse's legs together make only six legs," said some. "Let's say he arrives in a carriage drawn by two horses. Even then it makes only five pairs of legs in all," said others.

In the same kingdom there was a young man who decided he must have this princess as his wife. He arrived on a bullock cart at the palace.

"I've come on my thirty-five legs to marry the princess," he told the guards.

The raja rushed out with the minister.

"Show me your thirty-five legs," demanded the minister.

"Check for yourself," challenged the young man.

The minister could see the man's two legs and the four pairs of legs of the two animals drawing his cart. However, the other twenty-five legs were nowhere to be seen.

"Help," pleaded the perplexed minister.

"How many legs have you counted so far?" asked the young man.

"Ten," replied the minister.

"Did you count the spokes on the two wheels?"

Ah, the spokes! Two wheels on the bullock cart, twelve on each wheel, and twenty-four in all! But even then, the minister could only count thirty-four legs.

"You are still short by one leg," he said.

"Look carefully and you will find it," replied the young man.

The princess, watching the scene from the balcony, whispered to her maid, "Is the minister blind? Can't he see that the thirty-fifth leg is in the cart?"

The minister was at a loss.

"You counted everything, but missed the yoke. That is the thirty-fifth leg!" cried the young man.

"And so, the princess married the young man. He was not just lucky, but clever too! Naturally, all the other men in the kingdom and the fifty-six kingdoms around it were green with envy," concluded Thatha. ❖

the lecherous raja

In a certain town there was a Chettiyar, a very good man who kept to himself and never interfered in anyone else's business. One day his son came home with a wife, a stunning woman from the next village.

When the Chettiyar saw his beautiful daughter-in-law, he was shattered, for he knew the raja of his town was a horrible, lecherous man. He would lust after just about anything, even a stone pillar dressed in a sari. He would demand that whichever woman he fancied come to his palace, and if she refused, he'd abduct her anyway.

The Chettiyar's son had to go out of town on business for a few months. The Chettiyar began worrying about how to safeguard his daughter-in-law from the roving eyes of the raja. The woman had no clue about what was bothering the old man.

Every window in the house was kept shut. "Don't keep the front door open," he would say. "Don't come out of the house. Stay inside." He went on and on like this, until one day, very frustrated, she confronted him.

"What is the problem Maama? Have I done something wrong?" she asked.

"You are a young girl," said the Chettiyar. "You are very innocent. The raja of this town is a very lecherous man. If he as much as lays eyes on a woman, he'll carry her off like an eagle carrying away a baby chick."

The daughter-in-law burst out in loud laughter. "Is that all? You're scared about a stupid, amorous raja? It is only your fear that gives him so much courage. Let him just try and approach me. I'll chop off his little tail!"

This only multiplied the Chettiyar's fears. *What's wrong with this woman? This is the bravado of the very young. God only knows what will happen to her,* he fretted.

"Maama, I can read your thoughts from your expression," said the woman. "The raja can lust after me as much as he wants. Nevertheless, a man can't get very far without a woman's consent. An intelligent woman can battle almost anything and win. You stay calm."

The next day, the Chettiyar had to leave town on urgent business. Before leaving, he called the woman and told her, "Marumagale, I can't avoid this trip. I will try to be back before it gets too dark. Please be very careful until then."

Later in the day, the other women from the neighbourhood asked her, "We're going to the river for a bath. Do you want to join us?"

The thought of swimming in the cool river was irresistible. She accepted the invitation eagerly, hoping to be back before her father-in-law returned.

While the girls were engrossed in their water games, the raja was watching them from behind a bush. Of course, he did not miss the new beauty. *I don't think I've seen this one before!* he thought. He ordered his servant to follow the woman and find out where she lived.

That night, as the Chettiyar was getting into bed, a messenger from the palace arrived, asking him to come to the palace at once. Shocked, he asked the woman, "Marumagale, did you go out today?"

"Yes Maama. The neighbourhood girls were going to the river to bathe. They asked me to join. I couldn't resist the invitation. But I returned early," she said.

"Oh Marumagale, you have ruined everything. What will I do now?"

"What happened, Maama?"

"What did I tell you? I warned you so many times, but you paid no heed," he wept. "Those lewd eyes of the raja have surely fallen upon you. What will I say to my son when he returns? The raja has called for me now. I am sure I know what he wants..."

"Don't fear the worst, Maama. Whatever happens, we'll manage," she consoled him, and sent him off to the palace.

At the palace, the Chettiyar was given a royal welcome. Only he was not in a mood to enjoy anything. His heart was thumping hard— *gedhak, gedhak*. Finally, the raja asked him about the beautiful woman.

"She is my daughter-in-law, a very intelligent woman," replied the Chettiyar.

"Naturally, beauty is always followed by brains," said the raja.

"Please Raja, she is very innocent..." pleaded the Chettiyar.

"Fine. All she has to do is pass a test I will give her. Then I shall leave her alone," said the raja. "She must sow spinach on a rock and bring me those fresh greens after eight days."

"She will do it," promised the Chettiyar.

Outside the palace, the Chettiyar was shaken. *How does one plant spinach on rock? What can grow on a rock? Curse this raja! He is determined to have my poor daughter-in-law,* he lamented.

But when the woman heard about the raja's test, she scoffed. "Is that all? That's easy!"

She spread a thick layer of ash and cow dung over a rock. Then she sowed spinach seeds on it. In eight days, the greens had grown dense and lush. She plucked out a bunch, gave it to the Chettiyar and said, "Here, Maama. Give this to your raja."

When the raja heard about the trick the woman had played on him, he was amazed. *She is smart!* "She needs to take two more tests," he declared.

"Sure, tell me," said the now-more-confident Chettiyar.

"Here is the first test. After eight days, she must send me a whole pumpkin in a mud pot. Neither the pumpkin nor the pot should be damaged."

At home, the daughter-in-law asked the Chettiyar to fetch a new mud pot. She took it to the backyard and gently put a new young pumpkin, along with the creeper, into the pot. On the eighth day, the young squash had matured into a huge pumpkin, but it was safe inside the pot. She cut the vine at the mouth of the pot and sent it with her father-in-law to the palace. Though the raja was surprised, he gave the Chettiyar a brass jug and said, "Tell her to fill this jug with bull's milk and return it to me."

Back at home, weeping sorrowfully, the Chettiyar handed his daughter-in-law the jug.

"Stop worrying, Maama. I just have one request: please don't step out of this house for the next few days."

On the third day, a messenger came from the palace. "The raja wants to know why Chettiyar has not come to see him."

"I'm sorry," said the woman. "He can't come out of the house because he's menstruating."

"What?" squawked the messenger. "A man having his period!? Do I repeat this to the raja?"

"Certainly! After all, this is a magical town where bulls can give milk. Why can't a man menstruate? Go tell your raja what I just said. He will understand," replied the clever woman.   ❖

vittalabattar

Long, long ago, there lived a man named Vittalabattar, a total lazy bone, who hated to work. The only work he did all day was entering the house to eat and coming out to the thinnai to sleep.

Naturally, his wife found this very irritating. *Why is my husband like this? Doesn't every other man in this town go out to work? Why am I cursed with this lazy one?* she moaned to herself.

One day, she decided not to cook. Vittalabattar, dozing on the thinnai, was not aware of this. At lunchtime, he went in to eat.

But there wasn't anything in the pot for the ladle to scoop!

"Why is this pot empty? Where's my rice?" he demanded.

"If I keep serving you rice, you'll keep gobbling it. If you keep sleeping on the thinnai forever, where will the rice come from? Shouldn't you start acting like a man and find some work? Only if you bring in some money will you get any more food in this house," she declared.

Poor Vittalabattar! What could he do? He had been like this since childhood. His body was accustomed to idleness, but his brain was all the time ticking, even without his permission. As the saying goes, sloth breeds the most active mind. It is only when a person doesn't know how to use it that he gets into trouble.

Vittalabattar left his town and began wandering. He walked from town to town, eating free food served by some charitable souls and finding places to rest his head and sleep.

Somehow, though, it didn't seem right. So he returned home.

It was morning. His wife was working inside. Vittalabattar knew her daily routine. So, he sat on the thinnai and listened to what was happening inside.

This was her hour for making dosais. After a minute, he heard a *surrr* from inside the house. That meant she had just begun. He decided to count the number of dosais she was making. There would be a *surrr* when she poured the dosai, and another *surrr* when she flipped it over.

That was how he kept count. Two *surrr*s for each dosai! There were ten dosais in all.

The wife came out for some reason and saw her husband on the thinnai.

"When did you come?" she asked.

"Oh, just now," he replied. "I went to learn a craft, like you wanted me to."

"Really?" she exclaimed. "What did you learn?"

"I studied astrology!" he declared proudly.

Nothing great, she thought. *But still better than nothing at all. He has made some effort, at least.* He saw that she was silent.

"You think I'm lying?" he asked. "Okay, you were making dosais right now, weren't you?"

She laughed aloud. "I make dosais every day at this time. You don't need the help of astrology to tell me that."

"Yes dear wife, I know that," he said sarcastically. "But shall I tell you how many dosais you made?"

"Ah? So tell me then, how many?"

"Go in and count. You made ten dosais. If I'm wrong I'll chop off both my ears right now," he said.

She was truly surprised. She knew she had made ten dosais, not one more, not one less—exactly ten! Delighted, she came running into his arms. "Go bathe and come have the dosais while they are still hot," she said.

When Vittalabattar was bathing, the dhobi woman arrived to collect the dirty clothes. "Amma, so Aiya has come back, has he?" she asked, seeing that the wife looked very excited.

The wife, needing someone to share her happiness with, cried, "Yes, and guess what? He had gone out to learn astrology. He travelled to many far-off places to learn from real experts." She also told the dhobi woman about the dosai incident.

It was good fortune! The dhobi woman had been searching for an astrologer. It was almost as if she put her hand out and there it was, the magical herb to solve her problem.

"Amma, I am looking for someone to tell me where my donkey is," she said. "I looked all over the place yesterday, but I still haven't found it. Please, will you ask Aiya where my stupid donkey could be?"

Vittalabattar, who was coming out of his bath wiping his ears with a wet towel, heard the dhobi woman and remembered a proverb. "When a donkey goes missing, it will go to a ruined wall!" he said.

The dhobi woman rushed to a nearby ruined wall. There it was, her donkey, peacefully lying in the shade, munching on the green, lush grass!

Finding her favorite donkey convinced the dhobi woman that Vittalabattar was indeed the best astrologer in the area. She made it a point to tell everyone in the village.

There was a severe drought in the region. The rains had failed for three consecutive seasons, and the fields were almost drying up. The people just needed one good shower to revive their crops. When the village headman heard the news from the dhobi woman, he decided that Vittalabattar must have the solution. And so, the people of the village gathered at his doorstep.

"Will there be rain to save our crops?" Every man of repute in the village had assembled at Vittalabattar's house with the same question.

He had no clue what to reply. *This is serious! I'm in over my head,* he lamented. *It's one thing to trick my wife and the dhobi woman. But the village elders? Who knows when it will rain or when a child will be born? Only God knows these things. What do I tell them? If I promise rains, and there are none, they will have my head instead! Chee, what began as a joke looks to have become my death knell!*

Forgetting the audience in front of him, he mumbled to himself, "I must vacate this town by tomorrow night."

The crowd saw him mouthing the words "tomorrow night" and were satisfied that that was the prediction. They hailed Vittalabattar's glory and left happy.

Vittalabattar was now truly petrified. He dragged his wife in and began packing his belongings.

When the villagers saw that Vittalabattar was busy packing, they too decided to follow suit. No sooner had the entire village packed their things than the sky broke loose and it began to rain. It rained continuously for several days and several nights. The village was flooded; water seeped into all the homes. The villagers were happy that they had packed up all their important things because of Vittalabattar. The crops were saved, and a bountiful harvest was ensured.

Finally, by God's grace, it stopped raining. At once, the villagers gathered again at Vittalabattar's house. This time it was not only to thank him for the rains, but also for saving their belongings.

Eventually, Vittalabattar's fame reached the ears of the raja.

The raja wanted to meet Vittalabattar. If he was as great as people said, the raja planned to appoint him as the court astrologer.

Now this raja was a good raja, but extremely short tempered. He insisted on correct predictions. If any prediction proved wrong, he would chop off the astrologer's nose, pluck out his eyes, and abandon him deep in the forest. So every astrologer dreaded being appointed to the raja's court.

Just as the raja decided to send for Vittalabattar, news came from his private chamber. The rani had taken off all her jewels to bathe. When she returned, all the jewels were there except for her diamond nose stud. She had searched but could not find it. She knew the thief must still be on the palace premises, but didn't know who it could be.

When the raja heard this, he was so angry that the tip of his royal nose quivered. "Go!" he bellowed. "Fetch Vittalabattar at once!"

Vittalabattar, realizing that he would not get away with his pretence forever, was terrified when he saw the royal messengers at his doorstep. But what could he do? The call was from the raja himself! He went in to his wife, confessed the truth and begged, "Adiye! I am off. Forgive me for lying to you. I have no idea what will happen next. Now, only God can save me." He wiped his tears and left with the messengers to the palace.

At the palace, Vittalabattar had a regal welcome. But when he heard the raja's demand, he began trembling.

"Who could have stolen my dear rani's nose stud?" asked the raja.

Who knows? Maybe she just lost it, and here I am paying for her carelessness! he cursed silently.

"Oh Raja! Give me a number between one and ten," he asked humbly.

"Two," replied the raja.

"Then two people are involved in this theft," declared Vittalabattar.

"Name the two!" commanded the raja, grinding his teeth in rage.

"I need some time to do that."

"How many days will you need?"

"Perhaps... three days?"

"Fine! You may have three days. Until then you may not venture outside this palace. If you don't come up with the thieves' names in three days, then I shall chop off your nose, pluck out your eyes and abandon you in the forest," ordered the raja and left.

The soldiers dragged Vittalabattar to a luxurious room and locked the door. The room had every comfort imaginable. A most lavish prison!

His meals came from the palace kitchen, his snacks from the raja's private chamber. But Vittalabattar did not even spare a glance for any of these. He could only worry about losing his nose and eyes.

Now the royal maids who brought him food were named Mukaayi and Kannaayi. The rani referred to them as Mukee and Kanee, and they were known in the palace by these nicknames. They were very puzzled by Vittalabattar's behavior. *We bring him such tasty dishes, but he doesn't even look at them!*

Not only that; he had not even bothered to look at the pretty maids! He just seemed to be mumbling something to himself all the time.

One day, they hid in the room to get a closer look and find out what he was saying. They were shocked to discover that he was saying their names!

What Vittalabattar was mumbling was, "Oh curse my *muku* [nose] and *kannu* [eyes]!"

In fact, it was these two maids who had stolen the diamond nose stud. They had believed they were safe, and now this astrologer had found them out!

They fell at Vittalabattar's feet weeping, and confessed to the theft. Vittalabattar gathered his wits at once and guffawed arrogantly, "You measly maids! What did you think of me?"

"Aiya, we never imagined you would catch us. Please save us. We'll give you whatever you want," they begged, clinging to his feet.

Vittalabattar felt sorry for the young maids. "Alright, where is the nose stud?" he asked. They produced it. "Take it to the rani's bathroom and hide it in the drain."

Now, Vittalabattar was hungry. He wolfed down the delicious feast that Kanee and Mukee had served him. The food was scrumptious. Had he known that the food was going to be this heavenly, he would have asked for more time.

In any case, the three days went too fast.

On the third day the raja knocked on his door and demanded, "Well sir, can you tell my where my rani's nose stud is?"

"Oh Raja, the nose stud is nowhere but down the drain in the rani's bathroom," he replied modestly.

Lo and behold! The nose stud was there! The raja was delighted. He gifted Vittalabattar with many costly jewels and appointed him as the court astrologer.

When the other astrologers of the region heard this, they were green with jealousy. "Who is this Vittalabattar? Under whom did he train? How can someone who is incapable of doing simple sums call himself an astrologer? This is unfair, an insult to astrology!" they fumed.

Their grumbles reached the minister's ears, who took this grievance to the raja.

"You are right, minister. I will put Vittalabattar through one more test," said the raja.

Months passed. The raja decided to set his test for Vittalabattar. He caught a *vittal puchi* [moth] and hid it in his palm, and then went in search of Vittalabattar with the minister on horseback.

When Vittalabattar saw the horses, he wondered if he was in for another test. The raja rode up to him, extended his closed fist and asked, "Oy, how are you? Out on your constitutional, are you? Good! But tell me now, what have I got in my hand?"

Vittalabattar was sure his game was up. He shook his head slowly, and whispered to himself, "Oh Vittal, you are caught! You cannot escape now!"

The raja could not believe his ears. "Kudos, Vittalabattar! You have proved yourself once again. I should have never listened to those other idiot astrologers," he yelled, hugging him.

Vittalabattar raced back home and told his wife to pack. "Adiye, we cannot stay in this town even a moment longer. Or else I'm sure to be dead!"   ❖

peys & pisaasus

anjinaan and anjaadhaan

In Arasanallur village, there lived two brothers: Anjinaan, whose name meant *fearful*, and Anjaadhaan, whose name meant *fearless*. Anjinaan, the elder brother, would go with the other shepherds to graze his goats and bring them back to their pen at dusk. Anjaadhaan, the younger brother, cooked and took care of the house.

One day, as usual, Anjinaan took the goats to the foot of the hill to graze. There was a pey that lived there, which saw Anjinaan and craved to drink his blood. So it changed its form to that of an old woman, and approached him.

"Thambi, Thambi," it pleaded. "I am very old. I have a terrible itch on my back. Could you please scratch it for me?"

Anjinaan obliged, but just as he started to scratch the woman's back, the shepherds returned with their herds, and the woman ran off.

The next day, the pey came again with the same request, but just as he started to scratch it, it ran away hearing some noise.

On the second day, Anjinaan noticed that the old woman disappeared instantly as soon as someone came. *Perhaps it's really the ghost of a dead person*, he thought, frightened, and suddenly felt a severe chill in his bones. He hurried his goats back home.

Surprised to see him home so early, the younger brother asked what had happened. When he heard the story, he told Anjinaan, "Anna, you stop worrying. I shall take care of this tomorrow."

At high noon, the pey came again. It told Anjaadhaan, "Thambi, my back has been itching for a long time. Yesterday a young lad scratched it for me, but I don't see him today. Will you please scratch it for me?"

Anjadhaan asked it to turn around and sit on the ground. Once it was seated, he slashed the back—*parack, parack*—with the shards of glass he had brought along.

In terrible pain and bleeding profusely, the pey ran off once again. This time it stopped at the Veera Aiyanaar temple and yelled, "Veera, cure my wounds, and in two days I shall bring you cartloads of offerings!" With that, it soared into the air and flew off.

At home, Anjaadhaan told Anjinaan what happened and warned him that the pey would be back in two days for its revenge. "So, before it comes, let's go hide in the Veera Aiyanaar temple and chase it away."

On the second night, Anjaadhaan removed the idol of Aiyanaar and sat in its place. He told his elder brother to hide behind the temple with a huge iron pestle.

After a while, the pey arrived with cartloads of rice, grains, fruits and vegetables.

Anjaadhaan, pretending to be the Veeran idol, sat with his mouth wide open and tongue hanging out. The pey peeled a few bananas and dropped them in his mouth. It kept ringing the temple bell, *ga-ning*, *ga-ning*, and went on feeding Veeran's mouth. Seeing that the fruit was just slipping down the idol's throat, the pey sang out:

What is this? (ga-ning, ga-ning)
The idol is swallowing bananas! (ga-ning, ga-ning)

It began a frenzied dance.

Anjaadhaan had had enough bananas, and couldn't bear the pey's loud screams. He poked it hard with the trident in his hand.

Scared, the pey wailed:

I told you then, (ga-ning, ga-ning)
Please let me go! (ga-ning, ga-ning)

and it turned to run. The brothers chased after it for a while, brandishing the trident and pestle, then came back and collected all the offerings in the cart. They took them home, got married to nice girls, and are happy now.   ❖

Ki. Ra.: There are many stories in Tamil Nadu about peys and pisaasus. In most of the stories, the humans emerge victorious over the pey. This is probably a story told by adults to children, to teach them not to be afraid of ghosts; the *ga-ning, ga-ning* sound effect is clearly meant to appeal to a younger audience.

P.K.C.: I have used *ghost* and *pey* interchangeably in this story, but the pey is a little different than the English understanding of a ghost.

Peys are usually genderless; as in this story, they can become male or female as they wish. Though a pey is sometimes the lingering spirit of a dead human, more commonly it is just a supernatural spirit, often of evil disposition (see the next story for an unusually benign pey). English ghosts rarely have material presence, but peys are able to take a totally physical form. The English ghost floats a short distance above the ground; the Tamil pey often does the same, but may also touch the ground or fly high in the air. Peys are very strong, and flexible in size; they may frequently expand into huge smoggy clouds. They live in trees (most commonly tamarind, banyan, and murunga trees) or dilapidated buildings.

As Ki. Rajanarayanan and the storytellers explain in the following tales, there are different types of peys, some which do have a specific gender, or trouble humans of a specific gender. The term *pisaasu* is also used, especially when possession of a person's body occurs.

Usually, a *vethaalam* is a sphinx-like being which hangs from the lower branches of a tree in a cremation ground and poses riddles to humans. Depending on their response, it either rewards or devours them. But the vethaalam in the story in this chapter is very different.

Two more types of supernatural being, *munis* and *kaatteris*, are worshipped as gods in folk traditions even today. When the devotees do not express their gratitude sufficiently, these beings can turn malevolent and then must be appeased.

Though the Hindi *booth* is fairly close to the English ghost, the Tamil cognate *bootham* is very different, more like the Arabian djinn in that it needs to be kept occupied with tasks. Boothams often appear with pot-bellies and stumpy legs (though they too can change shape), and live in caves or abandoned wells where they guard treasure.

hey, you have a nail driven into your head!

There lived in a village a merchant and his wife. The merchant's work involved frequent travel to faraway towns. His wife was a very bossy woman. Every maid who came to work in the house would quit after a few days. She had yet to find a single maid she was satisfied with.

Once, when the merchant was returning home through the forest, a pey called out to him.

"I have a nail driven into the top of my head. If only you could pull it out, I would be freed from my curse. I promise to give you whatever you wish for. Please help me," wept the ghost. The brave merchant stepped up and plucked out the nail in one tug. The pey, grateful, asked him what he would like in return.

The merchant thought for a long time. After all, this ghost must surely possess many magical powers—and here was he, unable to keep any domestic help because of his wife's attitude. Gathering his courage, he asked, "I'm not able to find a maid willing to stay with us and help my wife around the house. Will you come and work as our maid?"

"Yes, I can do that. Why don't you drive that nail back into my head, so that I can change myself into a woman and then come with you?" said the pey. The merchant complied, and the pey changed into a woman. He brought the woman to his wife and said, "I've found a woman who can work like a pey. You can give her as many chores as you want."

The wife had a great time ordering the ghost-maid around. "Winnow the rice." "Cook me a full dinner, with vadai and payasam." "Clean the house." "Wash my entire wardrobe." Finally, the wife ran out of chores to give the ghost-maid. "You truly work like a pey!" she exclaimed.

One afternoon, after a long day's work, the wife and ghost-maid had just lay down for a nap when the wife asked, "Woman, will you please go shut the front door?"

Without getting up, the ghost-maid stretched her arm all the way across the room from the bed to the front door, and slammed it shut. The wife could not believe her eyes.

"How did you do that?" she whispered, frightened.

"That's just a trick I learned as a child. I'll teach it to you some-time," laughed the ghost-maid.

A few days later, the wife noticed that the ghost-maid was scratch-ing her head all the time, and suspected that she might have lice. So that evening she made the ghost-maid sit down and began to check her head for nits.

"Hey, you have a nail driven into your head," she said, surprised, and tugged it out.

The pey, thus released from its human form, grew larger and larger until it almost touched the roof. It bent down to the woman and screeched, "My God, woman, no wonder you can't keep a maid longer than a few days! You often told me that I worked like a pey—and in fact, I am one. But even I cannot handle this work any more. Thank you for pulling the nail out and releasing me. I'm really tired. I need to go sleep." And with that, it flew back into the forest.   ❖

the kaniam-pey

Once, there was a kaniam-pey in a village. What is a kaniam-pey, you ask?

There are different types of peys. The mohini-pey is one type, and the kaniam-pey is another. This type of ghost, if it happens upon a beautiful woman, will not let her go. It will take her away, drink up all her beauty and only then release her. A kaniam-pey generally does its rounds from midnight until about two in the morning. This is not a time when people normally venture out of the house. So, on nights when it cannot find any woman, it will rattle on a grinding stone with a pestle, *ghadaghadaghada.*

The people of this particular village did not know how to get rid of the kaniam-pey. They had prayed to every God they could think of to chase it away, but to no avail.

The summer nights were sweltering hot. But no one dared to sleep out in the open. If any couple did, the kaniam-pey would lift up the husband, tear him in two, and throw him away.

What do you mean, lift up the husband? Wouldn't he feel it and wake up, you ask?

That's just the point. One can never feel a pey's touch; it will be as though one has been tranquilized.

Is that right? So what happens next? you want to know.

What next? It will charm the wife away to its lair, and use her body over and over again until she can take no more, and then discard her. After that she will be in extreme pain for four or five days. Even after that, her body will ache, her limbs will be numb and she will be unable to do any work. Only divine intervention will be able to return her to normal.

One morning, a young and not-very-beautiful woman named Puvaayi from a neighbouring town got married to a man from the village. Her family travelled to the village to leave the bride in her husband's home. By the time they reached, it was almost night. They left her there and returned.

Late in the night, perhaps because of all the heavy feasting, Puvaayi's stomach was very uncomfortable. Or maybe it was just because she was alone in a strange home, with strange people. Her mother-in-law and sister-in-law were fast asleep, exhausted after all the celebration. Her husband was lying on the thinnai outside. (He, of course, was still awake. How could he fall asleep with a fresh new bride inside? But in those days, newly married couples did not talk to each other for the first three months. They needed this much time to get to know each other.)

Though her stomach was upset, Puvaayi did not know where to go to relieve herself. After all, she could not very well go right in the middle of the room! Her mother-in-law would use that as a reason to shame her in front of the whole village! On the other hand, she didn't want to ask her husband, or wake up the other two women in the room either. She didn't want to get in their bad books on her very first day in the new home.

She decided to handle the situation by herself. So she opened the front door and ran towards the bushes outside.

Just then, the kaniam-pey entered the village sniffing the air for a whiff of a woman's scent. The moon was not very bright. And there was Puvaayi squatting near the fence.

Remember that Puvaayi was a new bride, with her hair decked in jasmine and aromatic herbs, her body smeared with sandalwood paste and turmeric. A heavy cloud of fragrance enveloped her. The pey caught her scent even from many feet away. It found its way to her, completely aroused. But after getting a close look at her face, it became very angry. *Here I am throbbing with lust because of all those perfumes, and there she squats, looking ugly as a witch! How dare she mislead me?* Losing its temper, the pey tipped her over with its big toe.

She almost fell on her face. Luckily, she somehow balanced herself and fled home.

When the husband saw his new wife come running into the house, he wanted to ask what her problem was, but didn't. Remember, he was not supposed to speak to her for three months!

The next morning saw Puvaayi down with a high temperature, shivering. She was moaning aloud in pain. The mother-in-law, sister-in-law and husband were worried. This was her first night in the new house; what would they say was the reason for the fever and fits? So, they sent for an exorcist.

The kaniam-pey possessed the exorcist and sang out the reason for the new bride's fever:

I, with oiled hair
Smelling divine
Singing an amorous song
Was on my way.
There she was,
Neither a manly man
Nor the trunk of a castor tree
Nor a womanly woman
Nor even a shit-smeared stone.
How aroused I was
When I approached her!
See how my body still throbs!
My fevered heart
Was driving me to frenzy!
My anger swelled;
And while she squatted, I
Tipped her over
With my big toe.
With the breaking of a coconut
My passion will abate
And I shall go away.

The husband broke a coconut as ordered, and the kaniam-pey went away. Puvaayi became normal again. But the husband was still very angry with the kaniam-pey. Puvaayi might have seemed ugly to it, but she was his wife; to him, she was beautiful! How dare the pey not only lust for her, but also publicly humiliate her with a dirty song!

Three months passed. Once the husband got Puvaayi to love and trust him completely, on a new moon night, he told her to bathe in perfumed water and deck herself up in aromatic herbs and jasmine. He smeared her neck and arms with sandal.

"Why do you want me to do all this?" she asked, puzzled.

"Just do as I say," he ordered.

She did everything as she was told.

Midnight!

The husband took a heavy iron rod in hand, and along with Puvaayi, started down the path used by the pey.

Some distance down the path was a tamarind tree, in which the pey lived.

The husband stood Puvaayi under the tree. Then he went off to the side, lit a fire, heated one end of the iron rod, wrapped the other end with a sack cloth, handed it to her and whispered something in her ears. Then he ran to hide behind the bushes.

The pey, getting a whiff of the flowers and sandal, came down from the tree towards her. Puvaayi immediately began swinging the hot iron rod with all her strength. Loud screeches filled the air. She could not see the pey, but kept slashing at the air where she thought it must be.

Every leaf on the tree shook and rustled loudly. Giant winds rose from nowhere and threw dust all around. After some time, the screeching, the breeze and the dust settled. All was quiet.

The husband brought the now tired Puvaayi home.

As day dawned, the entire village gathered under the tamarind tree. There was a charred monkey-like form hanging on the bottom branch.

The village has been peaceful ever since.

the kanni-peys & the diamond necklace

Once upon a time there lived a woman named Gomathi. At dusk, she would finish her housework and then go to chat with her neighbours.

One evening, her neighbour Parvathi asked her, "Tomorrow early morning, my husband and I have to leave town to attend a wedding. Will you please lend me your diamond necklace?"

"Sure," replied Gomathi. "Come over tomorrow before you leave. I'll give it you then."

Now there was a kanni-pey close by that overheard this exchange. As everyone knows, all kanni-peys love jewels. And this was a diamond necklace!

Next day, early in the morning, the kanni-pey took the form of Parvathi, knocked on Gomathi's door, and called out, "Gomathi, we're about to leave. Please, can I have the necklace?"

Gomathi had no idea it was a pey. Still half-asleep, she came out and gave it the necklace, believing it to be Parvathi. "Be careful with it," she told the pey and went back to bed. The kanni-pey took off with it.

A little while later, Parvathi herself came to ask for the necklace. Gomathi, now fully awake, could not believe it. "What do you mean, give you the necklace? You already took it!" she said, irritated.

"Oh dear! What's happened? I have only just now come. Did you give the necklace away to some stranger?" asked Parvathi.

Only then did it strike Gomathi. "Yes," she said in a scared tone. "Now that I think of it, the Parvathi I saw didn't have her feet planted on the ground. She was floating a few inches above it."

"Don't worry then," consoled Parvathi. "It must just be some jewel-crazy kanni-pey. All we have to do is find it. Then we can get your necklace back."

The next day, at high noon, the two women went to the river to fetch water as usual.

From an orchard close by, they heard voices singing an eerie melody, and the sound of bells—*jull, jull*—from young girls' anklets.

"Give me the necklace that Akka gave you!" *Jull, jull...*

"Give me the necklace that Akka gave you!" *Jull, jull...*

Cautiously, the two women crept into the orchard to take a look. There they saw no fewer than seven kanni-peys dancing, with their loose hair flying around wildly, and not a scrap of clothing to cover their bodies. They were taking turns wearing the necklace and admiring themselves.

Parvathi dragged Gomathi out of their sight and whispered in her ear. "This is right moment. You go dance with them and wait for your turn to wear the necklace. I'll run back to the village and bring back some men with me. If we return with burning torches, the kanni-peys will run away scared."

At first, Gomathi felt too shy to strip naked and dance. Still, it was her diamond necklace! So she had to do it.

She stripped off her sari, loosened her hair and joined the peys in their dance. When her turn to wear the necklace came, she put it on and then quickly ran to her sari and wrapped herself in it. The peys came chasing after her, but then they saw a huge crowd heading towards the orchard carrying burning torches. Scared, they all flew away.

Gomathi returned home with her diamond necklace.   ❖

Tamil Editor's Note: Ki. Rajanarayan has recorded a few variations on this story. In one version, it is not a diamond necklace but a necklace made of gold coins. In another, it is a younger sister of the woman who joins the kanni-peys, singing, "Give me the necklace that Akka gave you." In yet another version, it is the husband of the sister who goes and dances naked with the peys to get the necklace. The person who told the version given here claimed that the incident really happened.

the muni

Once upon a time there lived a mother and her young daughter. The girl was at the right age to be married. The mother would constantly grumble, "If only I can get you married to a good man, then I can rest in peace."

Now, there was a muni on the roof of their house that overheard this. It had a look at the girl, and decided it must have her. So, it took the form of a young man and approached the mother. "I am very rich," it told her. "Get your daughter married to me. I shall see that she is kept very happy."

The mother was totally won over by the man's charm, and sent her daughter off with him at once. If the poor mother only knew the truth!

The muni brought the girl to a forest, where it left her in the care of an old Avvaiyar woman. "Ayah, ayah, take good care of her," it told the Avvaiyar woman. "I will come in the evening to fetch her," it said, and left.

Though half-blind herself, the old Avvaiyar woman could not help feeling sorry for the young girl's plight. She beckoned her close and whispered, "Girl, couldn't you find anyone else to marry? Did you have to choose a muni? It has gone to hunt for meat. If it doesn't find any then it will kill you and eat you!"

The young girl thanked the Avvaiyar woman for saving her life, and escaped back to her home.

In the evening, the muni returned, angry because it had not found any meat. "Where's the girl?" it asked.

"I'm half-blind. How would I know where she has disappeared to?" said the Avvaiyar woman.

The muni marched to the girl's house.

The clever girl had been expecting it. So she had made a doll out of rice flour and jaggery that resembled her, placed it on the doorstep, and shut herself inside.

The muni arrived and saw the doll. "Aha! I knew I'd find you here," it crowed. It picked up the doll and swallowed it in one gulp, and went away satisfied.

The very same night the mother and the daughter moved to a faraway town. ❖

the jadaamuni

In the village of Kaattuputhur there lived three brothers: Big Kaathaan, Middle Kaathaan and Little Kaathaan. They took turns tending and watching the fields.

One night, it was Big Kaathaan's turn. He packed his food and went off. In the field, there was a jadaamuni who saw him and wanted to scare him. It took the form of an old man and begged, "Big Kaathaan, Big Kaathaan, please give me some of your rice."

Big Kaathaan gave the jadaamuni some rice. After eating, it asked him, "Big Kaathaan, my head is full of lice. Will you please pick some of them out?"

Big Kaathaan agreed, sat down, and started to check his hair. The jadaamuni chose that moment to whip around and reveal its true, monstrous form. Scared out of his wits, Big Kaathaan ran home screaming, and told Middle Kaathaan what had happened.

The next night, it was Middle Kaathaan's turn to watch the fields. Just like the previous night, the jadaamuni came, begged for rice, then asked for its head to be checked for lice, and then revealed its true form. Middle Kaathaan, too, ran home in terror, and told Little Kaathaan what had happened.

The next night, it was Little Kaathaan's turn. Before setting off to the fields, he gathered ten iron claw-rings, three iron nails and an iron rod.

Late that night, the jadaamuni arrived and begged for rice. Little Kaathaan fed it rice into which he mixed some sleeping powder. Soon, the jadaamuni felt very drowsy, but still it asked Little Kaathaan to check its head for lice. Little Kaathaan was ready with his iron claw-rings; he ripped at the jadaamuni's scalp, grabbed its hair by the roots, and pulled it out in big clumps.

While the jadaamuni was still screaming in pain, Little Kaathaan nailed its hair and hands to a tree. Then he lit a fire using his flintstone, heated the iron rod, and branded the jadaamuni.

"Little Kaathaan, please let me go," begged the jadaamuni. "I shall give you a magic carpet, on which you can fly anywhere you wish."

Little Kaathaan snatched the carpet, heated the iron rod again over the fire, and branded the jadaamuni again.

"Little Kaathaan, please let me go," it wept. "I shall give you a magic bowl, that will provide a huge feast whenever you want it."

Little Kaathaan took the magic bowl, heated the iron rod again, and branded the jadaamuni yet again.

"Little Kaathaan, please let me go," it sobbed. "All I have left is a magic rope and a magic stick. At your command, the rope will tie up your enemies and the stick will beat them. Take them please, and untie me. I promise to go away forever."

Little Kaathaan took the magic gifts, warned the jadaamuni never to return, and let it fly off.

The three brothers put their magic gifts to good use, got married to nice girls, and lived happily ever after. ❖

Ki. Ra.: Jadaamuni tales in Tamil cannot be clubbed along with regular pey/pisaasu stories. This particular tale is a very old one, dating from the time when fire was still lit with flintstones.

In olden days, men, as well as women, used to have very long hair. It was considered natural, in those days, when someone you were fond of sat next to you, to gently feel their head for lice. Even today, in rural areas, it is common to hear the following lines in an oppaari (lamentation song for the dead): "Amma, only yesterday you made me sit by your side, caressed my head, and felt for lice!" Animals groom each other in much the same way.

A jadaamuni is a supernatural being that has long dreadlocks not only on its head, but all over its body.

Even today, during an exorcism, a possessed person may be nailed to a tree. There are lots of theories about which sorts of twigs should be used to drive out which sorts of pey, and which percussion instruments should be played during the session to control them.

the vethaalam

Once upon a time there was a raja who had four sons. But he and his rani longed for a daughter, and they tried propitiating the gods in all sorts of ways.

One day a saamiyaar visited the palace. "Raja, Raja, you look sad. Is there a problem?" he asked.

The raja told him of their longing for a daughter.

The saamiyaar pointed to a mango tree, and instructed him, "Pluck the tiniest fruit from the lowest branch of that tree, and share it equally with your wife. You will soon have a daughter."

After the saamiyaar left, the raja went to look at the mango tree. The fruits on the lower branches were all quite small, but there was one mango on the top branch that was very big and very ripe. The raja had his servants cut down the big mango, and he shared it with his wife.

As the saamiyaar had predicted, a baby girl was soon born. Had the raja followed the saamiyaar's instructions, the baby girl would have been a human child. Instead, it was a vethaalam. But no one knew this yet. She looked like a normal baby, and she grew up to look like a normal young girl.

Now, this raja had everything in thousands: a thousand horses, a thousand elephants, a thousand goats, a thousand cows, and a thousand hens. One morning, this stock was found to have been mysteriously reduced by a hundred; there were now only nine hundred of each animal.

That night, the raja sent his first son to watch over his livestock.

The son stood on guard, but around midnight, he fell fast asleep. He did not notice his sister thunder out of the palace into the grounds and quickly gobble up a hundred horses, a hundred elephants, a hundred goats, a hundred cows, and a hundred hens. In the morning, there were found to be only eight hundred of each animal left.

The second night, the raja sent his second son to guard the livestock. He too fell asleep at midnight. The next day, there were only seven hundred of each animal left.

The third night, the third son was sent. He too fell asleep at midnight. The next day, there were only six hundred of each animal left.

On the fourth night, the fourth and smartest son was sent to stand guard. He ate a heavy dinner before dusk, had a good nap, and then woke up at midnight to begin his watch. Just after midnight, he saw his sister thunder out of the palace into the grounds and quickly gobble up another hundred horses, a hundred elephants, a hundred goats, a hundred cows, and a hundred hens.

The fourth son was shocked. *Is this the daughter my parents longed for?* he wondered.

The next morning, he reported what he had seen to the raja.

"You sinner!" shouted the raja. "How can you say this about my only daughter? Get out of my palace! You have no place here!" And he chased him off.

The fourth son left the raja's kingdom and walked for days into the forest. One night at dusk, he climbed up a tree and fell asleep.

A little later, a tiger saw him, and stayed lurking beneath the tree, hoping to eat him up.

Just above him in the tree was a monkey who was making a bow and a few arrows. When the monkey saw the tiger, he thought, *What a shame it would be if the tiger killed this boy!* So he notched an arrow in his bow, and shot the tiger dead.

Startled awake by the tiger's dying roar, the fourth son sat up. The monkey told him what had happened.

Now this monkey was a king of the forest, and he too had everything in thousands: a thousand jackals, a thousand bears, a thousand rabbits, and a thousand of every other species of animal. The monkey king invited the fourth son to live with him.

When the boy had grown into a man, the monkey king abducted a simple farmer's daughter, brought her to the forest, and got him married to her.

Years passed. One day, the fourth son decided he wanted to see his parents again, and set off from the forest. But when he entered the kingdom, he saw that the entire land had turned into a cremation ground. Not even a worm or an ant was left; the vethaalam had eaten everything up, including his entire family.

In the empty, ruined palace sat the vethaalam, waiting to eat the fourth son. Sensing that he had come, it came thundering out of the palace to the gates. The fourth son took to his heels, ran back to the forest, and told his wife and the monkey king what had happened to his land.

The monkey king wanted to put an end to the vethaalam, but he didn't know what to do. Then the simple farmer's daughter said, "I have a sword. Wait; I will put a spell on it, and with it, you can kill the vethaalam. But make sure that you attack it from behind. If you try to attack from the front, you too will be eaten up."

So the fourth son went back once again. Knowing that the vethaalam would probably be waiting at the palace gates, he went in the rear entrance. He could see the vethaalam at the gates, deep in meditation. He crept up silently behind it and gave it one strong chop on the head with the enchanted sword.

The vethaalam gave a final roar and dropped dead.

After that, the monkey king moved all his animal subjects, along with the simple farmer's daughter, into the fourth son's kingdom, and they all lived happily ever after.   ❖

alamelu and the pey

Once upon a time there was a pey that lived in a tamarind tree. The tree was in the middle of a village, and people had to pass under it on their way to work in the fields, or to gather wood in the forest.

A young woman named Alamelu was one of those who had to walk under the tree every day. She was a very good looking woman, with a strong, fit body and skin blackened by the sun, who could do the work of five men. The pey fell deeply in love with her. One day as she went past, it touched her.

One auspicious Friday, Alamelu had taken her head-bath and was on her way to the temple when the pey whispered to her, "Alamelu, I am residing in your body. Please do not go to temple. I can't put up with all those gods."

"What good does it do me, you being in my body?" she demanded. "My family will keep beating me with neem leaves and dragging me off to exorcists, and the village folk will say I'm possessed! No, I'm going to temple. You get out of my body." And she took a couple of steps towards the temple.

"Please, Alamelu. I can do you great favors."

"You're a pey! What favors can I expect from you?"

"I'll make sure you never fall ill—not even a headache. If you have to carry a load, I will bear the weight. While you are reaping grain in the field, I will help you to cut twice as much as you could otherwise. Besides all that, if any scoundrel tries to tease you or misbehave with you, I will finish him off."

"Fine," she conceded. "I will not go to temple."

One day, Alamelu's elder sister came to visit, along with her husband. As their parents were no more, her sister had assumed the responsibility of getting her married. After considering alliances from various places, they finally decided on a young man in the same village, who lived alone with his mother.

The marriage was fixed.

Alamelu told the pey, "See, I'm going to be married soon. After that, I will have to go to temples with my husband when he wants to pray. I will have to light lamps, camphor and incense in my house. Go; it is better if you leave my body now."

"If I am to leave your body, then you must offer me the life of someone in your family," demanded the pey. "If you fail, then I will take the life of your husband."

"I have no parents. After so many years of living alone, I am finally getting a husband of my own. How can I give up my thali? Please ask me for something else!"

"Fine. What I love most in world is sweet sugary panniyaram. Every new moon night for the next one year, after the rest of the village has gone to sleep, you must bring seven panniyarams to the tamarind tree. If you do this, then I shall never trouble you again. But you must keep this deal a secret."

She agreed, and took seven panniyarams to the tamarind tree each new moon night for the next few months. She kept it a secret from her husband, too.

Just four months before the end of the year, she discovered that she was pregnant. Her elder sister insisted that she come stay at her house till the baby was born.

Alamelu went and told the pey that she had to leave. She also told her mother-in-law that she must deliver the seven panniyarams at the tamarind tree every new moon night for the next four months. She promised to tell the reason once she returned.

The mother-in-law delivered the panniyarams for two new moons. After that, she told her son, "Aley, son, do you know that you're not the only man in your wife's life? She has someone else, too."

"Why do you say so?" asked the son.

"All these months, she has been taking panniyarams to the tamarind tree every new moon night, without our knowledge. Just before she left to her sister's, she asked me to continue doing this for her. I did it twice. Both times, I checked the next day. The panniyarams had disappeared! So not only is that chap having an affair with your wife, he is also stuffing himself with our panniyarams every month!"

"Is that so? Then she shall no longer be my wife," swore the son. He sent word to Alamelu's sister, telling her to not to send her back.

When Alamelu heard this, she rushed back to her husband's village, even though she was full-term pregnant. On her way, she stopped at the tamarind tree, called the pey down and said, "I'm not giving you any more panniyarams. Instead, you may take my mother-in-law's life in two days' time."

When she entered her husband's house, both the son and mother were spoiling for a fight. They insulted her and cursed her no end. Finally Alamelu told her husband, "Your mother is falsely accusing me. I have no relationship with any man except you. If what I say now is a lie, may I fall dead in two days time. But if what I say is the truth, then may your lying mother fall dead. In any case, you will know the absolute truth in two days. Until then, leave me alone."

On the second day, the pey arrived as promised, and took the mother-in-law's life.

Triumphantly, Alamelu asked her husband, "You gutless fool, at least now do you see the truth? It was your mother who was having the affair all along. She blamed me instead so that you wouldn't doubt her. See which one of us is dead!"

The man could do nothing but accept what she said as the truth, and they lived happily ever after. ❖

the kaatteri

Once upon a time there was a kaatteri that lived in a forest near a town. It was abducting all the first-born boy children from the town, and was keeping them to be sacrificed to Kali. No matter how much trouble the parents went through to safeguard their sons, the kaatteri somehow managed to steal them away.

So the parents of the abducted children assembled at the raja's court to appeal for help. The raja tried his best to capture the kaatteri, but was unsuccessful. As a last resort, he told his messenger-drummer to announce in the town that he would give half his kingdom, and his daughter as a bride, to whomsoever managed to kill the kaatteri and bring back all the first-born sons.

Several brave, strong men rushed to the forest... but they all died. The kaatteri had an elephant guarding its hill. The elephant tossed all the men into the air and then trampled them to death on the ground.

In the same town lived a humble farmer and his wife. They had a son.

The son fell at his parents' feet, took their blessings, and said, "I shall go and kill the kaatteri and return safely. Please give me your permission."

"Son, it will not be easy for you kill the kaatteri," said the mother. "But I shall suggest a way. At the edge of the forest is the temple of Angaalamman. She has been our family deity since the days when we were only bonded labourers. She will definitely protect you. So, go and pray to her before you enter the forest."

The obedient son stopped at the temple and prayed. At once, Angaalamman appeared in front of him and said, "My son, I shall give you an elephant. This elephant will lead you to victory. Remember this: there is a small shining black pottu on the kaatteri's forehead. Before you attempt to kill it, you must wipe off the pottu. Then the kaatteri will diminish in size, and you can easily defeat it."

The young man rode off on his elephant. On his way, a baby monkey called out to him, "Brave man, brave man, where are you going? Can I come along please?"

So the young man took the monkey on top of his elephant. When they reached the forest, the young man got down with the monkey. He could see the kaatteri standing on top of its hill, towering into the sky. The kaatteri's elephant sentry rushed from the hill to trample him, but the young man's elephant charmed the kaatteri's elephant and lured it away.

When the kaatteri saw this, it came thundering down the hill itself, livid with rage. The baby monkey, scared by the noise, scampered up a nearby tree.

While the son and the kaatteri were fighting, the monkey silently reached down from his tree branch and wiped the pottu from the kaatteri's forehead.

At once, the kaatteri became so tiny that the son picked it up in one hand, sacrificed it at the Kali temple, rescued all the first-born boy children, and returned home victorious.

The raja, true to his word, gave the young man half his kingdom and his daughter. Today, everyone is happy.   ❖

Ki. Ra.: Even in these modern times, there are various superstitions concerning the safety of the first-born, especially if it is a son. It is believed that a first-born son's skull can be used by sorcerers for their black magic. The black pigment made from this skull will enable the sorcerer to win over all his adversaries and become super-powerful. The pottu on the kaatteri's forehead in this story is made of this pigment. This is why, if a first-born son dies at a young age, his relatives will stay behind at the cremation ground to ensure that his bones and hair are fully burnt to ashes. Bloodthirsty goddesses like Kali are also partial to first-born sons.

avittam and the priest

There once lived a priest in a village. He was such an effective priest that all the gods would do whatever he asked. Whether he was performing an exorcism with neem leaves or smearing holy ash on a sick person's body to heal him, everything he did worked.

One day, the priest visited a nearby town, where he spent the night at a friend's place. As usual, he was given a royal welcome and served a grand dinner. That night, he threw down his mat on the thinnai outside and went to sleep.

In that same house, not too long back, someone had died on the day of Avittam, the twenty-third of the twenty-seven stars of the lunar cycle, which manifests as a huge, grotesque demon who lives in the cremation ground. Usually, if someone died on that day, Avittam itself would visit the house every month on the same night, at midnight, for the next few years. The people of the house would spread some sand on the thinnai as a bed, and keep out a bowl of rice, and some water in a snail shell. Avittam would come and eat the rice, drink the water, roll for a bit on the sand bed, and then go away.

However, on this particular night, the people of the house had become preoccupied with the priest, and had forgotten that Avittam was due that night. The spot on the thinnai where the priest had chosen to sleep was just the spot where the sand bed should have been laid down for Avittam.

At midnight, Avittam set off from the cremation ground. Its bells rang through the town, *jaal, jaal, jaal*. The people of the house heard the bells and at once remembered. "What do we do? The priest is asleep in Avittam's place, and we have forgotten to keep out the rice and water! By God, it will burn down the town in anger! What do we do? What do we do?" they whispered, terrified. But nobody dared to open the door and warn the priest.

Plah! Something slapped the priest across the face, hard. He had been fast asleep, but woke up in a hurry. He heard the voice of the goddess Badrakali whisper urgently in his ears: "Aley, Avittam has just set off. What are you doing asleep?"

The priest thanked the Goddess fervently and went off to hide behind a haystack.

And then he saw! There was Avittam, towering into the sky, striding towards the town despite the ten lesser demons weighing it down, as the huge bells hanging from it swayed and rang *jaal, jaal, jaal.* "Dear goddess, it will destroy the town!" wept the priest, and began meditating deeply on Badrakali.

At once, Avittam felt the heat of hundreds of invisible torches burning at the gates of the town. Unable to bear the fire, it ran back to the cremation ground, dragging the ten demons along with it.

The next morning, the entire town fell at the feet of the priest in gratitude. ❖

Ki. Ra.: This is typical of the kind of stories that have been built up over generations by priests to exploit the superstitious fears of the people.

the bootham's task

Many, many years ago, there was a huge bootham that caused countless pains to the humans. No one knew when it would wake up and become hungry. It would sleep for days on end, and then suddenly wake up one midnight. As soon as it woke up it would walk to the closest village, grab the sleeping men, gorge on them and return to its dark mountain cave to fall asleep again.

Now, boothams are creatures gifted with magical powers. They can, if they wish, disappear into a tiny mustard seed, or grow so large as to grab at the moon in the sky, or grow lakhs of hands so as to accomplish in an instant a task that would take a crore of men six months to finish, or change their form into that of any living creature.

So our bootham had no reason to fear mere humans. It went on feeding on living things and sleeping as it pleased. It had started with eating up the birds and the beasts and the reptiles that lived in the forest, and now it had turned its eyes on the villagers.

The raja and the minister of the land consulted days and nights about ways to tackle the bootham. They searched for sorcerers who could annihilate boothams until finally they found a reliable one. He said, "You can feed this bootham till he becomes full, but you can never set it a task that it won't be able to finish in the blink of an eye. When it is done with its work, if we don't have another job ready, it will go mad and eat us."

The raja said very blithely, "As if we don't have plenty of work waiting to be completed! Go fetch me the bootham, and then see how I tire it out." So the sorcerer brought the bootham straight to the palace. It had taken the form of a tiny black monkey. The sorcerer brought it in on a leash, like a puppy dog. The raja gifted the sorcerer what he wanted for this service. Once the sorcerer left, the bootham turned to the raja and said mockingly, "So, you're the one who is going to keep me busy, are you?" Even its smile was terrifying. "Go on. Give me some work. Or else, I shall kick you and your palace like a football."

Naturally, the raja and the minister had drawn up a list of chores for the bootham to do.

The first day, they asked it to deepen all the reservoirs in the land, and strengthen their banks. "That's a snap," said the bootham, and promptly disappeared. It returned even before the raja could finish a yawn and asked, "And the next job?'

"Have you really unclogged all the reservoirs, deepened them, and strengthened their banks?" asked the raja.

"Come and check for yourself," replied the bootham, and it carried the entire ministry, along with the raja, on a single palm, and showed them the reservoirs.

They realized that the bootham was not lying. But how had it managed to finish in the blink of an eye? They had not expected it to finish so fast; they had hoped to keep it busy with this work for a few months at least.

The second job they gave it was to do the same to the rivers in the region, for during every monsoon, the rivers were flooding and destroying the fertile fields.

The raja and minister had no time to sleep, eat, or even brush their teeth. The bootham completed the chores so fast that they needed to constantly come up with more work.

Third, they wanted all the temples renovated.

Fourth, they asked for all the potholes in all the roads in the area to be filled in.

Fifth, they asked for new roads to regions afar.

The bootham finished each task in no more time than it took for them to give the order.

Just when the raja and the minister began to worry that they would soon run out of jobs for the bootham, and that there was no way to escape becoming its next snack, the rani decided to drop in.

The minister at once left them to their privacy. The rani was very hungry. She had just come out of a warm bath and was combing the knots out of her long hair as she entered.

"Why have you not come in for your dinner?" she demanded, and immediately the raja, as if waiting for her to ask this, poured out the story of everything that had happened. "We may as well skip our dinner, for soon we are going to be gobbled up by that bootham," he moaned.

The bootham chose that moment to enter and demand, "What is my next work?"

"Make me huge tubs and fill them with the water of the seven holy rivers of this land," commanded the raja. (It is auspicious to bathe in the seven holy waters just before breathing one's last breath, so as to attain instant nirvanam after death.)

As the bootham left to obey, the rani whispered to the raja, "Tell the bootham to come to me for its next chore."

When the bootham returned with the holy water, the raja went for his bath, asking it to take its next order from the rani.

"Bring me every pearl from the depths of every ocean on this earth," bade the rani. The bootham did so, in two minutes.

"Now, bring me all the precious coral from the reefs," she said, and the bootham did.

"Fetch every grain of gold from every mine," she exclaimed, and the bootham did.

All the while, as the rani gave her commands, she was removing the tangles in her tresses with her left hand. Finally, she gave the bootham one long strand of hair and said, "Take this hair to your cave, sit there and divide it into 108 exactly equal pieces. You are not to step out of the cave until you have done so."

The bootham left. The raja came from his bath.

"Can we go for dinner now?" asked the rani.

"But the bootham..." whispered the raja.

She told him about her order, to which he barked, "Are you nuts? Why only 108 pieces? He could even come back with 1008 pieces of your hair."

"I am not nuts. You are. The bootham will not be able to divide it into two equal pieces, let alone 108 equal pieces. After all, it is hair!"

One day passed, and another, and another, and several more. The bootham did not step out of its cave at all.

Of course, the wise rani was right. She had indeed saved the land and its people. The bootham is still stuck in its cave, puzzling over this chore.   ❖

husbands & wives

a queen among women

In a village, there was a woman. She was the head of the local gossip association. She could spend hours gossiping with the women of the neighbourhood. Whenever she wasn't eating or sleeping, she was making idle talk. If the session was very interesting, she would forget to make the kanji, cook the rice or cure the meat. When her husband returned home in the evening after a long tired day in the field, asking, "Why didn't you bring me my kanji?" she would come up with all sorts of innovative excuses. One day she would claim to have a splitting headache; the next, a raging fever or the runs. He would feel sorry for her and let her go.

One day, the husband was ravenous with hunger in the field. He waited for his wife to bring his kanji, which of course she did not. *I'm not going to tolerate this any longer. This evening, I'll whip her so hard, she'll weep and promise never to disobey me again,* he decided.

When the wife saw her husband marching towards the house brandishing his whip, she knew her game was up. So the moment he walked in through the gate, she fell flat at his feet, crying, "Oh please forgive me."

Somewhat mollified by her tears, he declared sternly, "Now, look here. This is your last warning. If you fail to bring my kanji to the field tomorrow, you're done for! I'll make you remove your thali, tie it to a tree and return you to your father's place for good. I won't put up with any more excuses!"

Early the next morning, the husband left to the field with his plough. The moment the husband had turned the street corner, she gathered her friends to gossip. The talk was so riveting that before she realized, it was already noon. Only then did she remember her husband's ultimatum. There was no time to soak the rice and prepare fresh kanji. What could she do? She took out a lunch box, measured a cupful of rice grains, dropped in a fresh lemon and shut it. She arranged the lunch basket on her head and left to the field.

In the field, the husband was gnashing his teeth at the delay. He was almost blind with hunger. He could see her at a distance, swaying along with the basket. *That bitch!* he fumed, hefting his whip. *What time did I ask for my lunch? What took her so long? This is it!*

Ignoring his angry stance, the wife approached him, took out the lunch box, put it on the ground, and looked up to the sky. "Oh Sun God, you who takes care to feed every bird and beast," she called out. "I plead to you every day for my husband's welfare, but still he doubts me. If I am a woman of honour, may the kanji I made turn to raw grains of rice, and the pickle turn back into a lemon!"

So saying, she opened the lunch box. Lo and behold! There it was: a cupful of rice grains and a fresh lemon. The husband was convinced she was indeed a queen among women!

She is back now, heading her gossip sessions.   ❖

the woman who made her husband carry her slippers

There once was a cruel, immoral man. His mother, worried by his wicked ways, asked everyone she knew to look for a bride who could tame her wild son. However, no parent in the neighbourhood would entrust their daughter to such a man.

Realizing how anxious the man's mother was to get him married, one young woman came forward. This woman's mother, unhappy with her daughter's decision, ranted: "Aiyyo, have you gone mad? That man is fully capable of murder! He will slaughter you as casually as though you were a cow or a goat, and bury you under the ground. Why do you want to marry him?"

"Don't you worry, mother," said the daughter. "Just wait and watch. In no time, I'll have him following behind me, carrying my slippers."

The man and the woman were married. They set up a home for themselves.

Every day, the wife would secretly cook rice and eat it all, but pretend to starve. Since the man was always out of the house, he had no idea about his wife's eating habits. One day he asked her: "Do you at least make yourself some kanji, or are you starving throughout the day?"

"I don't eat anything at all."

"Why not?"

"When our marriage was being fixed, the townsfolk told my mother, 'Why would you want to risk the life of such a beautiful daughter with a man like him? He is fully capable of murder! He will slaughter her as casually as though she was a cow or a goat, and bury her under the ground,'" she wept. "Since I don't want you to become a murderer by slaughtering me, I decided to starve myself to death instead."

"Is that what those motherfuckers think of me?" demanded the husband. "I'll show those assholes. I'll show them I can keep a home and wife, and father a dozen children too. Wife, you can stop worrying. From today on, you eat three meals a day, and be happy."

The wife wiped her wet eyes and said, "Just for these words of yours, I shall eat once a day. If you never make me cry, I shall start eating twice a day, and when I'm sure that we are the happiest couple in town, I shall eat thrice a day."

True to her words, she ate once a day in his presence (and twice in secret).

The man too began to temper his rowdy ways. He sought a job, brought home his wages and made an effort to make her happy. All this ecstasy meant that she was soon pregnant. The man was overjoyed.

I'll make those motherfuckers weep with jealousy when I walk down the street carrying my son! he swore. He lavished attention and care on his wife, as though she were precious gems and pieces of gold in his palms, in his eyes and in his heart.

The woman gave birth to a son. Gazing joyfully at the little child, the man begged his wife, "At least now, you should start eating three meals a day."

"Not yet," said the wife. "We must take our son to my mother's house, and show them that you have become as good as gold. Only then will I eat thrice a day."

He agreed.

The wife's mother's house was not far off, but they had to cross a small irrigation ditch to get there. The wife sent word to her mother about the day and the time of their visit.

As they left, the husband told the wife, "Your body is still tender. Don't walk barefoot; wear your slippers."

"Your wish is my command, dear husband," she said and put on her slippers. She normally never wore slippers, except when she went to the forest to gather firewood.

She carried the baby and walked ahead through the fields, as he followed behind. Across the field, she spied her mother and their neighbours watching them through the window. The water in the irrigation ditch was ankle-deep. As they approached it, the husband said, "Give me the baby."

"Oh no, the baby's head is not steady as yet," she said. "Men are not very good at carrying newborn babies. I'll carry him for now."

"How will you carry both the baby and your slippers as you cross the ditch?" he asked.

"Someone should hold my slippers for me while I cross it," she said.

"Right. And who will that be?" he asked.

"Who will carry my slippers? Why of course, the pair of slippers worn by the mother of your favorite son should be carried by—*you*," she purred softly into his ears.

"You sly bitch," he grumbled, swiftly looking around to see if there were any witnesses. Then he bent down, picked up her slippers and jumped over the ditch, while all the eyes peering from behind the window in her mother's house watched.

On reaching the mother's house, the wife asked her parents, "So, did you see your son-in-law following behind me and carrying my slippers?"

"Oh, we did! We did!" replied the happy parents.   ❖

the hunter's wife

Once upon a time, in a village, there lived a man and his wife. The man loved to hunt; he had to have meat every day. On days when no meat was available, he would simply starve, rather than eat vegetables. So every morning he roamed the woods until he managed to trap something—at the very least, a quail, partridge, crane, or rabbit. When he did find game, he would never stop with just one kill. He would make sure that he had one for himself and another for his dear wife. It was his practice to go for his hunt before dawn, bring home his prey, and then set off for work.

Now, the wife had a secret lover. Every day, when she made tasty curries from the quail or partridge that her husband brought home, she would serve her husband the bones, but would make sure to save the meat for her lover. The husband would return from work very late in the evening. By then the wife would have spent a long, passionate time with her lover, fed him well, and seen him off. The husband was completely unaware of all this.

One night, while he was eating his dinner, the husband asked, "What is this, my dear? Every morning I bring you two quails or two cranes. But see here, you only serve bones on my plate. What do you do with the meat?"

"Before our wedding, my parents consulted an astrologer, who said that I would meet my death if I were to eat a bone in my husband's house," she replied. "You are my husband, after all; you dearly want me to stay alive, don't you? That's why I eat the meat myself, and serve you the bones."

The husband thought to himself, *Naturally, she is the most important person in my life.* He told his wife strictly: "I don't want you to ever touch a bone."

Still, he had a nagging doubt: *Is it really possible that my wife manages to eat a full pot of meat every day by herself?*

One morning, the husband announced that he was off to work, but instead he hid in the backyard and watched. The wife finished her cooking as usual, cleaned the kitchen, had a perfumed bath and was waiting at the doorstep when the lover arrived. She shut the door and served him hot meat curry and rice, which he gobbled up in huge mouthfuls. They then moved to the bed, where they were lost in their lustful lovemaking. Later, after the lover had gone, the husband came in at his usual time, ate his bone curry and went to bed.

The next day, he made two elders from the village panchayat stand in the same place in the backyard to keep watch. They saw the lover come in, eat hot meat curry, and have fiery sex with the wife.

The very same night, they called for a meeting. There it was decided that if the lover wanted to continue eating half of what the husband brought in, then he should take care of the wife for half the month. The wife tried wailing and sobbing, but it was no use. "Once the panchayat has pronounced their judgment, there can be no change in it," said the elders. So she started off, behind her lover.

The lover turned round and snapped, "Are you crazy, woman? I have a beautiful wife and children at home. Why would I want to take you with me? I love meat, but I can't afford to eat it every day. I came running to you only because your curry was so tasty. Otherwise I have no love or affection for you." With this, he walked away without another look back. The husband walked off as well, relieved to be rid of her.

There was no one left in the village to care for her. I am told that even today, she wanders here and there, desperately begging for one mouthful of kanji.   ❖

the competition

In a small village there was a young woman. She had no mother, father, uncle, or cousin—no one. She was very poor and could barely afford to eat one meal a day. But God had blessed her with one boon, and that boon was her great beauty. She was beautiful beyond all comparison! Her nose and eyes were the work of a master sculptor, her waist and thighs made of refined sugar. She was fair-skinned, voluptuous, and had long curly hair. All those who laid eyes on her were left breathless for a whole hour; they would roam aimlessly, forgetting their duties, their thoughts full of mad fantasies about her. Each young man in the village secretly hoped to someday claim her as his wife, and so each harbored a secret enmity towards all the others.

The young woman was very much aware of this war of hormones her beauty was causing; she both enjoyed and feared it. *If I were to accept one young man's love and marry him, he would just make my life miserable with his undying jealousy. What is my way out?* she wondered. Finally, she called the young men and said, "I am going to give each one of you fifty goats and fifty buffaloes. Rear them for a year; then I will marry the one who sells them for the highest price."

The men agreed.

After that, the men concentrated on their fifty goats and fifty buf-faloes. They cut grass and tender shoots, ground up cotton seeds, stole grass from wherever it grew thick and soft, herded their animals all day long and all over the countryside, milked them, churned fresh butter and clarified it to make ghee, trekked to the remotest villages to sell it, and carefully saved every pie that they earned. They not only saved the money, but also counted it every day and found secret burrows in which to stash it.

It was around this time that a city man came to the village on a vacation. As he stepped into the town, the young woman had just finished washing her hair in the lake, and was sitting on the branch of a banyan tree, combing it with her fingers. Her long tresses were lying coiled in the dust at the roots of the tree.

The city man came to the lake to water his horse. There he caught sight of her, her long locks and her glowing beauty, and was bewitched. *The entire purpose of my birth on this earth will be fulfilled if only I can talk to her for one day; if not, I may as well be dead,* he thought, and began plot-ting how to introduce himself. He took off his precious nine-gemmed ring, dropped it on the ground, and hid himself behind the tree. When the sun's rays touched the ring, the gems flashed brilliantly, catching the attention of the young woman. She hastily tied her long hair in a knot, jumped down from the tree and eagerly picked up the ring. At once, he sprang forward, hugged her and confessed his love. She, too, found him very attractive. Indeed, he was tall, strong and handsome.

"I want you," she said. "However, if the young men of this village come to know of my attraction for you, they will peck and peck at us both and feed us to the vultures. Come back to this lake on the night before the next full moon, at midnight. I shall meet you here. Then we can elope to your city, and live there in peace."

The night before the next full moon was also the last night of the one year that she had stipulated to the young men. They were busy making trips to the nearby markets and shandies, bribing brokers with fifties and hundreds to get a better price for their cattle, and bringing back the money in sackloads to her. She took the sacks from each of them. Then she told them, "Go to the village temple and wait for me there. I shall count all the money, and place the one who has brought the highest amount in my heart. I will then go and bathe in the lake, dress myself beautifully and come to the temple just after dawn with my thali. I shall give the thali to my chosen. He will tie it around my neck. The rest of you must not start brawling, but be good sports, wish us the best and cook us a big wedding feast."

The men agreed and went to temple with the village elders. There they sat, patiently waiting for her to come. Each man's heart went *thidik, thidik* as he prayed that she would be his forever.

The moment the young men left to the temple, she threw all the money into a big sack, tied it up and carried the huge bundle on her head to the lake. The city man was waiting for her there on his horse. As soon as he saw her, he ran up to her and lifted her high in the air. He carried both the bundle and the woman and placed them on the horse's back. Hugging them both tightly to his chest, he galloped off towards the city at lightning speed.

At the temple, the young men waited for the woman to arrive at dawn with the thali, and the village folks waited outside for a chance to gaze upon her beauty once again. ❖

the quarrelsome wives

Once there lived a couple, with a grown son. The husband and wife could not stop quarrelling with each other. Even the most insignificant word could spark off a war, which would mean that both went without a sip of kanji for days. They would wake up at sunrise, remember last night's spat, and resolve not to speak to each other all day. The kanji from the night before would sit there in the pot, slowly going bad. The wife would be vexed because she couldn't ask her husband to go the market for fresh groceries. So she would just drink a glass of water and set off to work. When the husband woke up, he would look at the spoiled kanji, and long to ask the wife to make a fresh batch—but they were still not speaking to one another. So, he would quietly go to work on an empty stomach.

She's the woman; it's her job to make peace. If she can keep ignoring me, then I can keep ignoring her. I'm the man, after all, he thought. So he would beg for a quarter or half a cup of kanji from his aunts, but never ask his wife.

Finally, one day, fearing they would both die of starvation, he said to his wife, "Why should we go on quarreling like this? We live together in the same house, but don't even look at each other's face." To bring back some peace into the house, they found a nice, sweet girl for their son to marry.

On the day of the wedding, the wife told her daughter-in-law, "Listen, girl! I was raised the old-fashioned way. I was told to do whatever my husband wanted. I tried my best, but it has only earned me his disrespect. Now he gets angry at almost nothing. He'll refuse to eat the food I cook, go beg in his aunt's place, and talk badly of me all over the town. Let me give you this advice: be smart, and keep your man under your thumb."

The mother and her daughter-in-law soon became the best of friends. They joined together to tell their husbands, "If you're here when I ask you to be here, then you'll get your kanji. If you're late, then too bad!" Then they would turn around and go to sleep.

Both the father and son had to beg for their daily meals. The women would make gruel with whatever was available, eat it all themselves, wash the pot, and go to sleep again. The men's stomachs were emptier than ever.

The time came for the Thai Pongal festival. The husbands brought home new saris, shirts, rice, and dhal. "Let's clean and paint the house," they said. But they got no help from the women, who were too busy showing off their new saris to all the neighbours. After they finished painting the house, the men were very hungry. But as usual, there was nothing to eat at home. The son went in search of his wife and mother.

"We are hungry," he told them when he found them. "Can you stop gossiping, come home, and make us some food?"

The women paid no heed. When they finally did return home, they just boiled half a dozen eggs, ate them all themselves, and went to bed.

The men were starving once again. That night, they crept out of the house, and in a whispered conversation, decided that tomorrow would be their wives' last chance.

The next day dawned. The father and the son ate a bit of the spoiled kanji from the previous day, and left for work. When they returned for lunch, the two women were sitting outside checking each other's hair for lice and gossiping. The men went to the kitchen to see if there was anything to eat. The pots were empty as usual, but there was a smell indicating that something had been cooked. They went to their wives and asked, "Are you planning to feed us at all?"

The women said in chorus: "Oh, are you dressing us in such fine silk and gold that we should keep cooking for you every day?"

That was the last straw. The two men walked out, got married to the first women they met, and brought them back to the house as second wives.

From that day, the war has shifted from the husband and wife to the mother and daughter-in-law. It has not yet come to an end. ❖

moon, be my witness

The full moon of the month of Panguni was shining bright, almost milky white. Mukkaiya, lying on a cot out in the muththam, looked up at the moon and gave a loud guffaw. His wife, working in the kitchen, looked through the window at the sky, but could not see what was so funny.

"Why are you sitting there, laughing to yourself?" she asked.

"Oh, it's nothing," he said.

"Please tell me, what is that you find so funny?"

"Okay, come sit next to me," Mukkaiya said. "But you must promise never to speak about this to anyone, or we stand to lose our heads! Do you remember Muniyandi, from the house on the corner, who went to irrigate his fields four years back and disappeared without a trace?"

"Of course I remember!"

"Nobody in town knows what really happened. When Muniyandi came, I was already out there irrigating our field. Do you know what he did? He stopped me and wanted to divert the canal water to his field first. I asked him to wait till I was done, but he wouldn't listen. It started with harsh words, but soon the argument turned violent! He gave me a stinging slap on the cheek. My anger grew and grew until it filled my eyes and nose. I ran, picked up my spade and gave him a loud whack on the head. That was it! The man was no more!

"There was a full moon that night, just like tonight. As Muniyandi fell dead, he called out, 'Moon, be my witness!' I didn't know what to do. I looked around; thankfully no one had seen us. I dug a pit in our field, buried the body, and planted rice over it. Oh, I shiver when I think of it! But when I looked up and saw the moon, I thought of Muniyandi's last words and I couldn't stop laughing. What good was it, calling the moon to be his witness?"

The wife just sat there in stunned silence.

A few days later, Mukkaiya and his wife quarrelled. Angry words were volleyed back and forth by both. At the climax, Mukkaiya's anger again grew and grew until it filled his eyes and nose. He picked up his spade and charged at her.

"Aiyyo, he is coming to kill me, just like he killed Muniyandi from the house on the corner!" wailed the woman, running into the street. And that was how a secret that had been well-kept for four years became common knowledge in the town. ❖

night blindness

A young man who suffered from severe night blindness* was visiting his in-laws' home for the first time. He had not, of course, informed anyone about his affliction.

It was the sowing season. As the young man set off to check his father-in-law's fields, it began to rain and did not stop until dusk. The young man, having taken shelter in a shed near the well, could not see his way back. He was stuck.

In a little while, he heard a cowbell. He recognized the sound as the bell of one of his father-in-law's calves. Relieved, he followed the

---

* In the days before electric streetlights, night blindness was a serious handicap which would ruin a young man's marriage prospects. – P.K.C.

sound and caught hold of the calf's tail. The frightened animal bolted towards home, and the man scampered behind it, hanging on tight.

The folks at home, who had been worried, wanted to know why he was delayed.

"You have very irresponsible servants, Maama. They took off as soon as they were done with the sowing. Shouldn't they have checked the fields?" demanded the smart man. "This calf had strayed. If I had left with them, it would have been stolen."

His in-laws were very touched by the young man's concern.

It was Wednesday. When the man was setting off to the fields, his new wife whispered, "This evening you must have an oil bath. So return before it gets too dark."

It was his bad luck that it rained hard on that day too. The young man was stranded in the street. As he sat worrying about getting home, some creature brushed against his foot. He caught it. It was a nice fat rabbit, shivering in the cold rain.

Meanwhile, the anxious father-in-law had sent a servant with a lamp to look for him. The servant found the man standing with the rabbit. On recognizing the servant, the man shouted, "Is there not one responsible servant in my father-in-law's household? We all planned to have oil baths tonight, and we'll be very hungry afterwards. I know my father-in-law loves rabbit curry, and I managed to catch a fat one. What took you so long? Do you expect me, the new groom in this household, to carry it back myself? Here, go get a stick and tie it up." Making sure that he had a tight hold on one end of the stick, he followed the servant home.

After his oil bath, the man sat down in front of his banana leaf-plate to feast on the rabbit curry. A cat, drawn by the smell of the meat, was waiting outside the kitchen. The wife's two-year-old brother silently made his way to the man's leaf and took a mouthful. When the mother-in-law saw her young son eating off her son-in-law's plate, she giggled aloud. Hearing her, the man thought the cat had taken a bite from his leaf-plate. Sensing a vague form sitting next to him, he gave it a sound knock. The child yelled in pain and fell to the ground.

Realizing his error, the man said, "I'm sorry, but a growing child should not pick at his food; that can only bring bad luck to a house. I didn't mean to hurt him, but sometimes I get carried away when I'm angry."

The young man's bed was laid on the thinnai, outside. Nearby, a goat was tied to the grinding stone. Every time the goat bobbed its head, the bell around its neck chimed, *galeer, galeer*. The young man had been warned that the goat was ill-tempered, and butted anyone who went near.

The young wife was busy clearing the kitchen for the night. The man, waiting for her on the thinnai, was scared of the goat, which was jerking its head and leaping about.

In a little while he heard a *galeer, galeer* approaching the thinnai. Thinking the goat had broken its tether and was coming to butt him, he felt around until he found a heavy iron pestle. When the sound was very near, he swung the pestle.

His young wife fell down crying in pain. The poor woman had only come to show her husband her new pair of anklets!

The people of the house descended on the young man in a flash, demanding an explanation.

But our young man was not one to accept defeat; he was determined not to reveal the secret of his night blindness. He replied arrogantly, "Of course I hit her. Why should a woman from a good family have such loud bells on her anklets? What is she, a koothaadi street dancer? How is she going to make a good home for me, acting like this? I did warn you earlier about my temper, didn't I?" ❖

to whom do you think you belong?

There once lived a farmer who had no son. He told his wife, "You have to go out and find a man who can give you a baby. Only then will I take you back as my wife."

She chose a woodsman and got herself pregnant. She stayed with him till she gave birth. On hearing that his wife had had a son, the farmer went to take them back. The woodsman was willing to send back the wife, but would not give up the son. And so the dispute was taken to court of the raja. Each man stated his side of the case.

"Oh Raja," said the woodsman, "suppose I find a purse. Since it is empty, I put my money into it. When the owner of the purse comes to ask for it, I'm only obligated to return the bag, right? I don't need to give him my money!"

"That cannot be right, oh Raja," said the farmer. "Suppose I borrow a little curd to use as a base to set my milk. Can the person who lent me that spoonful demand my whole dish of set curd?

"Or, suppose I take my cow to a bull to impregnate it. When my cow delivers, the owner of the bull has to return my cow along with the calf, right?"

As both were adamant, the raja said, "This is a very difficult case. I will reserve my judgment for now. The three of you raise the boy together. When he grows up, get him married, then come to me and I shall give you my verdict."

The boy grew, learned the skills of both the farmer and the woodsman, got married, and returned to the raja with his two fathers, his mother, and his wife.

"Fine, my boy," said the raja. "You have so many to love you. Tell me, to whom do you think you belong?"

"Is there any doubt, oh Raja? I belong to my wife," declared the boy. ❖

Ki. Ra.: There was a time when it was socially acceptable to have the wife of an impotent man impregnated with another virile one. This is a habit that was very common among the royals. Readers must understand that this story is perhaps of that time.

And why did this wife choose the woodsman? Here is the reason: A queen will choose an intellectual man, because she wants the son she bears to be capable of governance. Similarly, a working woman will choose a strong man, because she wants her son to be good at physical labour. We take our cow to the strongest bull, don't we? Perhaps this wife was drawn by the woodsman's strong sinewy muscles!

I remember when I was young, in Ambasamudhram, before rice mills became common, overhearing old men sitting around the backyard openly admiring and discussing the firm breasts of the women who were pounding the rice.

three coconuts

Once, there was a couple who was very, very poor. The husband decided to meditate on God to relieve their suffering. God appeared before him and gave him three coconuts.

"When you break them, think of the thing you want most," instructed God.

The husband gave the three coconuts to his wife and said, "We can get whatever we want with these."

"Let's ask for a lot of gold," she cried.

"No! I always wanted a fruit orchard of my own," he insisted.

"Who needs an orchard? What we must have is a nice big house!"

And so they went on and on, each wanting different things.

Finally, exasperated, the husband threw the first coconut on the floor, yelling, "Mayiru*!"

As soon as he said the word, curly black hair sprouted all over the roof, ceiling, floor, walls, dishes, and furniture.

Aghast, he threw the second coconut on the floor and screamed, "All hair, please disappear!"

Immediately all the hair vanished... including their eyebrows, and all the hair on their heads and bodies! There they stood, like a couple of plucked chickens.

Only then did they realize how silly they had been.

The wife snatched the third coconut, smashed it, and pleaded, "Oh God, we promise to be content with what we have. Make everything normal!"

And everything went back to normal at once.   ❖

---

* The word *mayiru* generally refers to pubic hair, and is used as an insult, in the sense of "that's how much I value you." — P.K.C.

precious treasure

After a few days of being a guest at his in-laws', a groom was walking back to his house with his new wife. Along the way they passed a huge mango tree.

"What tree is this, machchan?" asked the woman.

"Don't you know what tree this is?" asked the man. "This area is full of them."

"I am my father's only daughter. I was the apple of his eye, his precious treasure, and I never had to leave the house. I have no clue what tree this is."

A little farther on, they passed a jasmine bush.

"Do you know what this is?" asked the man.

"I am my father's only daughter. I was the apple of his eye, his precious treasure, and I never had to leave the house. I have no clue what flower this is."

A little farther on, they passed a temple with a tall coconut tree in front of it.

"Do you know what this is?" asked the man.

"I am my father's only daughter. I was the apple of his eye, his precious treasure, and I never had to leave the house. I have no clue what tree this is."

Slightly frustrated, the man stayed quiet till they passed a cornfield. *Okay, woman, you eat this every day. You must know what this is!* he thought.

"Do you know what this is?" he asked.

The woman repeated the same docile reply.

Totally exasperated, the man marched into the corn field, pulled out a stalk, walked back and gave her a sharp blow in the centre of her back.

"Oh!" she wailed, and broke into a song:

Mango tree, jasmine bush, coconut tree, and corn stalk,
I know them all: please do not whack me any more, machchan!

And the poor "precious treasure" went back to sobbing.   ❖

the magic fish

Once upon a time, there was a couple. The husband was a very nice man. He would go fishing every morning, leave two fish from his catch with his wife to make curry, and take the rest to the market. With whatever he earned, he would buy rice and vegetables. By the time he reached home, he would be tired, and go straight to sleep.

His wife was a glutton. She was always looking around for something to munch on. Her jaws never stopped chewing. When the husband gave her the fish in the morning, she'd clean out the guts, chop it into pieces, make a pot full of kozhambu, and as soon as it began to boil, she'd pour it all over her rice and eat it up before he returned home. Even though her husband was slaving throughout the day, it never occurred to her to boil water for his bath, or to ask how his day had been when he came home. She was satisfied as long as her stomach was full. She would leave him just two handfuls of rice and a tiny portion of kozhambu with one fish head and a tail, then wipe the pot clean with her fingers and lick them.

Around this time, all the rivers and ponds in the region were drying up. There were not nearly as many fish to be caught as there had been before. The man knew no other job apart from fishing. Still, he would manage to catch a few tiny guppies, give them to her, and see that she ate her fill. He would go to bed with his stomach half-empty.

One day, he was lucky enough to catch a really huge fish. He was thrilled; this would earn him three or four days of rest!

But as he picked the fish out of his net, it began to sob.

Is this a joke? thought he. *A fish caught in the net normally tries to jump back into water! It doesn't lie around the bank and weep!*

"Fish, fish, why are you crying?" he asked.

"My entire lineage is going to die with me. You will find no more fish in these lakes or rivers."

"What do you mean? If there are no more fish, how am I supposed to earn a living?"

"Take me to a perennial river and throw me in. I will make sure we increase in number," promised the fish.

"It's all fine for you to say 'Throw me in a river'. When I go back home empty-handed, my wife will strip the sari from her waist, tie it around her head like a turban, and dance around me in a rage!"

The fish, understanding the man's predicament, gave him a gold coin and told him to come back for more if necessary. The man took the fish and threw it into a river that he knew would not dry up, even in the cruelest summer.

When he got back home, he gave the wife the gold coin and told her everything that had happened. The wife was livid.

"You useless man! You come home with a single coin, acting so proud of yourself! Why couldn't you demand all the gold it had?" She was leaping furiously between the sky and the earth.

He said not a word in return. He quietly ate what she left for him, and went to sleep.

The next day, the wife gave him a huge wooden trunk.

"Here, go to the fish and ask it to fill this trunk with gold coins."

He did.

A few days later, she gave him an even bigger trunk, and told him to get that one filled, too.

He did.

This went on and on and on for many days.

One day, he was sitting frustrated at the riverbank, when the fish saw him and asked him what the problem was.

"As long as my wife is around, you and I will never find any peace. Can I join you in this river?" he implored.

"We fish are born to live in water. How will you survive here? Go home and do as I say," said the fish, and whispered something in his ear.

He returned home and flopped on his mat. His wife begged him to have dinner.

"No! I don't want any dinner. I am going to hang myself tonight," he declared.

"What? What happened? Please don't kill yourself," she wept.

"What else can I do? All these days the fish gave me treasure after treasure. Today it said I have to return it all, with steep interest. Or else I have to agree to be its husband! It says that if I refuse, it will go appeal to the raja for justice," said the man. "Is it not better to just hang myself?"

The wife's stomach churned. Gold and money could be earned any day. But could one get a husband so easily?

"I don't want the gold anymore. Return everything the fish gave you. I shall help you pay back the interest," she cried.

Today, she runs around busily, working through the day. The couple, of course, is going to live happily ever after.   ❖

the man with two wives

There once was a man with two wives. He alternated between them every month. One wife lived on the ground floor, and the other up above. There was no stairway to go up—just a ladder.

It was mid-summer, the end of the month of Chiththirai. The downstairs wife was thinking that the next day would be the first day of the new month, Vaigasi, and her time with her husband would end; he would have to move upstairs. But she did not want to let him go.

Then her neighbour happened to say, "Did you know that Chiththirai has 32 days this year?"

I have one more day with him. Why should he run away so early? she thought, and just as he was climbing the ladder, she caught hold of his legs.

Now do you think the upstairs wife was about to let go of her man once he had already stepped onto the ladder? *If you wanted so badly for him to stay one more day, shouldn't you have watched the almanac?* the upstairs wife thought. She told the man to raise an arm so she could drag him upstairs. Now there was one wife pulling him down and one pulling him up. He was caught in between, begging, "Let go of me, let go of me...!"

Finally, both wives tired out and let go, and the poor man fell from the ladder and broke both his legs.

The wives decided that each of them would take care of one leg.

The upstairs wife was rich. She called a doctor, who treated the leg that was hers, and almost mended it.

The downstairs wife was not so well-off. She depended on poultices, herbal compresses, and fomentation. The leg that was hers did not heal well.

The husband could not go up the ladder with his broken legs, so he stayed downstairs. The upstairs wife was anxious for him to recover fully so she could call him up. She yelled to the downstairs wife, "You're not caring for him properly. Look at me—I had *my* leg set right in a few days!"

The downstairs wife became very angry. That day, she had washed her hair and was just combing it when a thought struck her. *In a few days, he is going to be fine. Perhaps he will decide to spend more days upstairs to make up for the time he missed. If I even want to see him, I will have to go up there to her house. Oh no! That won't do. I must not allow him to be completely cured.*

With a *chatack, chatack* from her wooden comb, she gouged his healed leg. He yowled in pain. Hearing the screams, the upstairs wife ran down, and saw that the leg she had treated was bleeding. "You sinner!" she yelled. "You've wounded the leg that I healed. You're going to pay for this!"

She ran up the ladder, heated an iron ladle, came down and branded the man's other leg with it. He screamed, of course, and the other wife came in to scratch him again with her comb. And so they went on and on.

This is how the man with two wives died.   ❖

the last dosai

Once there lived a husband and wife. They longed to eat dosais. But to make dosais, one needed rice and black lentils. There was rice at home, but where would they get the money for black lentils?

One day in the month of Purattaasi, the husband had an idea. With his very last pie, he bought some castor oil, stripped down to his loincloth, and smeared the oil all over his body.

Then he went to a general provision shop, where there were black lentils spread out on the ground outside to dry.

There, he rolled on the ground like a pious Vaishnavite, crying "Govindha, Govindha!", four times back and forth.

His body was now covered with black lentils!

He rushed back home. His wife brushed the black lentils off his skin and soaked them. Then she ground the rice and the lentils for the dough.

"I shall go and cut banana leaves," said the husband, "and we will eat together. You make the dosais." He went to the backyard with the knife.

The wife began making nice, round, soft, huge dosais.

As she took the first one out of the pan, she thought she would have a taste. That was it! She ate all the rest of them, steaming hot, as soon as she took them off the pan. Finally, there was just enough dough to make one tiny dosai that she kept aside for the husband.

The husband returned with the leaves, and she served him the tiny dosai.

"What happened to the rest of the dosais?" he asked.

"I ate them."

"How?"

"Here's how!" she said, and picked up the tiny one and popped it in her mouth. ❖

i'm just a punching bag!

Once upon a time there was a husband who was usually a very timid man. But one day, he flew into a rage and beat his wife black and blue.

The next day, neither of them went out to work. The wife's body was covered with bruises. They stopped speaking to each other.

But a husband and wife cannot go on like that forever. The wife broke the silence first, speaking so quietly she was almost muttering to herself.

"Everyone in town is cooking pork today. We could do so, too. It would soothe my aching body, and help me lactate better for your child. But who am I to demand? After all, I'm just a punching bag!"

The husband sat pretending he had not heard anything. In a little while, he stepped out of the house and returned with a cut of pork.

The wife studiously ignored the meat. She spoke again, so quietly she was almost muttering to herself: "I have washed the meat-pot and dried it in the backyard. I've even sharpened the knife. I've put the ingredients for the masala next to the grinding stone. All that's left to do now is cook the meat. But who am I to demand? After all, I'm just a punching bag!"

The husband ground the masala and cooked the meat, and soon the curry was ready.

After a while the wife spoke again, so quietly she was almost muttering to herself: "I have washed the rice, and it's ready to be steamed. It would be nice if someone could do that. Ah, Amma! My body is sore. I can't even move. But who am I to demand? After all, I'm just a punching bag!"

The husband steamed the rice. Now the wife was expecting her husband to call her to eat. But he remained silent.

Just then, Vellachi, their dog, sniffing the meat, started to whine.

"Oh shut up, you stupid cur. I don't want any meat," she snapped at the dog.

The dog just stood there, wagging its tail.

"Oh, all right! If you won't leave me alone till I eat..." she said. She got up and served two plates of pork and rice, one for her husband, and one for herself.

Both of them threw a few pieces of meat to Vellachi, too.   ❖

how can you doubt me?

Once upon a time there was a man named Karuppan, who was very hard of hearing. He lived with his wife and his widowed mother. Since he was deaf, his wife did not give him much respect. She treated the mother even worse, almost like a dirty weed. She didn't feed her properly, or even give her decent clothes to wear.

The mother wanted to cry about her plight to her son, but could not, for he was deaf. If she were to shout loud enough for him to hear her, then the wife would also hear her, and things would only get worse.

Karuppan noticed that his mother was growing increasingly thin, and wondered if she was not being fed well.

So, he called his wife and asked, "What di, are you feeding my mother properly? Call her here. Today she will sit next to me and eat."

The wife realized that the husband was suspicious of her.

She shed some false tears and said, "Aiyyo, how can you doubt me? Come, I shall ask your mother to eat. See her reaction for yourself."

She took her husband along to his mother and whispered in her ears, "Aithe, would you like some turmeric to smear on your face, and some kohl to decorate your eyes?"

Since the mother was a widow, she would never put on turmeric or kohl.

"Aiyyo, what are you saying?" she screamed at her daughter-in-law. "I don't want anything. Leave me alone."

"Did you hear that?" the wife asked the husband. "At least now, you should believe that I am a very generous woman."

Of course she is, thought the foolish son. *How can she help it if my mother is being difficult?* ❖

Ki. Ra.: Tales about mother-in-law/daughter-in-law conflict abound in folktales. In almost all of these stories, the oppressor gets taught a lesson in the end. Strangely, in this tale, the oppressor winds up the victor. There are two possible reasons: either this is a tale made up by an extremely victimized daughter-in-law, or else the story is incomplete.

the lying wife

Once there were two brothers, who lived with their wives in separate homes. Their mother lived alone. The younger brother's wife was a good woman, who cooked, cleaned and brought her husband his kanji on time. The elder brother's wife was terribly selfish. She only looked after her own interests, and ignored her husband completely. She ate her three meals a day and slept well.

The younger brother's wife knew what kind of woman her brother-in-law's wife was, and tried to tell him. "When you return home, ask for your kanji and see what your wife does."

He did so, and his wife replied, "How do you expect to get kanji, when I have no rice in the house?"

"Fine then. Go ask my mother to give you some kanji."

She went to the mother and said, "Your son is hungry. He wants some kanji."

The mother gave her a pot full of kanji, which the wife promptly ate up herself. She returned the empty vessel and went home empty-handed.

She told her husband, "Your mother has no rice either. She wants you to give her some."

"Then go ask at the neighbour's house."

She went to neighbour's house. When she was given some kanji, she again ate it all up herself and returned home with nothing.

"I was coming home with the kanji when I tripped over a cow's tether, and spilled it," she said.

Chee, I don't want to live with this woman anymore, thought the husband and took her back to *her* mother.

"Oh no! We don't want her either. She's always been a terribly selfish woman. Do what you want with her," said the mother.

So the husband tonsured her head, cut her in three, painted red and black spots on her face, sat her facing backwards on a donkey* and chased her out of the village.   ❖

---

* This is a rural method of shaming someone, analogous to tarring and feathering (usually without the cutting in three!) —P.K.C.

seven crane heads

Once upon a time, all wives were very moral; this is a story about how they learned to tell lies.

A very long time ago, there was a cruel husband. His wife was very innocent, fearful of most things in the world.

Every day, he went out to hunt and came home with a sparrow or a crane, which she made tasty curries with. Each time he brought home a bird, she whispered, "Please, Machchan. Do not kill a life."

"Are you criticizing me? Eh? Who do you think you are, to give me advice?" he snarled. He added a few more choice curses, too.

One day, he came home with seven cranes, gave them to her to cook and went to bathe in the river. As she was cleaning the birds, she saw that the seventh bird was still breathing. Not wanting to kill it, she spread turmeric paste over its wounds, and let it fly off. The other six, she used to make a curry.

When the husband sat for his dinner, he counted the number of crane heads in the curry.

"Why are there only six heads? What happened to the seventh?"

"It was still alive. I did not want to kill it. So I let it go," she said.

"What's this insolence?" he barked. "Go at once! Catch the seventh bird and cook it for me. Or else you'll have no place in this house." He dragged her outside and banged the door shut.

Not knowing where to go or what to do, she walked aimlessly, weeping, soaking the earth she walked on with her tears. She saw an old well and climbed onto the wall, intending to jump in.

An old Avvaiyar woman, who was passing by, saw her and stopped her before she could jump. She asked her why she wanted to die at such a young age. The wife, between heart-rending sobs, related her story. The Avvaiyar woman cackled with laughter.

"You stupid girl, you wanted to kill yourself for that? The only way to remove a thorn from your foot is with another thorn! Drumstick flowers only come for a short season, you should fry them only in the best ghee! If your husband is an asshole, don't try to play the saint. You have to learn a few tricks and lies to survive."

"So what should I do?" asked the wife.

The Avvaiyar woman took her home, packed some chicken curry she had made and said, "Give this chicken head to your husband and tell him it is the crane. He will not know the difference."

At home, when the wife served fresh hot rice with the chicken curry, the husband reached out, touched her hand gently and praised her. "There you are. I knew my wife would never disobey a single word of mine."

Since then, wives have learned to tell a few lies, and keep some secrets of their own.   ❖

the wonder-child

This satire, more a character sketch than a real story, was told by a septuage-narian named Arasaatha, who in turn was told this by her mother, Raaku.

Once there was a man who was a hard worker, but whose wife was idle and lazy and loved to gossip. She was incapable of even a simple job like raising a goat kid. Every morning, after the husband left for work, she would make herself some hot kanji, and then keep busy sparking quarrels between neighbouring mothers and daughters.

It was now six years since the couple had been married, but they still had no children. The women of the town would whisper, "Look at her! She doesn't have any brats at home, so she goes around the town as she pleases. Can't she get herself a job?"

The wife was longing to become pregnant.

Well, even if I can't get pregnant, I can tell my husband that I haven't had my head-bath, since I missed my period. Then he'll make sure the whole town hears of it, she decided.

That evening, the husband returned tired after a day of field work and asked, "Adiye, give me my kanji."

She served the kanji in a bowl and lay down on her mat.

"Adiye, I need salt for my kanji," he said.

"I'm sorry. I haven't had a head-bath in forty days. My period is late. I cannot bend down to give you your salt," she moaned.

The husband could not contain his joy. He drank his unsalted kanji, covered his wife with a sheet and said, "You take rest, my golden princess! I'll go inform your mother and be back soon."

On the way, he told everyone he saw, "My wife is pregnant. She hasn't had a head-bath in forty days. Her period is late!" He reached his mother-in-law's house, told her the good news, and ran back home.

There he found his wife, fresh from a head-bath, with her hair wet.

"Oh no, what happened?" he asked.

Waist and thighs like your younger brother,
Nose and face like your elder brother,
The baby slipped out
When I went to pee,

she wept.

"Aiyaiyyo, I didn't even get to see this wonder-child of mine!" he exclaimed, tied a rope to the ceiling, put a noose around his neck, plucked out his tongue and died on the spot. ❖

mendicant madness

Once there was a man who had sworn never to eat without first feeding a mendicant. But it's not every day that one happens upon a mendicant! You might go for days without ever seeing one. Our man would search high and low without finding anyone begging for alms. This meant that he had to go hungry, and that his wife had to stay hungry too.

Once in a blue moon, a mendicant would stray into the town—but would usually eat at the first house that offered him food, and then leave. Even if one of them stayed on for a nap, he would refuse to get up for a second invitation. "Get lost, I'm not hungry," he would snap and turn around to go back to sleep.

If the man insisted, the mendicant would demand a fee to eat. Our man would plead, "I can only afford one rupee."

The mendicant would laugh. "You expect me to eat again for a single rupee? Those days are gone!" Our man would by now have gone hungry for two or three days. He would be desperate, ready to fall at his saviour's feet. Hell, he actually did fall at some feet! The people of the town could not understand why the man was possessed with this "mendicant madness".

One day, having starved for several days, after yet another fruitless search, he fell faint in the street. The town elders decided to take matters into their own hands. They revived him, and after a long debate, finally got him to agree that he would eat if he was hungry, and *then* search for mendicants.

His wife had detested his "mendicant madness" from the start but had kept quiet till now. Even if a mendicant were to wander by while he was ploughing in the field, he would stop his work, abandon the plough, and rush over to find out if he had eaten. If the answer was "no", our man would drag him home, and his wife would have to cook and serve him food.

One day the wife had just finished her lunch, cleared the kitchen and lay down for a short siesta when our man barged in with not just one, but *four* mendicants. He joyfully called out to the woman, "Adiye, get up. Start cooking. I have to feed these men. They are very hungry."

"They can eat what's left over. Go cut some banana leaves from the garden for them to eat from," she said.

The man told the mendicants to take a seat on the thinnai and went to the backyard with a knife.

The moment he disappeared, the woman picked up a thick iron pestle and smeared it with turmeric and sandalwood paste. The mendicants watching this were puzzled and asked her what she was doing.

"Oh, nothing much!" she replied. "A few years back, my mother-in-law came down with a severe infection in the nape of her neck. The medicine man asked us to smear a pestle with turmeric and sandal and then give her a blow on the nape. Unfortunately, she died before we could complete the treatment. After that, every year on her death anniversary, we invite mendicants home, feed them, give them a blow on the nape and then present them with a pestle as alms. Today is her ninth death anniversary; that's why my husband brought you home. Please wait, I must hurry with the cooking."

Even before she finished her tale, the mendicants had hurried off. She was wiping the pestle clean as her husband returned with the banana leaves and found his precious mendicants missing. "Where are they?" he asked.

"Please, don't even ask me," she said, sighing. "Those men refused to eat unless I gave them this pestle. But how could I? I got this as part of my dowry."

"Are you an idiot? What is so great about this pestle? If you had to give it to them, I would have bought you seven better pestles! You had to chase them off for a silly pestle?" he asked in a rage. "Give me the bloody pestle. I'll follow them, fall at their feet, apologize and bring them back."

He snatched the pestle and ran behind the mendicants. The four men, hearing his footsteps, turned around to see our man racing after them, heaving the heavy pestle in his hand. They broke into a run, and the man raced after them. The chase went on for some time. The wife stood watching the show from the gate, howling with laughter. ❖

the unwanted shave

Once there lived a barber with his wife and five-year-old son. There was a terrible famine in the village, and the frustrated people were so busy foraging for their daily food that they stopped shaving. Every man began sporting a long beard, and the barber had no one to shave. So one day he decided to migrate to a more fertile town.

The barber's family packed their belongings and left, leaving behind a lit oil lamp*. Not knowing exactly where they were headed, they travelled through hills and forests. After seeing no one for a long time they came across an ascetic meditating under a tree in a sparse wood. His long beard was flowing around him all over the ground.

---

* It was once a custom in the villages to leave behind a lit lamp, so that the next person to take over the house would not enter into darkness. – Ki. Ra.

The couple decided to rest under the tree for a while. The cool breeze made the son fall asleep. The wife left him behind with her husband, and went to look for food.

The barber sat looking idly at the ascetic's beard.

My hands are itching to give him a good shave. Why don't I just do it? I think he'll be happy, when he comes out of his meditation, to have a satin-smooth cheek.

Once the idea had sparked, he did not stop to think. He quickly got ready and began to shave the ascetic. As a clean smooth face slowly emerged, he smiled to himself: *Aha! Now this is what I call a handsome face!* He finished shaving the cheeks and trimming the hair. But the ascetic's head was bent and his chin was tilted downwards. So he gently lifted the ascetic's face and drew his knife upwards along his throat. At this point, the ascetic was jerked out of his meditation. He stared disbelievingly at his long beard, now fallen in a pile on the ground. He felt his chin; not a hair there!

"Dey," yelled the enraged ascetic. "What have you done to me? Hear my curse!"

The barber stood there, not understanding why the ascetic was mad.

"Dey, here I am in deep meditation, begging God to rid this world of hunger and starvation. I sat here for months without moving an inch. Just as I was connecting to God, you disturbed me! How am I to meditate now? I'll have to begin again from scratch!"

"I could have cursed you to turn to dust and dirt, but I lack the strength now that you've disturbed me," he continued. "So tell me, how do I punish your misdeed?"

"Oh Swami, forgive me," cried the barber, raising his folded arms high in the air and falling to the ground. "I had no idea that you would be so angry. You can punish me any way you choose."

"Leave your wife with me," ordered the ascetic, and the barber agreed.

When the wife returned and heard about the curse, she wept, "Oh Swami, how can you say this? How can I live without my son?"

"Your son may stay here as well, if he wants to," said the ascetic.

"I want to stay with my mother," wailed the son.

The barber left behind his wife and son and went on his way. After a little while, the son began crying with hunger. The woman could not see what the ascetic wanted with her: after all, he could do nothing to feed her or her son. She looked around for fruits and vegetables. She came upon a busy line of ants. She followed the line to the spot where they were burrowing. She dug the earth there, and found a pot full of grain. She took it out and made a tasty gruel; she fed her son and left some in front of the ascetic. Then she went to look for her husband.

Unable to find him after a long search, she returned to find that the ascetic had eaten his share of the gruel and had left some for her.

"I don't want that," she snapped. "What do I need food for when my husband is wandering the forest with no wife or child?"

"Forget that man who abandoned you," smiled the ascetic. "I am your husband now. Make me happy."

"The only mistake my husband made was to give you a shave. It's just a stupid bunch of hair—give it three months and it'll grow back. Just for that, you take away his wife for a lifetime? If you were a true ascetic, you would bless him and let us live in peace."

"I'd be crazy to let you go, woman," laughed the ascetic. "You are resourceful enough to find grain and cook a meal in the middle of a wild forest!"

"You can have me only if I am alive!" she declared.

She picked up her son and ran to the river to drown herself. The shocked ascetic jumped up and stopped her, apologizing profusely. He searched through hills, shrubs, forests, cities, villages, and jungles until he found the barber and brought him back to the clever woman. ❖

two brothers and two boiling pots

Once there lived two brothers, who were both married and lived in adjacent houses.

The elder brother was a very generous man, who refused nothing to the needy. His limitless generosity soon reduced him to penury.

The younger brother was a miser; if you asked him for a few coins, he would put them in a gunny sack and shake them, and give you whatever got filtered out. His wife was just the same.

One day, an old man arrived at the elder brother's house.

"Aiya, I am hungry. I haven't eaten for days. Please give me a mouthful," he begged.

The elder brother was already so poor that he was hungry himself. But, not wanting to send the old man away with nothing, he asked for his wife's thali to pawn. The old man secretly listened to the whole conversation.

Once the elder brother left, the old man told the wife, "Amma, I never eat without bathing first. Can you heat up a big pot of water for me?"

The wife set a huge pot of water on the stove.

When the husband returned, the old man told them, "The two of you lift me by the shoulders, and put me inside the pot of boiling water."

Petrified, the couple refused. The old man insisted, promising that nothing bad would happen. Hesitantly, they picked him up and gently lowered him into the pot. The next moment, the old man and the water disappeared and the pot was suddenly full of gold coins. Happily surprised, the couple once again became generous with their bounty.

When they heard about the elder brother's luck, the younger brother and his wife could not rest. The wife pestered the younger brother until he went out and dragged an old man home off the streets. At the mention of food, the old man came willingly.

At home, the husband and wife lifted the old man to drop him into a pot of boiling water. The old man was hollering loud enough to rouse the whole village. But was the couple going to let go of this divine chance to get rich? No way! They flung the old man in.

What then, you ask? The old man boiled to death, of course. The raja's soldiers handcuffed the younger brother and his wife and threw them in prison. ❖

friends & family

tricks of the trade

It's impossible to concentrate on two different things at the same time, and the person who knows this best is a pickpocket. Just before picking a pocket, he will distract his mark's attention and then finish the job in the blink of an eye. First either the pickpocket or his accomplice will bump up against you in a crowd. While your thoughts are preoccupied with the bump, you lose your wallet. Even if there's no crowd, that doesn't deter the pickpocket. In this case he may employ a woman whose only job is to stand so close to you that you can smell her. Almost able to touch her, you won't want to move back an inch. And ta-da! Your money has vanished!

There once was a pickpocket who was an expert in his trade, a karma yogi fully devoted to his profession. No one would imagine that he was just a petty thief; he carried himself and dressed like a gentleman. If he were to stand next to you, perhaps *you* would be taken for the pickpocket!

He had but one sorrow. His only son had shown no aptitude for his trade. His only interests were playing marbles with his friends and climbing trees.

One day, the pickpocket called his son and said, "You stupid boy, how can you be so irresponsible? How do you expect to learn anything if you go about playing marbles and climbing trees? Shouldn't you learn your father's trade? Suppose I die tomorrow…"

"Oh no, Appa! Don't say such things," wailed the son.

"Fine. Suppose some unlucky day I get thrown in prison for six months. How will you feed yourself and your mother?"

"Don't worry about that Appa. Amma has lots of 'uncles' who can take care of us."

"You nitwit, you should learn my profession," said the pickpocket. "It's no ordinary work. It takes a great deal of concentration and expertise. We don't pick a pocket when the mark is fast asleep. Instead, we have to pick his pocket while he's wide awake. That calls for real intelligence."

One day the pickpocket took the son along to the woods for his first lesson. "We are now going to steal a bird's egg from its nest. Not while the parents are away hunting for food—that's amateur stuff. I'm going to teach you to take an egg from under the mother while she's sitting on her batch."

The son nodded.

"Follow me and watch carefully," he said and stealthily scampered up the tree. The father and son slithered across the branches like snakes. Not a word was whispered; they communicated only with their eyes.

As they approached the nest, the pickpocket made a tiny sound. The alerted bird looked around cautiously. While its attention was thus occupied, the pickpocket removed an egg from under it and tucked it behind him in his dhoti.

As they were sliding down the tree—carefully, so as not to alarm the bird further—the son picked the egg out of his father's dhoti and put it in his pocket. Once they were back down, the father looked at the son and demanded, "Did you see that, my son? You should wait for the right moment, and steal it quick." He felt for the egg and was surprised not to find it. He felt his son nudging him, and looked down to see him grinning widely, holding out the missing egg.   ✦

sweet or spicy

In a village was a couple with three daughters. One day the mother died. The father concentrated on raising the three girls, who were as dear to him as his own eyes. The third girl was very intelligent and good looking. If she were told to go and fetch a fruit, she would return having chopped down a whole tree. She feared no one, and would call anyone's bluff, even her father's or her elder sisters'. The father and sisters resented this.

One day, the father returned home with boxes of sweets for the girls. But the third girl said, "Why did you have to bring so many sweets? How am I to fill my stomach? If you had brought something salty or spicy, then I could have had that, and drunk some water, and then felt full. What am I to do with only sweets?"

"See girls," said the father, "I brought these sweets with so much love, and still she finds fault in me. One can go without spicy food, but sweets are a must! Don't you agree with me?"

"Of course Appa," the older sisters sang in chorus, "you are right. We don't want anything spicy! We want only sweets!"

The third daughter said, "If you are so sure, then let's make Appa eat only sweets for the next two days."

"Are you trying to kill our Appa?" demanded the two sisters.

"That's exactly what she wants! She will not rest until she sees my smoke*," said the father. "We should not have her here any longer. Chase her out of this house."

"Where will I go?" cried the third daughter.

If we just let her go, she will head into town and spread stories about us. Let's put her in a basket and throw her into the sea, they decided. She wept and wailed, but it was no use; at midnight, they put her in a basket and threw her into the sea. There, she sobbed until she fell unconscious. The basket gently floated into the dawn.

A raja was out on his morning stroll by the sea when he saw the basket floating towards the shore. Inside was a beautiful sleeping girl. At once, the raja decided he wanted to marry her. He carried her home and got his palace physicians to treat her. On waking, the girl remembered what had happened, and began to cry again.

"Do not weep, woman. You have nothing to fear. I want to marry you," said the raja.

So the two married, and lived happily.

Back in the village, the father had begged and borrowed the money to get his first two daughters married. Once wedded, they wanted nothing more to do with the old man, and threw him out of the house.

I would not be in this sorry state, had I but kept my third daughter, he thought in tears. He roamed here and there until one day, he arrived in her country, at the palace doorstep.

---

* The phrase "...will not rest until she sees my smoke" —*pogaiye paakaame*— here means she wants to see his corpse burn to its last on the funeral pyre. The reference is to the komberimookan (scarce bridal snake, or common bronzeback). In folklore, this snake is not satisfied with just killing its victim; it will climb onto a tall tree in the cremation ground to watch him burn. – Ki. Ra.

"Amma Thayee, my hunger is killing me… please give me a drop of your kanji…" he called.

Hearing the familiar voice, the daughter looked out, saw him and knew at once who he was. But he did not recognize her; she was dressed in the finest silk and decked in gold jewelry, and looked completely different.

She sent her servants out with plates and plates of sweets: boonthi, jilabi, halwa, and more!

"I do not want any of this. Please give me a cup of your salted kanji and some chili," he cried.

"I thought you liked nothing but sweets?" asked the daughter, from behind the palace door.

"Who is that?" asked the father, looking up.

"It's me, your third daughter—the one you threw out of your house because I asked for something spicy or salty."

They hugged each other, and wept torrents for all the lost years. ❖

three things to share

Once there were two brothers. The elder was very clever, and the younger extremely innocent. They only had three possessions between them: a cow, a mango tree, and a blanket.

The elder one hatched a scheme.

"Thambi, Thambi," he said, "we have only these three things, which we must both share. Let us divide all three equally. You take the front portion of the cow and the roots of the mango tree, and you can use the blanket the whole day. I get the rear portion of the cow, the top of the mango tree, and I'll only use the blanket at night." The younger brother, being naïve, agreed.

So, the younger brother took care of the front portion of the cow; he fed it with grass, hay and corn husks. The elder brother got the milk, the dung, and the money from the dung cakes. The younger brother got to water the mango tree, while the elder brother got the money from the sale of the fruit. While the younger brother got to cover himself with the blanket during the sweltering daytime, the elder brother snuggled in it to keep warm at night.

Only months later did it slowly begin to dawn on the younger brother that he was being exploited.

One fine morning, as the elder brother was milking the cow, the younger one whacked its horn with a thick staff. The cow, startled, kicked the elder brother with its rear leg.

Then, when the elder brother went up the mango tree to pluck the fruits, the younger one began chopping at the trunk with an axe.

"What are you doing?" asked the elder brother.

"I am only chopping my end of the tree, Anna," replied the younger brother.

In the evening, when he went to the river to bathe, he took the blanket along and rinsed it. When the elder brother looked for the blanket that night, he found it soaking wet.

"It is mine during the daytime," said the younger brother. "So I washed it."

The elder brother realized that his game was exposed. He begged to be forgiven and went to the panchayat, and with their help decided a way to share all three things fairly with his younger brother.   ❖

Ki. Ra.: There are countless folktales about feuds between brothers. We can safely assume that when the concept of ownership came into existence, jealousy and disappointment followed close behind.

When it comes to division of inheritance, feuds arise even today. This is almost a social custom.

There are similar stories across Tamil Nadu. In most of them, the wronged brother finds justice through a stroke of blind luck.

rabbit roast

There was a saamiyaar who lived in a forest who loved rabbit roast and ate it every day. If he missed his rabbit roast, he wouldn't get peaceful sleep that night.

Now, rabbits are creatures that move with great speed, and the saamiyaar was too old to race behind and catch them. He had a special way around this problem. He would apply a little *something* on his forehead and instantly become invisible. In fact, even if he were to walk up to a lion and give it a sharp knock on its head, the stupid animal would be clueless about his presence.

But the saamiyaar did not waste his talent on this kind of childish prank. He used it exclusively for trapping his daily rabbit. Whenever he spotted a chubby rabbit grazing on a patch of grass, he'd apply the *something* to his forehead, walk up to it silently, pick it up by its ears, strip off its skin, clean the meat, stuff its belly with freshly ground masala and roast it on an open fire. Even as the meat cooked, his mouth would water and his stomach would growl. When the meat was half-done, he'd break off a leg and begin to chew on it.

Our rabbit-loving saamiyaar also had a disciple, whom he had taught all his knowledge and skills, including his method of trapping rabbit and the best recipe for the roast.

One day, he ordered the disciple to go catch a rabbit and roast it by the time he finished his bath. He also gave him a little of the *something*.

The disciple caught a rabbit and was halfway through roasting it. Wanting a taste, he broke off a leg. It was delicious! He was just reaching out for a second leg when the saamiyaar returned.

The saamiyaar counted the rabbit's legs.

"Where is the fourth leg?" he asked the disciple.

"I don't know. It had only three when I caught it," swore the disciple.

"What? Only three legs? I have never seen a three-legged rabbit!" exclaimed the saamiyaar. He knew what had happened to the fourth leg, but wanted the disciple to confess voluntarily.

All through the day, while tutoring or gardening, the saamiyaar asked casually, "How many legs did your rabbit have?" The disciple's reply was a prompt, "The rabbit I caught had only three legs."

The saamiyaar was irritated. He starved the disciple the whole next day, then woke him up in his sleep and demanded, "Dey, how many legs did your rabbit have?" The answer was the same, "The rabbit I caught had only three legs."

The next day he sent the disciple to fetch a rabbit, but said he would do the roasting himself. The disciple, who had starved the previous day, was ravenously hungry.

On the same day, the raja of the land had come into the forest for his annual hunt and a break from his kingly duties. The famished disciple strayed into this camp. Because he had applied the special *something*, no one could see him. As the raja was eating his elaborate lunch, the disciple took his seat opposite the raja and began eating off the plate.

Now, everyone knows that when you eat at an outdoor picnic, you eat twice as much as you normally would. Even so, the raja's cook was surprised at the amount of food that was disappearing from the raja's plate. The raja's appetite was never this huge; even he himself was astounded. "I didn't realize I was *this* hungry. Look how fast I am finishing your food!"

Once the disciple had gorged himself, he set off immediately to hunt for a rabbit and brought it back to the saamiyaar. The saamiyaar cleaned and roasted it. Before eating, he broke off a leg, gave it to the disciple and asked, "Tell me again, how many legs did your rabbit have?"

"The rabbit I caught had only three legs," replied the disciple.

Kid, you're done for, cursed the saamiyaar.

The disciple had no appetite for the roasted rabbit leg after the huge feast from the raja's plate. He repeated his culinary expedition for several days, though the saamiyaar continued to starve him. Over the days, the raja became thinner and thinner and the disciple kept gaining more and more weight.

One day, the raja visited the saamiyaar. "What happened, oh Raja? You have gone very thin. Are you unwell?" asked the saamiyaar.

"I cannot understand what's happening. I seem to eat three times the normal quantity, but I'm still losing weight. I desperately need help."

Instantly, a thought flashed in the saamiyaar's brain. *Perhaps I have the answer right here next to me. Here is my disciple ballooning, and the raja obviously becoming thinner. There must be a connection between the two,* he thought.

"Raja, from tomorrow, when your food is served, insist that it is piping hot. The steam from it must be heavy. Believe me, you will know what is ailing you in a couple of days," he advised the raja.

The raja's lunch the next day was grand and hot, with thick steam rising from the food as it arrived at his plate. The disciple was intently concentrating on the rabbit, deer, and fowl curries. He was busy blowing on the meat to cool it down. He was unaware that the special *something* smeared on his forehead was slowly melting because of the hot steam, and running down his nose. He was gradually becoming visible to the silent, stunned audience.

The raja finally understood why he was getting thinner. He ordered his soldiers to capture the disciple and chop off his head.

On the day of the execution, the saamiyaar paid him a visit.

"My dear disciple, I can still save you," said the saamiyaar. "How many legs did your rabbit have?"

"The rabbit I caught had only three legs," replied the disciple stubbornly.   ❖

the rich man who never told a lie

A saamiyaar was visiting a remote town. People of the town pestered him every day with invitations for lunch and dinner.

"I will eat only once in any one house," said the saamiyaar. "That too, only in a house where no one has ever told a lie!"

A very rich man stepped up and said, "Come to my house, oh Saamiyaar. No one in my home has ever told a lie." The saamiyaar accepted the invitation.

Before going, the saamiyaar inquired about the rich man and learned everything he could about him.

Walking along with the rich man, the saamiyaar asked, "How many children do you have?"

"Only one son," replied the rich man.

What? The people of this town said he has three sons! Why is he saying he has only one? Is he lying? wondered the saamiyaar. *But I should not be too hasty to judge him. Perhaps he is telling the truth. Let me wait.*

"How old are you now?" asked the saamiyaar.

"I am ten years old," answered the rich man.

There he goes again! His hair is gray, his face wrinkled, he can barely walk, and he says he is only ten! No, no, I should not come to a rushed conclusion. I shall give him one more chance, decided the saamiyaar.

"How many acres of land do you have?" asked the saamiyaar.

"I have only six feet of land for myself," said the rich man.

This is like trying to hide a whole pumpkin in a spoonful of rice! thought the saamiyaar. *This man is indeed the king of liars! How can I eat in his house? Will it turn me into a liar as well? No, let me see how far he can go...*

When they arrived at the house, the rich man told his wife, "Adiye, we have a special guest today. So, make him your best lunch. I'll take him to the river to bathe. We'll be back soon."

On their way back from the river, they passed an orchard. The rich man plucked two ripe mangoes, and cut a bunch of ripe bananas and some banana leaves.

"Whose orchard is this?" asked the saamiyaar.

"This belongs to The Ones Who Do Not Sleep a Wink at Night," replied the rich man.

The saamiyaar could make no sense of this answer. *Wait and see, you fraud! I shall sit at your feast, chop of your nose, lay it on your leaf-plate and walk out,* the saamiyaar grumbled to himself.

At the house, the wife had laid out the dinner. "Please come and eat," she said.

"No. I need to clarify a few things before I dirty my hand with your food," declared the saamiyaar.

"What is it?" asked the rich man.

"I know you have three sons. Why did you tell me you have only one?" demanded the saamiyaar.

The rich man immediately called for his three sons and gave them a task. The eldest and the youngest both said, "Oh go on, Appa! You are forever ordering us around." Only the middle son promptly agreed to obey.

"Did you see that, oh Saamiyaar?" asked the rich man. "I do have three sons, but only one of them truly listens to me. The other two are mere wastrels," said the rich man.

"Fine, but why did you claim that you were only ten years old?" asked the saamiyaar.

"I am over sixty," replied the rich man. "But for the last ten years, I have devoted myself to a spiritual life. I believe that only since then, I have truly lived," replied the rich man.

"Excellent answer!" applauded the saamiyaar. "But you own thousands of acres of fertile land. Why did you claim to have only six feet?"

"I have acquired thousands of acres of land. I did every trick in the trade to become this rich. But it has only made my sons proud and arrogant. What use is all this wealth to me? When I die, the six feet of land where I will be buried is all that will truly be mine," said the rich man.

The saamiyaar sat down to eat. Actually, after all this fuss, he ate really well. As he was taking his leave, he asked the rich man, "What did you mean when you said the orchard belongs to The Ones Who Do Not Sleep a Wink at Night?"

"I do own the orchard and work hard tending to my trees. But at night, I am so tired that I fall fast asleep. Meanwhile the thieves, who stay awake all night, steal most of my yield. So in truth the orchard belongs to *them*, The Ones Who Do Not Sleep a Wink at Night!" said the rich man. ❖

the most skilled in the world

Once there was a man who was the best archer in the land. He was extremely proud of it, too. In fact, he thought there was no one in the entire world who could match his skill.

Every morning, as his wife was cleaning the front doorstep and drawing her kolam, he would pick up a piece of straw, notch it in his bow, and aim it at her pierced nose. The straw would fly straight into the tiny hole and stick there.

This daily demonstration, staged even before the sun had fully risen, irritated the wife no end. She was also scared that one day his aim would go awry and her eye might be hurt. But her nervousness only made him double over laughing.

Finally, one day, unable to take it anymore, she burst out, "Don't be so sure you are the most skilled in the world. There is bound to be someone better."

The argument escalated into a full-blown fight, and in the end, she marched out of the house to her brothers' place. Seeing her distress, her brothers told her, "You stay here in our house for a while. We'll go and search for a man who is more skilled than your husband, who can cut him down to size." With that, they marched off to meet their brother-in-law and challenged him: "Dey, are you really so arrogant? There's bound to be someone better skilled than you."

"Is that right? Then show him to me. In fact, I'll come along with you to look for him," smirked the archer.

They left together. On the way, they met a man carrying a huge load of palm leaves who was running westwards, against the wind.

"Where are you off to in such a hurry?" they asked.

"I carry this load every day from the point where the sun rises to the point where it sets, before dusk falls. There is no one in this world who is a faster runner than me," replied the man.

Oh God! Imagine, to make it to the point where the sun sets, and then run back at night to the point where it rises, and then begin the trek all over again the next day! Adeyappa! the brothers marveled.

But the archer mocked him. "Don't assume that you are the best," he said. "There is bound to be someone more skilled than you."

"Is that right? Then show him to me. In fact, I'll come along with you to look for him," said the runner, and joined their search.

They travelled to many towns and villages. One afternoon, in a remote village, they chanced upon a man lying on a cot, out in the open, gazing unblinkingly at the blazing sky.

The group of men looked up too, but they saw nothing except the sun burning into their eyes. *Perhaps he is mad,* they thought, and shook him hard to get his attention.

"You idiots!" snapped the man. "Why do you have to choose the most inopportune moment to disturb me? What do you want, anyway? Out with it! I don't have time. They have just laid Lokidhasan on the funeral pyre."

"But why are you lying on your cot in middle of the road, blocking everyone's way, staring at the sky?"

"Oh, you poor near-sighted things!" said the man pityingly. "Up there in the heavens, the devas are putting on a stage production of the life of Harichandra, for Lord Indran. I watch it every day, at this time. And you had to call me right at the climax!"

"Aha, this man is indeed the most skillful of all!" applauded the whole group, except for the runner, who said, "What is so special about him? There is bound to be someone even more skilled."

"Is that right? Then show him to me. In fact, I will come along with you to look for him," said the man with incredible eyesight, and joined the search.

The journey continued until the group reached a land where the raja's young son had just died of snakebite. The royal physician announced, "There is a special herb which grows only on Karumamalai. If anyone can fetch it by tonight, then I can bring the prince back to life."

The gathered crowd was shocked. "Karumamalai? How is that possible? That hill is thousands of miles away from here. How could anyone go there and return in one day?" they murmured.

Hearing this, the runner called out, "Who says it cannot be done? I shall do it!"

"Oh good," cried the physician. "However, you might not be able to get the herb so easily. It grows atop a rocky ledge, as long and as tall as ten-palm trees. How will you possibly climb that? And don't think of rappelling down by a rope, either—then the pythons would swallow you. So, how will you fetch me the herb?"

"Stop worrying," said the archer. "We have amongst us a man with incredible eyesight, who can spot things from miles away. I am capable of aiming my arrow at the farthest target. You give us directions and describe the rock. We'll take care of the rest."

The physician gave a detailed map of the path they would have to take, the treacherous ledge, and a description of the herb.

The runner sped away, faster than the wind. The others gathered on the palace terrace, seven storeys up. The man with incredible eyesight spotted the herb hanging from the centre of the peak of the ledge. The archer notched an arrow with a crescent-shaped arrowhead in his bow, and aimed it. The arrow shot through the air like a silver streak of lightning and cut through the stalk of the plant. The herb fell into the palm of the waiting runner, who returned to the palace in a blink.

The raja's young son was brought back to life.

The raja did not know which of the three skilled men he should reward. The brothers and the crowd began to argue amongst themselves: "This one is the most skilled!" "Oh no, it is that one we have to thank!"

Finally, the raja's minister announced, "All three are to be rewarded, for such a feat could not have been achieved by one without the help of the other two."

The raja thanked them all and gave them many precious gifts.

Cleansed of their pride and arrogance, the three men and the brothers returned home in peace. ❖

P.K.C.: The idea that the story of Harichandra is being staged in daily installments for the gods in Devalokam is just a flight of fancy specific to this tale. Harichandra is a character referred to in both the *Mahabharatham* and the *Ramayanam*, who was famous for his adamant refusal to tell a lie. Lokidhasan is Harichandra's young son, who dies of a snakebite.

gnanamma's goats

There was once a widow named Gnanamma. One day a young boy came to her doorstep, pleading. "Please, I am starving. Give me a little kanji...," he cried. He looked so pathetic that Gnanamma called him inside and fed him some plain rice kanji with fried, salted chili. As she mixed salt in the kanji, she questioned him and learned his story. To him, the salted rice kanji tasted like manna from heaven. His burning stomach was somewhat cooled. He wanted to do something for her in return.

There was a she-goat tied to the tree outside. Since she was kept tethered, she had missed the mating season. She had been not grazing properly, and was looking weak. The boy went into the woods, cut some fresh grass, and fed the goat. She had not seen fresh green grass in days. She happily munched it down and looked up expectantly. So the boy went and got some more.

Gnanamma let the boy stay with her and take care of the goat, which he fed daily with fresh green grass. He became very fond of the animal. Gnanamma continued to feed the boy with rice kanji and fried, salted chili. When she gained more trust in him, she let him take the goat out to the woods to graze.

Good food and the company of fellow goats made the blood flow fresh in the goat's veins. Now she was fat and skippy. Naturally, this attracted the males of the herd. Very soon, the goat was pregnant and gave birth to two chubby she-goats.

Now, the boy took all three goats for grazing, and Gnanamma continued to feed him with rice kanji and fried, salted chili. The boy grew up into a strapping youngster and the herd increased to two hundred head. Butchers from villages all around sought out Gnanamma's goats. Gnanamma was now rich in her own right, but continued to feed the boy nothing but rice kanji and fried salted chili, even on festive days. She did not want to give him anything tastier, for then he might learn to want more.

The boy took his herd to the open hills, along with the other goat-herds in the village. Every afternoon, they would sit as a crowd under the tree to have their lunch. While the other goatherds would bring a variety of side dishes, the boy would only have his rice kanji and fried salted chili. The rest teased him mercilessly for this. But the boy kept quiet and never was provoked.

Soon it was time for Chiththirai Thiruvizha, the Spring Festival. Every household feasted on mutton and chicken. But mean old Gnanamma still only gave the boy rice kanji and fried salted chili. This time, he felt hurt.

The next day, the other boys all brought fresh rice, not kanji, along with meat for their lunch. When they saw his simple meal, they asked sarcastically, "You idiot, you built a herd of hundreds from a single goat. At least yesterday, couldn't you get fresh rice and a piece of bone?"

He remembered the scene at Gnanamma's house the previous day. He had held a fat goat as it was being slaughtered. Mutton legs and liver were roasted; minced meat was fried; ribs were added to the soup and some of the meat made into a tasty curry. The meat that wasn't cooked immediately was cured with turmeric and salt and strung out in the sun.

Today, he could not stomach his kanji and fried salted chili. He put it aside. The other boys offered to share their lunch with him, but he pleaded severe stomach cramps. They told him to go home, and offered to graze his herd and bring it back. But he paid no heed. When they moved their herd, he stayed behind with his.

As the sun went down, he stopped every stranger who passed by, and gave them two of his herd. By sunset, he had given away all the goats.

It was now very dark. Gnanamma, worried about her missing goats and the boy, came looking for them. On her way, she met the other boys, who told her that he had stayed behind under the tree. She hurried on.

There she saw the boy lying curled on the ground, his lunch untouched and the goats gone. She was shocked. She did not pause to ask what was troubling him. She simply shook him awake and demanded, "Where are my goats? Boy, answer me! Where are my goats?" again and again.

The boy looked at her intently for a long time, before whispering with a sob,

For my tasteless kanji
And fried salted chili
I slogged tirelessly, Gnanamma – your goats
Have gone on their way, Gnanamma...

And he broke down with a loud wail.   ❖

the chasing wave

Once upon a time, there lived a brother and a sister. Now, the elder brother had a lustful eye set on the sister. She soon came to realize his shameful intent, and felt that her peaceful world had been turned upside-down. She went to plead for mercy from every god that she knew of. "Save me from this great danger. Please make my brother understand that his thoughts are immoral," she wept. But no god came forward to help her.

One night, the brother silently approached the sister's bed to touch her. She woke up at once. Stopping him, she said, "Don't you know what it means to be brother and sister? How can you be so horrible? Will God forgive you for even thinking such thoughts?"

The brother was in no mood to listen to her advice. Do the adamant ever see the right path? He fought her down and tried to molest her. The sister jumped up and ran out of the house, with the brother chasing behind her. The sister kept running, not caring whether it was day or night, whether she was running on ground or over water. The brother continued to chase her.

In her haste, the sister tripped and fell into a puddle. Seeing his chance, the brother stretched out his hand to grab her.

At that instant, she prayed, "Oh Iswaran, Iswari: Make these hills and this earth, these rivers and these lakes change into one giant ocean." Then she ran into the ocean as a wave. In the next instant, the brother followed her as another wave.

And so, for ages and ages, the lecherous brother-wave has been chasing the sister-wave. On that fateful day when he catches up with her, the ocean will swell forth and destroy the Earth completely.   ❖

Ki. Ra.: There was a time in human history when there was no discipline in the sexual union between man and woman. Mother and son, elder brother and younger sister, elder sister and younger brother... all such unions occurred. At some later period, this was deemed wrong, and moral codes were formulated. But it must not have been easy to enforce these codes at first, for it is extremely difficult to change a habituated man.

Versions of this story are common amongst people who live near the seashore. It was probably invented by some imaginative soul who saw a smaller wave as a woman and a bigger wave behind it as a man. The belief that the world will be destroyed when the brother-wave catches the sister-wave is common among the fisherfolk community.

the unlucky potter

Once there lived a potter, who was very lazy and equally unlucky. The day he chose to go out and collect clay, it rained and the clay became too wet. The day he chose to light his kiln, it flooded and the firewood became too damp. The dejected potter decided, *Fine! If this is how it is going to be, I shall make no more pots.* So he became a farmer.

However, the people of the village assembled at his doorstep and begged him. "Potter, potter, this is not the right work for you. If you stop making pots, what will we do? After the harvest, what will we cook our rice in?"

The potter was irked. *No way am I going back to pottery,* he decided. *Instead, I'll have a harvest that makes these idiots green with envy.*

He sowed his field with sesame seeds. The plants grew green and lush. "Look at my field! Imagine my rich harvest," bragged the potter to everyone he met.

After the harvest, he took the seeds to extract oil. The miller gave him fresh oil in a huge clay pot.

As the potter walked back with the oil he started daydreaming. *I shall sell this oil,* he thought, *and with the money I will buy more land and sow more sesame seeds and make more oil and become really rich. Then I will build the biggest mansion in this town. I'll employ all these idiots to work in my fields. Then Lakshmi Devi, goddess of wealth, will invite herself into my house!*

Just then, he was passing the spot where he used to put down the clay for making his pots. Forgetting momentarily that his head-load was now a pot of oil instead of clay, he dropped it heavily to the ground. The pot of oil shattered and spilled all over the slushy ground. The people around exclaimed gleefully, "Potter, potter, you should have listened to what we said. Go back to making pots!"

The potter returned to his pottery.   ❖

Ki. Ra.: Actions which are done habitually start to become involuntary. The hands and feet start to operate on their own.

There was once an old man who, after his constitutional walk every day, used to remove his footwear, place it in a corner, hang his walking stick on a hook, hang his towel on the coat-hanger and flop on his bed, tired. One day, he came home and hung his walking stick on the coat hanger, put the towel on the hook, placed his footwear on the bed and flopped in the corner, tired. People at home knew at once that something was wrong.

Strange things are bound to happen when one lets go of the firm grip on one's memory.

P.K.C.: There is a casteist tone to the above story (distasteful, to me) which does not come through in the translation. The word for potter, *kuyavan*, is a caste name, and the "moral" is that people should stick to their caste trade.

the address change

The city was getting too busy and noisy. A music lover, who was getting sick of the hustle-bustle, bought himself a house well away from all the traffic and moved in.

"But what use is it having a big luxurious comfortable house if you can't sleep at night?" asked Thatha as he gazed at his listeners' eager faces.

Why couldn't he sleep? wondered the children. Perhaps he was unwell, or had a headache, or was just unaccustomed to the new place, they thought to themselves.

"There was a loud noise which kept up all through the night. Ludd, ludd, ludd," said Thatha.

"So what did he do?" the children asked.

The music lover, who had not been able to sleep a wink for several nights, got out of the bed one morning with fiery red, burning eyes, called his servant, and told him to find out the source of the *ludd, ludd, ludd.*

The servant returned with a grin and said, "You have two carpenters as your neighbours on either side."

Oh my God! After all my efforts to get away from the noise, why did I have to wind up with this house? How can I get out of this situation? wondered the music lover.

He did not want to move out. The price had been steep, but the house itself was very satisfactory—except for that *ludd, ludd, ludd.* Now he knew why the previous owner had sold it.

I'll have to use my brains, decided the music lover.

First, he sent for the neighbour on the right. He learned that he did not own the house, but was only a tenant. "I'm willing to give you a thousand rupees to move to a different house," he said to the neighbour.

Why should I lose out on a thousand rupees? thought the neighbour. "Okay! I'll look for a new house and let you know soon."

"You don't have too much time. You'll get the full thousand only if you move by tonight. If you wait until tomorrow, you'll get only seven hundred and fifty. The longer you wait, the less you'll get."

"I'll be back in a jiffy," said the neighbour, and ran out. *Who wants to say no to Sridevi, the goddess of good luck, when she is inviting herself in?*

Next, the music lover sent for the neighbour on the left, and told him the same thing. This neighbour was happy and troubled at the same time. It was not easy to find a new house in a day. But he, too, reluctantly agreed.

That evening, the music lover saw carts being loaded at both the neighbours' doorsteps. He paid them both and waited eagerly for the long overdue night of sleep.

And in truth, that night's sleep was probably the best he had had in a long time.

The following night, the music lover had just switched off the light and laid his head on the pillow, when it came: *ludd, ludd, ludd...*

"Aargh! Don't tell me two *more* carpenters have moved in! I should have been more careful," he groaned.

He tossed and turned in his bed, waiting for dawn. Finally, restless, he decided to go for a walk to tire himself out. As soon as he stepped out onto the street, he saw one of the carpenters working in his shed. The music lover could not control his anger. "What are you doing here? I paid you good money to move out!" he yelled.

"I did exactly as you told me," the carpenter coolly replied. "I had just set off to look for a new house when I learned that the man on the other side of your house was doing the same thing. So we exchanged homes. You asked us to move, but you didn't specify where."

"The music lover didn't know whether to laugh or cry," said Thatha, *finishing his tale.*   ❖

the gold bracelet

"Isn't it very cloudy today?" asked the man of house, pointing at the sky, a gold bracelet on his wrist. The labourers, weeding in the field, promptly looked up at the sky. No one noticed the new, flashing gold bracelet. The man was very disappointed.

He had been coveting the gold bracelet for a long time. Only now had he been able to afford it. But what was the point if no one appreciated it? He wished even one person would stop to say, "Hey, nice bracelet! I haven't seen that before. Is it new? How many carats is it? How much did you pay? Where did you buy it, or did you have it made?"

The man with the gold bracelet stood with his hands on his waist and announced, "The crops have grown well. It is time to harvest."

"Not really," murmured the labourers amongst themselves. "It can grow some more. It needs at least one more rain."

They were looking at the crops, not the bracelet. The man with gold bracelet left the fields, frustrated.

That night, there was a fire; the haystacks along the field were burning. Every man and woman gathered to pass pots of water to put out the blaze.

The man with the gold bracelet was ordering the queue. "Take the water to that end… take the pot to this end!" he shouted, waving his hands wildly in the air.

Even in that rush, one old woman paused to ask, "Thambi, when did you buy that new bracelet?"

"Damn it, why didn't you ask me that this morning?" demanded the man with the gold bracelet. "These haystacks need not have been burnt in vain."

"You cursed man!" yelled the old woman, cracking her knuckles at him. "You should rot in hell, for sure!"   ❖

the story of the lamps

Mother would always become extra busy on Friday evenings. The cleaning and washing down of the house would begin in the morning, and by the time the sun went down, she would be running around in full speed. She would clean the main doorway with good, fresh water. Then she would draw a kolam—not like the elaborate ones drawn during Markazhi, but a neat four-lined one—and then come in to light the oil lamps in every room.

During the lamp lighting she would not put up with a single disturbance. If the children cooperated in this act, her face would bloom and she would resemble Lakshmi.

Her curious children one day asked Thatha, "Why is it, Thatha, this happens only on Friday evenings?"

"There is a long story behind this," said Thatha and began telling it.

Long, long ago, there was a very rich shipping merchant who had two children, one boy and one girl. They were very close all through their childhood. The brother and sister would whisper to each other, "When we grow up, even if we are married off, we will never drift apart. If you have a daughter, he should wed my son. If I have a daughter, he should wed your son. That way we will become in-laws and live next to each other as neighbours."

When they grew up, they were married off.

We've already said that the father was a rich merchant. So you can imagine the grandeur of the daughter's wedding! The man she was married off to was an even richer shipping merchant. For her dowry, her family gave a whole ship full of precious jewels and fine silk. The wedding itself went on for seven days. The expenses skyrocketed, and the girl's family ended up spending more than they had planned.

On her way out to her new husband's house, at the doorstep, she told her brother, "Remember: If I have a daughter, she should marry your son!"

A few years later, the brother's ship was wrecked in a storm. All the men and the goods on board sank deep into the ocean and were lost forever. The loss of his ship, so soon after the huge expense of his sister's wedding, reduced the brother to abject poverty. He sold what little he had left to pay off some of his debts, and moved his family into a tiny rented house.

By now, the brother had two sons, and the sister had two daughters. Because he had lost all his wealth, the brother no longer had any connection with his sister's rich family.

On some evenings, the sister would sit by herself, silently crying. Her daughters noticed this and wanted to know the reason. When they persisted, their mother finally had to tell them about her dear brother, who was now very poor, and the promise they had made to each other when they were young.

"Why can't you keep your promise now?" asked the daughters.

"How can I? My brother's family would need a very tall ladder to reach our status. You two have been brought up in luxury. You wouldn't last a day living the way they have to!" the mother exclaimed.

After some years, the elder daughter got married. The groom, as you might expect, was also a rich shipping merchant. The poor brother and his family were not invited for the wedding. Even if he had been, it is doubtful whether he would have accepted the invitation. How could a poor man feel comfortable among so many rich folk?

After a few more years, when an alliance was being sought for the second daughter, she announced to her mother, "I refuse to wed anyone except your brother's son!"

"Di, but you have not even seen your uncle, let alone his son!" said the mother.

"I do not care what they look like. I want to marry him because that is what you promised your brother when you were young," said the daughter.

This second daughter was born adamant. She would refuse to eat her food without lots of rich ghee on it. After finishing every meal, she would demand to have a fruit juice. Before going to bed, she would demand a glass of milk with saffron. Seeing that she was going to be just as stubborn about her marriage, the mother agreed. But naturally, she was worried about sending her daughter to live in such poverty.

The younger daughter arrived at her husband's house, which she found decorated with nothing but scarcity. The girl had not imagined that they would be this poor.

This was the family's only source of income: they would go together at dawn, gather banyan leaves, and stitch them together to make leaf-plates. By selling these in the market, they managed to earn enough to feed themselves a single meager meal at night. The next day, they would be off to gather more banyan leaves.

It was a big change for the young woman, but she did not lose heart. She joined in the hard work with her husband and his family.

One day, the raja of that land was about to have his oil bath, and had just removed his jewelry, when a crow swooped down and flew off with his signet ring. The raja's men searched high and low, but could not find the ring.

For any raja, the signet ring is just as important as the scepter. The raja could have tolerated losing any of his other jewels—but the signet ring had to be recovered.

Soon after stealing the ring, the crow came to perch on the branch of a tree in the second sister's backyard. The young woman happened to look up and saw something shining in its beak. She shooed away the crow, which dropped the ring as it flew off.

The young woman picked up the shiny thing and saw the insignia of the kingdom. She knew immediately that the ring must belong to the raja, and that she would not be allowed to keep it.

A little while later, a messenger-drummer of the raja came, announcing to the people that whoever found the lost signet ring and returned it to the palace would be rewarded with a huge sum of money and gold.

The young woman took her husband along and went to the palace with the ring. On the way, she told her husband that she would do the talking; he must not say a word.

When the raja saw his ring, he was overjoyed, and asked the young woman what she wanted for a reward.

"Oh Raja, I do not want gold or money," replied the young woman. "I just ask one small favour. You must decree that this Friday evening, no house in this kingdom—not even your palace—should light an oil lamp. I alone should be allowed to light the lamps in my house. This is my only request."

The raja agreed, and issued the decree to the entire land.

That Friday evening, the young woman gave her house a thorough cleaning. She placed lit oil lamps all over the house. Then she made her husband stand at the front door, and told him not to let anyone enter the house. If anyone insisted on coming in, he was to let them only if they promised never to leave.

Next, she made her brother-in-law stand at the back door. She told him that if anyone wanted to go out of the house, he was to let them do so only after they promised never to return. And once they left, he was to padlock the door immediately.

The sun set, leaving the entire kingdom in darkness—even the palace.

As she sat meditating in the puja room, she heard a woman's voice inside the house, grumbling and spitting in disgust. "Chee! Thoo!* Who would want to live in a house that reeks of cleanliness like this? I'm leaving. I refuse to stay another second."

A wild woman, with her clothes in disarray and her hair flying all over the place, was demanding to be let out the back door.

"Who are you?" asked the brother-in-law.

"I am Mudevi, goddess of poverty," she said proudly.

"Oh!" he said. "You may go—but only if you promise never to return to this house."

Mudevi swore, and went off in a huff. The brother-in-law immediately shut the back door and boarded it with two huge bars of wood.

A little while later, a group of eight beautiful women approached the front door, and asked the husband to be let into the house.

"Who are you?" asked the husband.

"We are Ashtalakshmis, the eight goddesses of wealth," they said.

"Aha!" said the husband. "Please come in. But there is a condition: if you enter, you must never leave. Do you agree?"

"Yes, we agree," they said.

Ever since that Friday night, the pots in that house that held the gold, money, and grains were always full!

---

* The interjections "chee" and "thoo," used to indicate spitting, are traditionally associated with Mudevi.—P.K.C.

"Now do you understand why oil lamps are lit on Friday evenings? It is to protect the house from Lakshmi ever leaving it," said Thatha.

"Now we understand why Amma is in such a hurry to clean the house on Fridays and light the oil lamps," cried the children.

Thatha laughed, bobbing his head up and down.   ❖

thatha's coconuts

Thatha was on a roll. "It's not enough just to have coconut trees," he said. "You have to know how to climb them, and pluck the fruit."

"How is that possible, Thatha?" demanded the children. "Every grove owner can't bring down all his coconuts by himself."

"I don't know about possible and impossible and all that. Let me tell you what happened yesterday in my own backyard," said Thatha.

"What happened?" chorused the children.

Thatha began his tale.

Now, Thatha did not know how to climb any tree, let alone a coconut tree. The day before, he had wanted two coconuts. But there was no one around.

Just then a stranger passed by. He was a big, strong man, and an expert climber too. Thatha called the man over.

"Can you climb up this tree and get me two coconuts?" he asked the man.

"What can you do with just two coconuts?" the man asked flippantly.

Not wanting to get into an argument with the stranger, Thatha said, "Look, this is urgent. Please do me this favour."

"What's in it for the climber?" asked the man.

"Fine, you can take one too," agreed Thatha.

The man scrambled up the tree, kicked down five coconuts, and climbed down.

"Dey, I only asked for two!" exclaimed Thatha. "Within a blink of an eye, you've kicked down five!"

"Just wait, I'll do the accounts for you," replied the man and came over with four of the coconuts.

He seems honest, Thatha thought. *He has left only one behind for himself and is bringing me four. Good!*

"Now this is my fee," said the man. "One for going up the tree, and one for coming down. You offered me one *and* you said I could take one for myself. So, it's four coconuts for me altogether. The remaining one is for you. I know you wanted two, but you will have to make do with one," said the man, and sauntered away with four coconuts, leaving behind the one lying on the ground.   ❖

the buried chain

Once upon a time there were two girls who were inseparable friends. They were like the mortar and pestle, always found together, except when they were asleep. They always made sure to find work in the same place. The people of the town used to laugh, "Call one of them to work, and both will arrive!"

One day, the two girls decided to go up to the hills to gather firewood. On the path, they passed a chain, half-buried in the ground, glinting of gold. Both girls saw it, but neither wanted to reveal it to the other. They had walked a little way past it when one of the girls said, "Listen, you go on ahead and gather the wood. I think I am coming down with a high fever. I shall rest here for a while, and then go back home."

But the other girl was no idiot. *Adi chake, incredible! Does she really think she can send me away and walk off with the gold chain? I won't let her do it,* she thought. Aloud she said, "I'm not feeling well either; my stomach has been aching since this morning. Actually, I didn't even want to come gather firewood. I only came because otherwise you would have been alone. I think I'll rest here, too." With that she sat on the ground next to her friend.

Neither of the girls even opened their lunches. Each one just sat alert, waiting for the other to leave. Eventually, it started to get dark. They could not remain sitting there all night.

Let me start heading home, thought one of the girls. *She won't budge until I do. Once we get home, as soon as she goes inside, I'll come back and take the gold chain.* The other girl had exactly the same idea. On the way back, as they passed the chain, one girl dropped her head-cloth on it, as if by accident. The other dropped her lunch box at the same spot.

They reached home, and after a few minutes, each hoping that the other had gone to sleep, they both hurried back up to the hills.

That night a few men had come to the hills to trap monkeys to use in street shows. They saw the head-cloth and the lunch box, and realized that some woman must have been there earlier to gather wood. They figured that perhaps the woman had heard an elephant or a hyena, and had dropped her things in her panic to run. Just then, they heard footsteps, and quickly put out their torches and hid behind a tree.

First, the girl who had dropped her head-cloth .came. She lit matches, stick after stick, searching for the spot. Her golden earrings shone bright in the match light. Guessing by the design of the earrings that she was young, and had come alone to the jungle, the men sprang from their hiding place and grabbed her. "Shut your mouth. If you so much as make a peep, we'll kill you," they threatened her. They took her earrings and had just turned to run off when the other girl rushed up the path, like a dust storm. She, too, began to search for the spot using matchsticks.

Her golden earrings, too, shone bright in the match light. Guessing by the design of the earrings that she too was young, and that she too had come alone to the jungle, the men again sprang from their hiding place and grabbed her. "Shut your mouth. If you so much as make a peep, we'll kill you," they threatened her. They took her earrings as well.

"What are you two women doing out so late?" asked the men.

The girls had to come clean. When they told them about chain, the men relit their torches and started looking for it. But it turned out to be just a cheap, powdered-bronze chain! The men gave each girl two smart blows on the back, refused to return their earrings, and sent them packing.

At home, the two girls both complained of some fictitious ailment and kept themselves locked inside. But they couldn't hide forever. After a few days, they returned to work. All the other women asked them about their missing earrings. "Oh, we lost them when we were gathering firewood. We looked everywhere, but could not find them," they said.

The women of the town placed their hands on their cheeks and gaped at them in surprise. "We know they are thick friends. But both of them losing their earrings in the same place at the same time? This is too much!" ❖

the rich sister and the poor sister

An elder sister had married into a rich home, while her younger sister, unfortunately, had married into a very poor home.

On the elder sister's son's first birthday, a huge party was thrown. The younger sister's family, of course, was not invited.

"My sister is having a birthday party. Shouldn't we go over there?" the younger sister asked her husband.

"Why? We were not invited," he said.

"So what? She is my sister. I must be there! Look at the crowd that is there already."

"What does it matter who's there already? We have not been invited, so we will not go."

"I am definitely going!"

"If you are so determined, then you go alone. I am not coming," he declared.

"So don't come. I'll go alone, and stuff myself with vadai and payasam," she said, and set off.

By the time she arrived, the party was over and lunch was being served. The guests were already sitting in lines on the floor in front of their leaf-plates. She found an empty place in a corner and sat down to eat. During the second course, when rasam was being served, a rich woman looked at her and whispered, "She looks like a beggar-woman. Why is she eating along with us?"

"Oh no, she's no beggar. She's the aunt of the birthday boy," said the woman next to her. "The elder sister is blessed by Sridevi, the goddess of good luck, and this one by Mudevi, the goddess of bad luck."

"Is that right? But why invite someone like her to a party of rich people like us?" asked the first woman.

By now, the talk had reached the elder sister's ears. She came running.

"You impoverished bum," she shouted at her sister. "What are you doing here, eating at my feast? Get lost, you cur," she yelled and dragged the younger sister out of the hall into the streets.

The younger sister returned home in tears.

"Didn't I tell you not to go to a home where you've not been invited? You deserve what you got, and worse," her husband said.

"I was wrong not to have listened to you," she wept.

With the passing of time, things changed. Now it was the younger sister's turn to be blessed by Sridevi. She became very, very rich. Now she only dressed in silk saris and diamond bangles, diamond necklaces, diamond earrings, diamond finger rings, and diamond nose studs.

The elder sister's son was now getting married. This time, she did invite her younger sister.

"Come, let's go to the wedding," said the younger sister's husband.

"Chee, I don't want to. You go yourself," she declared.

At the wedding hall, seeing the husband alone, the elder sister rushed over to inquire about her sister.

"I asked her to come, but she refused," said the husband.

The elder sister immediately walked over to the younger one's house.

"You are still blaming me for the past. Please come. I want you there when my son is married," she begged.

"No Akka. I don't want to come. You will only feel insulted."

"Oh no! Please, you must come at once."

After a lot of cajoling, the younger sister dressed herself in all her finery and went to the wedding.

At the wedding hall, all the women guests were awestruck by the younger sister's adornments.

"Just look at those heavy diamond bangles!"

"Her diamond nose stud is stunning!"

"That sari must have cost a cool 1500 rupees at least!"

After the wedding, lunch was served. But the younger sister sat off to the side. The elder one noticed this and pleaded with her to join the feast.

So the younger one sat at her place, removed her jewels and placed them next to her leaf-plate.

"Eat, oh diamond bangles, eat well. Eat, oh diamond necklaces, eat well. Eat, oh diamond nose stud, eat to your heart's content..." she went on and on, in a loud, clear voice.

The crowd watched her in shocked silence.

"What are you doing? Why are you asking your jewels to eat?" demanded the elder sister. "How can they possibly eat?"

"All this kind reception is only for my jewels and wealth, not for me," replied the younger one, in a quiet tone. "Remember? When I did not have them, you threw me out."

Calmly, she walked out of the hall. The other guests, seeing the elder sister's true colours, also followed suit.

"Look what she has done to me," wailed the elder sister to her husband. "Now I have been insulted by the entire town!"

"I told you not to invite her," replied her husband. "You ignored her when she was poor. You called her this time just because she's now the richest woman in town. You deserve what you got, and worse."

Unable to stomach the humiliation, the elder sister moaned aloud for a very, very long time. ❖

the chettiyar's bullocks

"The bullocks kept on walking and walking, but the cart they were pulling did not reach home," said Thatha. "Do you know that story?"

"No, we don't. Tell us," the children cried.

Thatha opened the snuffbox, pinched out a little powder, took a loud snort, and began his tale.

The next day was the wedding. The landlord had to arrive in time for the auspicious hour. However, the town was quite far off. The landlord consulted his cart driver about the best time to leave.

"Well, there is not much moonlight. We start around two in the night, Aiya," said the cart driver.

The cart driver was a smart man, but a sleepy-head. Since he had to set off in the middle of the night, he avoided sleep and continued with his chores. The landlord stayed awake until about eleven, checking his accounts.

As he went off to bed, he called the cart driver and asked which bullocks he was using for the journey.

"The pair that the Chettiyar has for his mill would be ideal. They have good speed too," said the cart driver.

"Fine, I am off to bed. Get the cart ready and wake me up at two."

At two in the night, as ordered, the cart driver brought the cart out of the shed, fastened to it the Chettiyar's bullocks that he had borrowed, straightened the bed, adjusted the cushions, spread a silk sheet on them and then woke up the landlord.

The half-asleep landlord was aware only of walking to the cart and getting onto it. Once he settled comfortably on the soft bed amidst the cushions, he went back to sleep. The cart driver, who had been busy the whole day, was sleepy too. After all, he had stayed awake past two in the night.

The path to the town was well laid. Even at a steady speed, they would reach before dawn. The cart driver settled on his iron seat in the front. He had to go slow, so that the landlord's sleep would not be disturbed. He held his reins tight and set off.

The night was cool, with a pleasant breeze. He was not only an expert at driving, but also at napping while driving. Whatever the distance, he was capable of sleeping without tipping over. He leaned back comfortably and once the cart had turned onto the long road, he too fell asleep.

At this point, Thatha paused to chuckle. Those that had heard the story before also chortled. "What was the cart driver's plan? Even going slow and steady, they would reach the town before dawn. But things don't always go according to plan, do they?" he asked his audience.

From the road on which the cart was traveling, a tiny path veered off to the left, which led to the Chettiyar's oil mill. The bullocks were used to that path as they treaded it every day, plying the Chettiyar back and forth. Therefore, they took that path, reached the oil mill, and began going round the mill, as they were trained to do.

The bullocks went round and round the mill until dawn. The landlord and the cart driver, in their deep slumber, lulled by the gentle swaying, slept on, thinking that the cart was on the road.

The day broke. The Chettiyar, heading to the woods behind the mill for his morning ablutions, arrived. He was surprised to see the landlord's cart, with his bullocks walking round and round the mill. *Didn't the landlord borrow my bullocks to go to a wedding?* he wondered. As he got closer, he saw the cart driver leaning on the side of the cart, gently nodding his head to the rhythm of the cart's movement, and the landlord in his soft bed, fast asleep.

The Chettiyar could not control his mirth. With his huge paunch jiggling, he laughed—silently, of course.

Suddenly aware of something strange, the landlord snapped awake. "Dey, you wretched asshole, where is the cart going?" he demanded loudly.

The driver jerked up in attention. *Chee! It was a mistake to have set off with mill-bullocks.*

"Aiya..." he whined plaintively.

"Shut up, you impotent fuck! Stop the cart now!" raged the landlord.

Knowing the landlord's violent temper, the Chettiyar quickly hid behind his mill.

The landlord jumped off the cart. "Lock the bullocks to the mill, and drag the cart home. You're fired!" he screamed, and strode off. ❖

naughty & dirty

a jenny and ninety-nine jacks

"Dey, don't ever go near Thatha!" screeched Kittan.

"Why?"

"He tells stories with all kinds of dirty words in them."

That was the first I heard about Thatha. Mostly because I was told not to, I felt I had to meet him. But I was still very young then.

It was only years later that I gathered the courage to actually go and ask him for his "dirty-word stories". I realized then that he was a treasury of folktales, or, as Kittan used to say, an ocean — one I could keep on fishing from; the catch would never run out.

"Tell me Thatha. Don't children get spoiled when we use dirty words in front of them?" Kittan asked him one day.

We could tell from the twinkle in Thatha's eye that he was grinning under his moustache.

After a long silence, he said, "If someone's going to get spoiled, he'll get spoiled. He doesn't need the help of my stories. In fact, people who know a lot of 'dirty-word stories' are less easily spoiled than others. Do you know the story of Rishyasingar?" he asked. "Vibaanda Munni, father of Rishyasingar, was an idiot. He was sure that if he could raise his son completely away from the company of women, he would remain virtuous. And what did that blockhead's son do? He ran off chasing the very first woman he laid his eyes on!" Thatha finished with a laugh.

It's time I gave Thatha a proper introduction. Though "thatha" means "grandpa", he wasn't really such an old man. We all called him Thatha because his name was Thathayya Nayakar.

"I shall tell you a story about giving advice to morons," said Thatha.

Once, in a forest, there lived a hundred donkeys, out of which only one was a jenny.

Dogs, cats and donkeys have a particular "season". During the season, the poor female donkey would have a horrible time handling the ninety-nine randy male donkeys. *"Ngyaa, ngyaa..."* she would scream in pain, her pathetic braying echoing through the forest.

As you might expect, there was stiff competition among the jacks over which one would get the jenny. While the mighty were engaged in open warfare, the weak and scrawny would make a beeline for her, only to be butted away by the stronger donkeys.

"Are we not donkeys too?" the weak ones would protest. "Is this not the season for us, as well? Should we not be allowed to satisfy our desires? You are not the only donkeys here, you know!"

But what use is it trying to reason with brawny ruffians? Their word is the law.

And so, during the season, the forest would be turned into a huge dust storm.

A drongo was watching the whole drama from a tree nearby. *What kind of injustice is this?* thought the drongo as it watched the poor jenny fight off the amorous jacks. *Do they really think that this one jenny can service all of them?*

It flew down onto the jenny's back.

"Sister Drongo, do you see my plight?" wept the jenny.

The drongo looked at the tall lusty jacks standing all around.

"Go away, leave her alone!" screeched the drongo.

One of the jacks approached the drongo and said, "Look here, Drongo. Hear me out before you start screeching at us. We are not like you birds. We don't have the luxury to do it whenever we want. This is our only opportunity. The season only lasts a month. If we miss this chance, we have to wait around for a whole year."

"I understand, brother," replied the drongo. "What you say is true. But how can one jenny serve all of you? Is that not like trying to pound a grain of rice with a hundred pestles? How can the rice take it?"

The jack reared back in anger. "Hey, who are you to interfere? This is none of your business. Get lost." And it threw its front legs onto the jenny's back to mount her.

The drongo tried various ways to stop the brute, but to no avail. It didn't know how to save the jenny. It could think of only one method.

It quickly flew around under the jenny's tail, and tried to block the entrance to her dark cave.

The brutish jack did not notice this. He just thrust into jenny with all his might.

"What happened to the drongo?" asked Kittan.
"Think for yourself!" guffawed Thatha. ❖

newlyweds

Long, long ago, newly married couples were not allowed to speak to each other for the first three months. They were so young and bashful that they wouldn't even look up at each other's faces for that whole time.

One such young pair had just got married. The groom was invited to live in his mother-in-law's house for the first three months.

The members of the household, including the son-in-law, would leave every day to work in the fields. At night, tired out from their work, they would all spread gunny sacks or mats under the trees and sleep—except for the young couple. The young man would sleep out on the thinnai, and the young woman would sleep locked inside the house.

The young man yearned to talk to his wife, but he didn't know how to approach her. It wasn't so easy in those days as it is now; all this modern business of running around trees and singing love duets was not allowed. Even in broad daylight, as soon as he entered the house, she would run into another room to hide. He was restless with longing for his wife.

So one day, he complained of a severe stomach ache and stayed home from work.

The mother called her daughter aside and said, "Girl, we are off to work. You make ginger tea and kanji for your husband, and then join us in the field."

"Am I to be alone with him, until then?" asked the timid daughter, nervously.

"Of course you won't be alone. I'll tell our neighbour Alamelu to come and sit with you," said the mother.

The mother went next door and said to Alamelu, "Thayee, my daughter is alone with her new husband. God knows what can happen if they stay alone too long. Could you go and sit with her?"

"How can I, Akka?" asked Alamelu. "I would have to give up the day's wages."

"Don't worry about your pay. I'll give you the money."

And so, Alamelu came over as a chaperone for the daughter.

How do I get rid of this woman? wondered the young husband, out on the thinnai. *She's like a bear intruding while I'm doing my prayers!* The daughter told Alamelu, "Akka, will you wake my husband up and tell him to have his kanji? I have to join my parents in the field." But the husband refused to budge. He saw a chance to get rid of Alamelu. "My stomach is still rumbling, Alamelu. Go to the market and get some fresh ginger for my tea," he groaned.

Alamelu checked that the daughter was busy grinding chutney to serve with the kanji, and left to buy ginger. As soon as she left, the husband got up, went in, sat next to his wife and declared, "I'm hungry. Give me my kanji."

What do I do now? puzzled the woman. *I was hoping to have Alamelu here till I left to work. Where has she disappeared to?* She looked around for the coconut shell in which to serve him the chutney (not realizing that he had hidden it). He sat waiting for his food with an innocent look on his face. She stood there, not knowing what to do, holding the chutney in her palm. Grinning, he took a lick of the chutney right from her palm, and then took a sip of kanji.

The new bride, flustered by his touch, squirmed shyly. "Take some chutney and mix it with the kanji," she gasped.

Aha! I finally got you to say something, smirked the husband. "My stomach cramps are getting worse," he told her. "I think I'm dying. You are too young and too beautiful to become a widow so soon. When I die, get married to a good man."

"What do you mean?" she sobbed. "What can I do to relieve your pain? Tell me quickly!"

"I can think of only one way out."

"Tell me, tell me! What can I do to save you?"

"That old keethari, the cowherd, might know the cure. Will you go ask him? If you follow his instructions, then perhaps I may survive."

The wife rushed out to find the old man. In the meantime, Alamelu returned with the ginger. The husband sent her off to inform the girl's parents about his plight.

The wife came back in tears, removed her blouse from under her sari, put the blouse in a pot of water, and boiled it, as Keethari had instructed. Then she swabbed her husband's body with the water, using her sari pallu. He lay there, holding his breath, pretending to be dead. She gently touched his nose to see if he was still breathing. Not feeling any warm air, she fell wailing on his chest. He inhaled deeply as her soft, plump breasts brushed against his nipples, and hugged her tight.

"What happened after that?" you ask.

Well, what do you think happened? The wife, overjoyed to see that her husband was still alive, dissolved into his arms.

When the worried parents returned home, they could see that the young husband had finished his business to the full. *Oh well,* they thought, *they were going to get to this after three months in any case. Why were we trying so hard to keep postponing their pleasure?* So they went in search of a nice, fat chicken to cook for the son-in-law.

Ever since then, the custom has been to have the nuptial night immediately after the wedding.   ❖

the trained parrot

Once upon a time, there lived a couple who had a daughter, ready to be married. The parents sought alliances from many places, but the girl was in love with her neighbour. He was a smart young man, and very handsome. But the parents arranged an alliance for her: a man who was all skin and bones, and as a black as a pot. At the first sight of that man, the daughter wanted to puke. But what could she do? He was her parents' choice, so she had to accept him as her husband.

The wedding was conducted on an auspicious day. Then she had to move into her husband's house. Her parents and neighbours bid them a fond farewell, smearing vibhuthi on her head to protect her during her travels. She excused herself for a moment, saying she had to take a leak, and sneaked behind the house to meet her lover from next door.

"I am leaving to my husband's house," she sobbed. "But I don't like that man. I love only you."

"I love you too," said her lover. "I was waiting for the right time to speak to my parents about you. But before I could, your parents got you married. I think I shall die with my dreams of you."

"Do you think I will be any happier? I shall never be able to forget you."

They tried to think of a way they could be together.

It was she who thought of a plan first. "It won't look good if I keep leaving my husband to come to my parents' house so that we can meet. Instead, you come over to my husband's house at night. I know a way we can be together till dawn, and then you can return to your home during the day. When you come, bring a trained parrot with you," she said, and left to her husband's.

The new husband was thrilled to have gotten her as his wife. He longed to speak to her and touch her. He couldn't wait to get home.

At dusk, the girl bathed herself, smeared turmeric and sandalwood paste on her body, drew a huge pottu on her forehead, braided her hair and adorned it with lots of flowers. The husband softly crept to her side and gently touched her arm.

That was it! She sprang at him, dancing in wild hysteria. "Adey! I am Mother Maariyaatha, not your wife," she cried in a hoarse voice. "I have taken possession of her body. How dare you touch the body in which I reside?"

The husband and his mother fell at her feet and begged, "Amma, can we do anything to appease you?"

"There is! You must not go near your wife until I give you the sign. In fact, you can't even enter the house. I will come as a parrot, and be with her during this time. When the parrot leaves the house, you may safely assume that I have left her body as well. Only after that can you claim her as your wife, and lay your hands on her," commanded the wife/goddess.

"When will the parrot come?"

"When it gets here, your wife will inform you. Until then, do not even step into this house!"

The mother and son fell again at her feet, and rushed out to the thinnai.

That very night, her lover arrived with the parrot. She hid him in the backyard and ran out to anxious pair on the thinnai.

"Aithe, Athaan, listen to this! This parrot just fell into my lap, out of nowhere."

The mother and son fell at the parrot's feet and touched it with devotion.

"Mother Maariyaatha, you have paid a special visit to my home. I am blessed," whispered the mother-in-law. Then, she turned to the girl and said, "Woman, this is no ordinary wild parrot that flies around the woods. Mother Maariyaatha has come in this shape. She has taken possession of you. My son, unaware of this, got married to you and brought you here. You cannot be husband and wife while the Mother is in you."

"What is this, Aithe? It was you who chose me as your daughter-in-law. Now you say I cannot be a wife to your son!"

"What can be done, my girl? The Mother is in you now. We dare not disobey her command."

"But Aithe, how do you know that the Mother has possessed me?"

"My body trembles just remembering that miracle!" said the mother-in-law. "You were not conscious of the Mother speaking through your body this evening. You cannot stand here chatting with us, or the Mother may get angry. Go into the house, shut the door and be with the parrot. The day the parrot leaves you and flies off, then you may call in my son and be happy with him."

The girl prostrated herself at her mother-in-law's and husband's feet, took their blessings, went into the house, shut the door and called in her lover from the backyard.   ❖

the scorpion sting

In a village, there was a farmer with a very beautiful wife. Every man in the village would have given an arm and a leg to bed her. One man, in particular, had been watching her for a long time, as she went out for her daily shopping.

Let me open a shop in my house, he thought. *Then she will come here to do her shopping, and she will get to know me.* So, he broke down the wall of his house which faced the street, and converted one room into a shop. He stocked it full of everything he thought she might possibly want.

The farmer's wife saw that the new shop was much closer to her house than the one she had been going to. So she went there, carrying cotton seeds to barter for her daily provisions. Normally, shops would give one measure of grain for one of measure of cotton seeds. But this man gave her two measures of grain.

At first, she thought this was just a ploy to attract more customers to the new shop. But after a while, she observed that other customers were treated normally; she was the only one who received the double measure.

He was yet to say a word to her except "Take what you want." His throat dried up at the sight of her, and he kept his face averted.

Finally, one day, her curiosity got the better of her. "How come you're being so generous in your exchange?" she asked him. "Can you afford this?"

"I am not generous with everyone. Only with you," he said.

"Why?"

"I like you very much," he replied, shyly.

"Chee! Do not entertain thoughts like that about me. I will never come to your shop again," she declared and walked off.

After that, she went back to walking past his shop on her way to the old shop. He was inconsolable. The investment for starting the shop had been huge. He could not afford to shut it down just because she refused him. He sighed dejectedly, and went on running the shop with no active interest. His customers slowly dwindled.

One night, she desperately needed dry ginger for the dinner she was cooking. She went to her old shop, but they were out. On her way back, she saw that the man's shop was open. There were no customers; he sat there alone, like a monkey, staring at the naked yellow light bulb.

I hope he has dry ginger, she thought.

She stood there at the shop and called out, "Do you have dry ginger?"

He went on staring at the bulb. She stepped closer and called out again, "Do you have dry ginger?" Only then did he turn around, but he still didn't look at her.

"Are you unwell?" she asked.

When at last he saw it was her, his eyes became wet with tears.

"Why are you crying?"

He did not say anything, but simply put out his hand. She gave him the cotton seeds she had brought to exchange. He took them, then looked up to ask what she wanted.

"Dry ginger," she said.

He gave her plenty of it, the same double measure.

She came away, not saying a word. After that, she began frequenting his shop again.

Many days passed. There was not a word exchanged in this whole time. He did not even look up at her face.

One night, it was very late as she set out to shop. All the shops were closed, except his; he had stayed open waiting for her. As she gave her barter, he measured out the grain. Very slowly she stepped back into the street, and then turned round to ask, "Are you sick? Why are you getting so thin?"

"Because I cannot forget you," he replied in a quiet voice.

She didn't respond to that comment directly, but went on to talk about the goings-on around town. He answered only with distracted grunts.

Then, without warning, he asked, "Can I come to your house tomorrow morning?"

She smiled at him with the corner of her mouth, and left.

The next morning, her husband left to the fields early. After some time, a crow tipped over his water pot. *What is this nonsense? How am I to plough in the hot sun without water to drink?* he thought, and rushed back home with the pot.

When he got home, he saw that the front door was shut. Puzzled, he peeped through the keyhole.

There inside, he saw the shopkeeper sucking on his wife's breast!

The farmer banged against the door with all his might, until it sprang open.

The wife looked up and immediately gathered her wits.

"Thank god you're here! But for this man, I would have been dead by now!"

The farmer could not understand. He looked at the shopkeeper, who was standing silent with his head bent.

"What are you saying?" cried the farmer. "Tell me what happened!"

"How do I explain? I am so ashamed. I was out gathering cotton seeds when a scorpion jumped out from nowhere, landed on my breast, and stung me. I was in severe pain. I didn't know what to do. I'd been told that this man here knew how to suck out the venom from a sting. So I went to him. He refused, saying he would not come if the man of the house was not here. I told him, 'My husband will not think bad of you—please come!' I am better now, though my breast is still throbbing," she sobbed.

"It is all right. Don't cry. This could have happened to anyone," consoled the husband. "I came back because a crow tipped over my water pot." He thanked the shopkeeper for coming to his wife's aid, took his water, and went back to the fields.

Days passed. One day, the woman was cooking in the kitchen when her husband screamed from the front room. She rushed to him.

"Hurry woman! Don't stand there gaping. I have been stung by a scorpion. Go fetch that shopkeeper. He has to suck out the venom. Go!" he yelled.

Not knowing what else to do, she ran to the shopkeeper. "You have to come now, or else he will doubt both of us," she pleaded.

At her house, the shopkeeper asked the farmer hesitantly, "Where have you been stung?"

The farmer looked at him for a second, then dropped down his dhoti and pointed.

The shopkeeper could not protest. He bent down to suck out the venom!   ❖

pillayar, guard my wife

There were two brothers, named Ramu and Somu. Ramu's wife died suddenly. Utterly dejected, he journeyed off to regions unknown.

Somu's wife, Kaathayi, had a secret lover. Somu had a suspicion that his wife had something going on the side.

Once, Somu had to leave town for the harvest, but did not want to give his wife the chance to meet her lover. So, he went to the roadside temple and prayed to Pillayar. "Pillayar, Pillayar, I have to leave my wife and go away for a while. I am leaving you to guard her. Please take good care of her. I shall be back in three days."

Kaathayi, thrilled to have some time with her lover, sent word to him immediately. When he arrived, she told him, "Come in and rest for a while. I shall make you a hot lunch."

Pillayar, watching this from his temple, decided he would not betray Somu's trust in him. So he took the form of Somu's brother Ramu and knocked on the door. Kaathayi opened the door, but did not recognize Ramu, for she had never seen him.

"Kaathayi," said Pillayar, "I am your brother-in-law, Ramu. A few weeks ago, I wrote to your husband that I was coming. Didn't Somu tell you?"

Scared, she rushed in, shoved her lover under the cot and covered him with a blanket.

After lunch, Pillayar said, "Kaathayi, I shall sleep on the thinnai outside, to protect you." From under the cot, he picked up the blanket—with the lover still wrapped inside—and went out. On the thinnai, he beat the lover black and blue and chased him off.

The next day Pillayar left the house on some errand. Kaathayi, not wanting to miss out on this chance, called for her lover again. Pillayar, with his divine power, realized this and returned immediately, carrying sacks of rice.

This time, Kaathayi hid her lover inside the cone-shaped thombai where the grain was kept.

"Kaathayi," said Pillayar, "your husband will come back in the evening. He wants you to store this rice in the thombai."

Even as Kaathayi tried to stop him, he poured all the rice into the thombai and left.

In the evening Somu returned with *his* fresh harvest of rice. He opened the thombai and was surprised to find it already full.

He ran out to the temple and wept, "Pillayar, Pillayar, did I not ask you to guard my wife? Her lover has already gifted her a whole thombai full of rice!"

In answer, Pillayar told Somu everything that had happened in his absence.

Somu chased Kaathayi out. Then he found a nice woman and got remarried!   ❖

cat's scratch

Once, in a village, there lived two brothers. Every morning they went to the forest to gather firewood and hunt game, which they would sell in the town for a good price and then buy rice to make their kanji.

The elder brother, who was married, was a very jealous man. He didn't trust his wife or even his own brother. Every afternoon, as the brothers cut firewood, the elder brother would spit on the ground and order the younger brother, "Dey, go home and get the kanji that your anni has made before this spit on the ground dries!" The younger brother would sprint home and be back with the kanji in a jiffy.

One day, as the younger brother reached out to take the kanji from his sister-in-law, a cat leapt out of nowhere and scratched her chest. (In those days, women did not wear a top blouse to cover their breasts.) The cat's claw scratched deep and the wound began to bleed. The brother promptly gathered some herbs, crushed them and said, "Come here Anni, let me put some medicine on the wound."

"Please don't delay any further. You must return before your brother's spit dries up. I can bear my pain. Go!" cried the woman.

By the time the younger brother reached the forest, the elder brother was blinded by hunger and jealousy. He had no time to listen to excuses, and sprang on his brother with a sickle yelling, "You motherfucker! Are the two of you trying to cheat me?" The younger brother took to his heels.

That night, the elder brother spread out his mat, lay on it and beckoned his wife.

"Please leave me tonight. I am very sore," she said.

"Why? Did you have such rough sex with my brother?" he roared.

"Stop accusing me. It was a cat that scratched me," she snapped back.

"And the cat chose to land on your chest and nowhere else? How strange," he smirked.

"Do not throw careless words at me. My pallu has come down only for you," she swore.

"You expect me to believe that? I am going to chop off both of your breasts. You must not make a whimper," he growled as he pulled out his sickle.

She looked at him for a moment, and then stood with her arms raised high in the air. He slashed her left breast. As the breast fell off, he began losing sight in his right eye. When he cut off her right breast, he lost sight in his left eye and was rendered completely blind.

There she stood, arms above her head, strong as a copper statue, completely unhurt, still smiling.

He fell at her feet, hugged them and sobbed, "Save me, woman. I cannot be blind for the rest of my life. Do something!"

"Do not weep, husband. Spread some of my blood from the sickle on your eyes and you will regain your sight."

He did this, and immediately he could see again. He re-attached her breasts, which healed immediately, and once more he fell at her feet. "I now know how honourable you are. Forgive me. Let us bring back my brother."

Together they went in search of the younger brother.   ❖

two chopped noses

Once there was a goatherd. He had a wife who hated him from the very core of her being. She didn't like him even the least tiny little bit. The man generally left at dawn with his goats to the hillside, where he grazed them; at sundown, he would herd them back to the pen and come home when it was totally dark. But when he lovingly reached out to his wife, she would snap: "Chee! All I can smell is the stink of goat dung on you. Move away."

He did not mind his wife's attitude. He'd eat whatever she served, tell her what had happened to him that day, and then fall fast asleep—so fast asleep, it would be easier to wake a dead man.

Four houses down from the goatherd's house was the house of a cowherd and his wife. The goatherd's wife and the cowherd fancied each other. The moment the goatherd fell asleep, the goatherd's wife would shut the door and run off to meet her lover. The cowherd would tell *his* wife, "You sleep inside the house. I'll spend the night in the cowshed. You never know when a cow might snap its tether and wander off into the fields. Or which bastard is roaming around out there waiting for the right moment to walk off with the cattle."

After that, in the cowshed, the lovers would be in the throes of passion until dawn. At the first call of the rooster, the goatherd's wife would return home.

One night, the goatherd was startled awake by a nightmare. Waking, he saw that his wife was not there. *Poor woman, perhaps she has an upset stomach,* he thought, and went back to sleep.

The next morning, as he set off to the hill with his goats, he asked his wife, "Where were you last night? I woke up around midnight, and you weren't there."

She stood speechless for a moment.

"Where did I go?" she repeated. Recovering her wits, she said, "I went to the cowherd's house to help his wife gather cow dung. She spends the whole day gathering the dung and making cakes, and then takes them to the market to sell. Poor woman, she has no one to help. That cowherd is useless. He never listens to a word his wife says. He does whatever he pleases..." She went on and on like that, spinning a long yarn.

He gaped at her for a while, and then interrupted.

"How funny that your friend should call you to help gather dung at midnight!"

"Oh you silly man, how would you know what time it was? You're such a deep sleeper. I leave as soon as you're asleep, and return well before midnight."

Maybe she's telling the truth, he thought, and left with his goats. But a small grain of doubt kept nagging his brain. After that, he did not sleep as peacefully as before.

A few nights later, he again woke up to find the wife missing. He went out into the yard and looked up at the sky. It was indeed midnight. He came back inside, but could not get back to sleep.

The next night, he lay there with his eyes shut. The moment his wife shut the front door, he got up and stealthily followed her.

At the cowshed, he saw that his wife was not gathering dung with her friend. She was having fiery sex with the cowherd! He quietly snuck away.

The next morning, he told his wife, "I have to sleep in the goat pen tonight. Are you sure you won't be scared to sleep alone?"

She could hardly keep from laughing. *Why should I be scared? Even when you're here, you're no better than a corpse. As if I have to sleep alone tonight! As if I'll sleep at all!*

As soon as the goatherd left for work, she ran out in search of the cowherd and told him, "My husband is staying out in the pen tonight. I'm sick of lying in that stinky cowshed. Come over to my house. I shall cook a feast and we can enjoy ourselves till sunrise."

The cowherd was overjoyed. "Go start cooking. I'll tell my wife I have to go out of town tonight. I'll be over at your house at sunset."

She ran back home, cooked up a huge feast, bathed, and had just put on a fresh sari when the cowherd arrived. While they were eating their dinner and sharing betel leaves, the goatherd went quietly to the cowshed, selected two of the best cows, took them to a friend's house on the other side of the hill, and spent the night there.

The cowherd returned home after a session of heated lovemaking to find two of his cows missing.

Aiyyo, two cows have been stolen! The thief must have known I was not at home! When my wife learns about this she'll kill me, he thought. He picked up a thick staff and gave himself four hard blows, and then started screaming. "Aiyyo, the cow thief is beating me!" His wife, sleeping inside the house, came rushing out. "Adiye," he cried. "Some crook was untying our cows. I ran up to stop him, but he beat me up and left with two of them."

"You poor thing! You don't have to sleep in the cowshed alone any more. I will come and sleep there with you," she said.

He tried arguing with her, but it was no use; she insisted. The next night she came along with him to the cowshed.

That night when the goatherd's wife came over, she saw two figures sleeping in the cowshed. *What do I do now?* she wondered. She paced up and down, trying to figure out who the second person could be.

The cowherd's wife heard her footsteps, and got up. All she could see was someone pacing about. *That fucking cow thief has returned. Just like a dog can't stop licking and a hen can't stop pecking, a thief can't stop stealing either. He walked off with two of our cows, and he thinks he can walk off with more. But I won't let him get away with it. I'll teach him a lesson!* she thought. Picking up a sickle, she crept up behind the goatherd's wife, chopped off her nose, and went back to the cowshed to sleep.

The goatherd's wife was in unbearable pain. Not daring to cry aloud, she stumbled back home and hid behind the thombai. Just then, the goatherd woke up to check on his wife. Not finding her, he grumbled, "That slut, looks like she's gone off to fuck tonight, too. I shall catch the two of them in action!"

In the cowshed, the cowherd noticed that his wife was not there. *Maybe she could not bear the stench,* he thought. *Let me check if my lover is waiting on the road.* He had taken just two steps when he saw the goatherd hurrying up the path. Thinking that it was his lover, the cowherd rushed over, saying, "You've come! I was about to head to your house. My wife insisted on sleeping in the cowshed with me."

The goatherd leapt on him and chopped off his nose.

The next day the two lovers, with their chopped noses, had to invent stories to hide behind.

"When my husband had gone to the pen, some unknown person jumped on me and chopped off my nose!" said the goatherd's wife.

"The same dickless thief who stole my cows in the black of night came back. When I tried to fight him, he chopped off my nose!" said the cowherd.

The goatherd and the cowherd's wife both knew the truth, but they chose to keep quiet. ❖

two brothers, one wife

Once upon a time there were two brothers. Since there was no one to make kanji for them or take care of the house, the elder brother got married. His wife took good care of both of them.

Now, the younger brother wanted his sister-in-law. When his brother left for guard duty at the goat pen or to work in the fields for a couple of nights, he'd use the opportunity to make his moves on her.

"As your elder brother's wife, I should be like a mother to you. Wait for two years, we'll get you a wife of your own," she begged.

"You, like a mother to me?" he scoffed. "You're my elder brother's wife... so you're half mine! If you comply, I shall forgo the thought of marriage forever. The three of us can be together all our lives, like the palm and the back of a hand, one big happy family."

She was in two minds about it. If she pushed him away, and a new woman came into the house as his wife, that would only mean trouble. Instead, she might as well keep both men happy! So she returned his affections.

Four or five years passed. Now, she was a mother of four. The house was always crowded with whimpering children. She had no time to either sleep or talk with the younger brother. If she was not breastfeeding, then she was cooking, and if she was not cooking, she was singing lullabies—*ro, ro, ro.* How much things had changed!

The younger brother saw that it was only going to get worse, not better. She had no more time for her men. This was his elder brother's bad luck, not his! He didn't want to share a woman anymore; he wanted one of his own, to care only for him.

"Anna," he told his brother, "how much longer am I going to be working for you and your family? Should I not have any pleasure of my own? Please find me a girl."

"I will," promised the elder brother. "Wait till we finish the harvest. Then the next celebration in this house will be your marriage!"

The woman overheard this. One day, when her husband was not at home, she cornered the younger brother.

"You promised me that you would never get married, that we would always be together as a family. So how is it fair now for you to ask your brother to find you a girl?"

"What are you, mad?" he sneered. "Back then, I didn't want a marriage. Now I do, so I am going to marry."

"I believed you when you made all those promises. Now that I'm a mother of four children, you want to leave all the responsibility on me and my husband?"

"I like that!" he snapped. "I was young then. I didn't know any better. Shut your trap now, or I'll tell my brother everything that happened. I'll let the whole town know, too."

She realized that it was no use arguing with him, and kept quiet.

A month passed; it was time for harvest.

The brothers were busy at work in the fields, when the woman told her husband, "We are almost done here. Your brother and I can finish the rest. Will you please go help my mother for the next ten days? She is handling the harvest all by herself."

The unsuspecting husband left at once.

A few days later, she called the younger brother and said, "There is no more grain in the small thombai. Can you get into the big thombai, and hand me four measures of grain? I have to make kanji."

He opened the door in the top of the big thombai and went down the ladder.

As soon as his head disappeared, she pulled out the ladder and shut the door.

"Aiyyo, aiyyo!" yelled the brother from inside. "What are you doing? Please open the door. It's dark in here."

"Go on, scream louder," she said. "It was not enough for you to enjoy your brother's wife without his knowledge. Now you want a young, fresh bride, do you? Aha, but you can only get one if I let you out! I think I'll keep you in there and starve you until you learn your lesson."

And she left him there. He screamed for water and food, but she paid no heed. Four days passed. Too weak to protest any longer, he lay slumped inside the thombai. Hearing no further sound, she quietly opened the door and peeked in. When he saw the light from above, he pleaded with folded palms, promising never to think of marriage again.

She felt sorry for him, and slowly lowered the ladder in. He came out half-dead.

Now, it is said that he runs miles at the slightest mention of marriage! ❖

the secret lover

There once was a husband who knew that his wife had a secret lover. So, the husband pretended to go blind.

One day the news came that the wife's brother was getting married. The husband hurried home to ask her to make idlis for them to carry on the journey. She quickly made her lover hide in a huge pot, told the husband to guard the rice that was drying in the sun outside the house, and went to buy lentils for the idlis.

The husband was standing there near the rice with a big stick to chase away the crows, when he heard the lover coughing inside the pot. He quietly went in and beat him to death.

The wife, on her return, found the lover dead but still grinning widely. She secretly took his body to the cremation ground to burn. But before she lit the pyre, she was drawn in by his grin.

"Oh my lover, you may be dead. But your smile is still so beautiful!"

She bent down to kiss him. Suddenly, his teeth clamped down on her lips, and did not let go.

When the people of the town found her like that at the cremation ground, they smeared the poor woman with shit as punishment, and slammed her on the ground again and again, like a dhobi washes his clothes, till she died.   ❖

the replacement

Once there was a man who had just got married. In his game with the damsels, he was a champion indeed! But his new wife was still inexperienced and not used to his fast moves and passion. She liked it, but she was still bashful.

He left for work early in the morning and returned late at night. She'd serve him his kanji and stand at a distance.

"Is there anything to go with my kanji?" he'd ask.

"What is there except *this*?" she'd lisp, shyly, with her head bent.

"You do have *that*, don't you? Bring *it* here," he'd say.

"You have one yourself! Take a taste of *that*," she'd reply.

This game of words continued for several days. One day he came home with a vadai, tucked it between his thighs, and sat down to eat his kanji. The same game started again; this time, at her final tease, he put his hand between his legs, plucked something out, put it into his mouth, chewed and swallowed.

The wife stared at him, horrified. She thought he was acting, but it looked like there really was something in his mouth. She rushed to him.

"Please tell me you didn't eat *that*," she gasped.

"Why would I lie? Feel for yourself," he grinned.

And she did. (He wanted her to, didn't he?)

He had been telling the truth! There was nothing between his thighs.

"You told me to take a taste of *that*. I did. I found it so good that I ate it all up," he said.

"I must take a small detour here," said Thatha, "and tell you about a rural tradition.

"When I was a child, during Pongal celebrations, there was one day called Manjal Neerattu Vizha*. After the shower there would be a public dance called the cheththaandi attam (masked dance). Men with their faces disguised would dance in front of their women. In olden days, they may have just smeared their faces with dust or ash, but one needs variety to keep the entertainment going. So over the years, they shifted to masks.

"There was one dancer who wore a grotesque mask and a tiny bit of cloth covering his butt, but was otherwise naked. He had tucked his prick in between the cheeks of his butt, held it tight, and was writhing to the rhythm. His groin looked like a young girl's!

"This is exactly what our man in the story had done," said Thatha.

So naturally, the wife could feel nothing there. She burst into tears. But how long could she keep crying?

"Can you not do something for this?"

"There is nothing that cannot be mended. In fact I can get a new one that's even better than the one I had. But it will be a costly affair."

"Tell me how much, and I will ask my mother to give me the money," she said.

"Say, about a thousand…"

"That much!" Once again she dissolved into tears.

"You stupid woman, stop shedding false tears. No woman who wants her husband to have *that* would tell him to take a taste of it! Go get me the money, if you want the replacement."

---

* Turmeric-water shower: a festival where a girl will select the man of her choice, normally her favorite cross-cousin, by throwing a pot of turmeric water on him in public.

At her mother's she threw a tantrum till she got the money. He left with it.

Where did he go? On a long picnic, slept where he felt like, ate what he wanted to; in general, he was a rich, free bird for a month or so.

Meanwhile, the mother had come to stay with the daughter to help around the house and make sure she was safe. When the daughter left to work in field during the day, the mother stayed back to clean and cook.

Finally, the man returned home.

"Welcome home, Maappilai," said the mother, from behind the kitchen door. "Would you like something to eat?"

"I have eaten, thanks. Where is my wife?"

"She is at work; she'll be back in the evening. So, how are you now? Are you better?"

"Much better."

"Did it work out well? How much did it cost?"

"Yes, it worked out very well. Only the cost shot up a bit."

"That's alright. What does money matter, as long as the result is satisfactory," she said, peeking out of the door.

She looked eager to check *it*. Naturally, it was her money; shouldn't she know that it was well spent?

He showed her. She stared at it in awe.

"Not bad at all, Maappilai! It is huge, well built!" she exclaimed, gently caressing it. "It's a pity your father-in-law didn't have a chance to get a replacement like this. I must say the structure is beautiful and strong. I'm not exaggerating—it is truly awesome! Only a thousand? I wouldn't mind spending fifty thousand, for one like that!"   ❖

four hundred goats

A father and daughter were grazing their goats in the forest. There were four hundred goats in all.

Without warning, dark, heavy clouds raced in from the horizon and swept across the sky, with flashes of lightning and roaring thunder. The father stood gazing at the impending rain. He knew that a long heavy shower would spell doom for his herd. They could not stand exposure to extreme cold or dampness.

As the father wrung his hands, the daughter gathered the herd, lifted her skirt and, in a flash, shoved all the goats into the dark cave between her thighs.

The father gaped at her in shock. *Oh my dear God, I never knew she had one this deep! What do I do? Where do I find a man who can fill that and make her happy?*

Afterwards, the only thought that occupied the father's mind was finding his daughter a suitable boy. He spent considerable time travelling to far-off regions, searching.

He was returning from one such trip when he was caught in a raging storm. He had to cross a flooding river to get home. He knew there was no bridge, nor any boats which could take him across.

He was told that a few miles downstream, a kind soul had made a temporary arrangement for people to go across to the other side.

He walked until he found a log bridge, on which there were several people walking to and from the other shore. He joined them.

It was only at the other end that he realized what the bridge really was.

Aha! He is indeed the right man to keep my darling daughter happy forever, the father decided then and there. ❖

the donkey and the mullaikeerai

Once upon a time there was a very rich man, over sixty years old, but still with the looks of a strapping young buck. His first wife had no children. After a long time he married a younger woman, but she too bore him no children. As he grew older, his heart longed for a child of his own. So he left his first wife at home and took the second on a pilgrimage to Kasi, where he prayed for a son, and to Rameswaram, where he prayed for a daughter. A few days after their return, the second wife missed her period.

The rich man was overjoyed. Naturally, why wouldn't he be?

During her pregnancy the second wife started craving mullaikeerai. So, in the garden near the well, he sprinkled a few mullaikeerai seeds, laid down some manure, watered the patch and waited for the keerai to grow.

A week later, the keerai was lush, thick and green, ready to be plucked the next day!

Unfortunately, the dhobi's donkey chose that morning to stray into the rich man's kitchen garden and gobble up all the keerai. Just as it turned to leave, the rich man came to pluck the keerai for his wife. What he saw in the mangled patch made his stomach burn. He picked up a thick piece of firewood and whacked the donkey on its hind legs. Both the legs snapped and the donkey fell to the ground.

Some time later, the dhobi, who had been searching all over for his donkey, came there to find it lying on the ground with its hind legs broken. He read the situation immediately. His income was dependant on the donkey; he could not work without it. When he realized he would no longer be able to earn, he became enraged, and yelled out curses.

"Are you brainless? How could you do this to a helpless beast? How could you break its poor legs for a stupid bunch of keerai?"

The rich man was not in the house, but the second wife heard the volley of curses. She came out running with a broomstick to chase the dhobi off. She raised it to hit him, but he caught her hand. His grip was so tight that she tripped and fell on her stomach, causing her to miscarry.

What happened next? Total chaos. On one side was the entire community of dhobis, and on the other the whole kith and kin of the rich man. What a commotion! It was impossible to hear what anyone was saying!

The village elders tried to intervene and arbitrate the case. But nothing would placate the rich man.

"I am going to take him to a court of law and make sure he gets the punishment he deserves!" he declared.

The village elders tried telling him that this was too silly a case to take to the court; it would only result in his humiliation. But he would not listen.

At the court, the rich man stated his case:

"Your honour, I am getting old. I do not think I can manage to father a child after this. I spent so much time and money taking my second wife on a long pilgrimage to Kasi and Rameswaram to pray for a child. She had just become pregnant. But this cursed man has spoiled all my hopes!

"It's not like I went to his house, pulled the donkey out, and broke its legs. During her pregnancy, my wife was craving mullaikeerai. In the kitchen garden, I sprinkled a few mullaikeerai seeds, laid down some manure, watered the patch and waited for the keerai to grow. That stupid donkey raided the keerai patch. It was only then that I lost my temper and broke its legs.

"This man had the nerve to come to my house and shout curses from the street. My wife, to protect my honour, went out with the broom. He twisted her hand, tripped her to the ground, and aborted her fetus, thereby killing my only child!"

Then the dhobi stated his case:

"Your honour, I did not send my donkey to graze on his keerai patch. I had tied it up; I don't know how it broke loose. I had searched all over for it, when finally I saw it lying in his backyard, with its legs broken!

"There are all kinds of animals roaming around the town. What do they know about property boundaries? If he wanted to protect his garden, he should have fenced it.

"I am sorry my donkey ate his keerai. But what he should have done is come to me for compensation. He could have fined me. He could even have whipped me; I get that all the time from people like him anyway.

"Instead, he chose to take his anger out on the poor donkey. I have no donkey now. How can I do my work?"

At this point, he almost wept!

"The river bed is three miles off. How do I carry my wash load that far without my donkey? Am I to take it on my back? It's not enough that he's spoiled my income, his wife dared to come at me with a broomstick! I only caught her arm to prevent the blow. I did not trip her; she fell on her own and lost her child. I am innocent, your honour!"

"Can your donkey's legs be mended?' the judge asked the dhobi.

"Yes, your honour, if I can put the legs in splints."

"And how long will it take before your donkey is completely healed and can do its job?"

"Six months, your honour."

This was the judge's verdict:

The wash loads, for the next six months, should be carried by the rich man on his back to the river bed. The dhobi was the reason the rich man's child was aborted. So it was now the dhobi's duty to replace the lost fetus to the wife! ❖

the irusi

Once upon a time there was a couple. The wife was good-looking, but she was an irusi—a woman with the outward appearance of a female, but with a slit that was only good for taking a piss, not for anything else. On top of that, she was careless and hasty with the housework. She never bothered to do anything properly. When she served rice, it would either be mushy or half-cooked, and her dosais would be served in little torn pieces instead of nice and round. If her husband complained, she would just say, "You can't swallow a whole round dosai anyway. You have to tear it to pieces to eat. So eat it the way I give it to you!"

She is of no other use to me; at the very least I should get decent food at home! grumbled the husband.

After toiling all day in the hot sun, he would return home hoping that there would be some kanji to eat. There she would be, fast asleep, as though she were passed out drunk.

"This is the limit! I'm not asking you to come and work with me in the fields. Is it too much to expect some simple food?" he would demand.

"Will you die if you go without kanji for a day?" she would sneer.

One such day, a beggar came to their doorstep.

"Aiya, give me something to eat," he pleaded.

"I have nothing in the house to give you," said the husband.

"Please aiya, you must have something."

Frustrated, the husband rushed back in, dragged his wife out, pushed her at the beggar and said, "Here, this is all I have. Take her if you want."

The wife snapped back at her husband, "I'd rather be with a beggar than stay here as your wife!" She took the beggar by the hand and said, "Come along, let's go."

The beggar was shocked at first, but then became happy to get a woman. He took her along with him to the next town.

Along the way, the wife sat down under a shady banyan tree and told the beggar, "I'm tired. Let me sleep here for some time. Go get me some kanji."

"Of course, my dear," replied the beggar. "Have a good nap. I'll take good care of you, don't worry."

When he was single, begging from four homes in a day had provided him with enough to eat. Now, with a mate, he found he had to beg in at least ten homes to keep them both fed. In addition to her food, there were other expenses, like oil for her hair, saris for her to wear, betel-leaf for her to chew, and snacks for her to munch between meals.

He wouldn't have minded these expenses if only he could do something more with the woman. And what an attitude!

How can I get rid of her? he wondered.

Just then, a tribal forest hunter passed them, with baskets to sell.

"How much does a basket cost?" asked the beggar.

"You are my first customer of the day. Here, take a basket and give me whatever you can," said the hunter, with his eyes fixed on the woman. She was looking at him, too, admiring his strong, muscled body and his thick moustache. The beggar noticed her interest and told the hunter, "You can take her, if you wish."

The woman happily followed the hunter to his temporary hut in the foothills. There she fell asleep in the shade of a tree. When she woke up, she announced that she was hungry.

The hunter looked up from the basket he was weaving and said, "If you're so hungry, you can eat some mud. Get up and help me make baskets. You'll only get real food if you do some real work."

"If you can't even feed a woman, then why did you bring me here, you useless asshole?" she shot back. "I don't know how to weave baskets. Even if I did, I wouldn't."

"Is that right? You'll do as you're told, or I'll give you four whacks on your back!"

She leaned back, thinking he was only joking. But he grabbed her by the hair and gave her four stinging blows on the back. Unable to bear the pain, she screamed.

"Shut up," said the hunter. "I don't want to hear another peep from you. Or else I'll bury you alive."

Realizing that he was fully capable of doing just that, she shut up and sat down to weave. After a few minutes, he looked up at her and grinned.

"Wipe that irritating grin off your face. It makes me feel like someone's rubbing chili paste into my pussy," she retorted.

The hunter couldn't stop grinning. He threw his basket aside, pulled her onto his lap and kissed her hard. Then he rushed into the forest and returned with a honeycomb, tapioca, and a collection of fruits. He lit a fire and lovingly roasted the tapioca for her. Even before the sun had fully set, he dragged her onto his mat. Only then, to his great surprise, did he realize that she was totally useless. *She has no skills, she doesn't like to work, she can't even...! What do I want with her? All she's good for is eating and sleeping. She's a burden on the Earth!*

He waited until she was asleep and then quietly slipped away.

The sun rose high. The birds in the trees were twittering. The air was slowly warming up. She sat up and was shocked to see the man and his gear missing. She looked around for a while, and then burst into loud sobs.

A short distance away was a dilapidated mandap in which an old saamiyaar was meditating. He heard the woman's wails, and came looking. There stood a beautiful, ripe young woman, in tears.

"What happened, my dear?" he asked her. "Why are you crying?"

She told him everything, top to bottom.

"Do not worry, my dear," said the saamiyaar. "I have been an ascetic all my life. But I have not yet done enough good works. I shall now care for you as if you were my own child."

He hugged her gently and caressed her back reassuringly. She folded herself into his warm embrace, and fingered his long beard.

"Was your beard always this long?" she asked.

"I was born with this beard. To this day, not a single blade has touched my body," he replied, puffing up with pride.

"Is that so?" she asked, starting to laugh uncontrollably.

"What's so funny?" he said.

"If your beard is this long, then your hair down *there* must be just as long. Imagine, if I could comb out the tangles and braid them both together, you would have to stay doubled over for the rest of your life!" she said, giggling.

What a nasty, vulgar woman she is! She's insulting all my years of devotion! "Wait here for a minute, I've got a toilet emergency," he said, and ran off. ❖

the crab

Once, there was an old man with a son. When the son was old enough for marriage, and had proved that he was a responsible farmer, the father got him married to a girl from another district. One day, there was an important function at the girl's native home, which she absolutely had to attend. In those days, it was impossible to make that kind of trip by car or train; one had to walk the whole distance. But it was sowing time, and her young husband could not leave the fields to accompany her. She could not be sent alone on such a long journey, so her father-in-law decided to go with her to keep her safe.

When the two had been walking for a while, the father-in-law had to take a leak. Not knowing how to tell this to the girl, he said, "Thayee, you keep walking. I have to pick some herbs. I shall join you soon." The girl was smart enough to understood. "Fine Maama," she replied and went ahead.

Now, pissing is like yawning. When someone wants to take a leak, then immediately, everyone else does too. The girl too now felt the urge to pee. Since the old man was away, she looked around for a safe place to squat. She choose a nearby field that had just been harvested. As she was looking around, worried that her father-in-law might come back or a stranger might walk by, she did not notice that she was peeing on a crab burrow.

Once the warm piss entered the burrow, a stupid crab crawled out and entered *her* burrow.

Startled, she stood up and frantically tried to dig it out with her fingers. The idiot crab just crept further inside, with no intention of coming out.

True, it was just a tiny land crab. But its frenzied scrambling inside her was both arousing and bothering the girl. She tried sitting, bending over, standing, but nothing seemed to work.

The father-in-law returned and saw the girl looking disturbed. The sun was already going down. They would have to hurry if they wanted to reach their destination by nightfall. He waited for a while, but she just kept restlessly sitting, bending, and standing, not seeing him at all.

"Is there a problem, my girl? Is your stomach upset?" he asked, gently.

What could she say? How could she explain her predicament?

Somehow, in as few words as possible, she told him. He was an experienced man, and he understood.

"You just stay there, my dear. I will be back in a minute," he said, removing his top-cloth and turning to leave. "Don't be worried. I will solve this."

He went to a pond close by. Using his top-cloth, he caught four fish. He brought them over to her and told her to squat over the fish. She did.

In a few minutes, the crab, drawn by the smell of the fish, crawled out.

"Appa!" she thought, feeling as though she'd just got her life back. She got up and said, "Maama, it is alright now!" And they went on their way once again.

This is the original story.

Of course, the listeners will be caught up in the excitement and the novel experience of the woman. There are times when other living things enter human bodies, like ants that enter the ear and refuse to come out. It is common for leeches, also, to crawl into a woman's vagina when she is bathing in a stream. But since it's common, this is of no special interest for a storyteller.

This crab story has a few different versions. If the storyteller wants to stretch out the ending:

The crab comes out, drawn by the fish smell. Both the girl and the father-in-law watch to make sure.

The father-in-law then gently inquires, "You are sure that only one crab went in?"

"I think so, Maama. I am not positive."

"Relax then, let me check if there are any more," says the father-in-law, stepping forward to help.

If the fingers are not long enough and the audience wants more, the story can extend further!   ❖

jealous husbands

The panchayat had a new case to deal with that day. It was a divorce case, where it was the wife who wanted to end the marriage.

At the court, the wife was asked, "What does your husband lack? He is handsome, has a good job, and earns well. Why don't you want him? Be frank with us."

What could she possibly say? She was a Tamil woman, after all; she had to be diplomatic. So, after a bit of a hesitation, she said,

"If the water in a well is ten feet below the ground, how do you hope to draw it out with a rope just seven feet long?"

Even today, there are communities in some rural areas where after marriage, if either spouse is dissatisfied, they can separate and remarry. It is only those communities that do not give priority to sexual satisfaction that make human life miserable, especially for a woman with a "big appetite".

There are some husbands who understand the situation, and keep silent about their wives' discreet relationships. Then there are others who make a hue and cry about it at the panchayat. The experienced elders usually just laugh this off. "Oh get lost! This is not a haystack that will be depleted if someone else takes some hay."

There are many tales ridiculing these petty, suspicious husbands. Here is one:

Once upon a time, there was a man who had to leave on a trip. He drew a picture of a goat kid on his wife's pudendum, saying, "This sketch should not be tampered with till I come back."

When he returned, he found the sketch intact... only the goat now had horns!

"What is this?" he demanded.

"What can I do? You said you would return soon, but you took so long! A goat can't remain a kid forever, can it? It's only natural for it to grow horns," she said.

"You're right," he had to agree.

"You youngsters do tell lame stories, don't you?" sneered Thatha. "Wait till you hear this one.

"Once there was a bum who was over-possessive of his wife. Do you know what he did?" Thatha took a while to tell us, for he was too busy laughing. Finally, he gasped, "How do we seal a bottle of kerosene? With a ball of tamarind, right? When he left town, this dimwit used a lump of tamarind to seal his wife's that."

"What did she do if she wanted to pee?" asked Kittan in his screechy voice.

Thatha turned to me. "Where did you find this idiot?" he demanded. "Just as a storyteller must have a certain talent, the listener should have some basic etiquette as well. Don't ask stupid questions. You should understand that a folktale has neither head nor feet."

213

Now this husband was strong, like a soldier. He could single-handedly hold off any attack. But for all his strength, where it came to servicing women, he left a lot to be desired. He was useless below the waist. Perhaps that doubled his jealousy.

One day he left town, planning to return before nightfall. But in those days, one could not travel by car or train; one had to walk. By the time he came to his home town, it was well past midnight. He was truly anxious.

Now, there was a valid reason for his anxiety. Right opposite his house was the village mandap, which was the permanent hangout for all the young men of the town. They even slept there. Just the thought of it made his stomach churn.

He hastened home.

Inside, he saw his wife fast asleep as if she were dead to the world. Then he noticed that her sari had been lifted up to her waist.

He lit an oil lamp and quietly came closer to confirm his suspicions. Aha! The tamarind was missing!

I must find the culprit right away, he decided, and went out to the mandap. There were many men lying there asleep.

The husband went to each man in turn and checked if any of their organs tasted sour.

Here screechy-voiced Kittan, who had been listening with rapt attention up to this point, spat in disgust. "Chee, Thoo! Thatha..."

The husband found two that tasted sour. He shook the men roughly awake and dragged them to the house of the village headman.

The headman was asleep on his coir cot outside his house.

"Aiya," wept the husband. "You must give me justice. This is what happened." He told the story. "These are the bastards! I have proof."

"How did you find out?" asked the headman.

The husband explained in detail.

The headman slapped his forehead with his palm, *tup, tup, tup!* and collapsed in loud laughter.

"What's so funny Aiya? You do not believe me? You can check for yourself," cried the husband.

"Get lost, you dog! Why should *I* check? You're the idiot who was cursed to do this to every man in the village! Go away!" he chortled, and chased the man off.

You must be thinking this story is highly exaggerated. But, it is necessary for a storyteller to give the listeners a shock once in a while. ❖

labour pain

When God made the Earth, he also created labour pain, to be experienced by woman alone.

The women of Earth gathered together and appealed to God, "Is this fair? After all, man is also responsible for getting a woman pregnant. Why should only we have to go through so much pain? You are God! Now share half of this pain with the man who fathered the child."

"Of course," said God, and granted their wish.

After that, whenever a pregnant woman went into labour, the father of the child would also start rolling on the ground in pain, screaming, "Aiyyo, Amma, Appa...!"

Things were going very smoothly.

One day, a pregnant rani had just felt her first contraction. That meant the raja should have felt something too, right? But there he was, sitting as comfortably as a block of stone, chatting with his friends.

Suddenly, they heard a yell from outside the palace. "Aiyyo, Amma, Appa, I cannot bear this pain...!"

Everyone rushed out to check, including the raja.

There was the palace servant rolling on the ground, clutching his lower back, screaming.

And so, the women's demand for equality became an embarrassment. They joined together once again, and went back to God.

"God," they appealed, "please make the delivery pains exclusively ours. You can even triple the pain, we will bear it all!"

"Of course," said God, and granted their wish.

Since then only woman experiences labour pain; man has no share in it.   ❖

the raja and the servant

For a long time, the raja had harbored a suspicion. In his palace was a servant who looked exactly like him. Really—take off the raja's crown, his embroidered clothes and his jewels, and he would be indistinguishable from the servant.

Actually, it was the rani who noticed the resemblance first. Only after checking himself in front of the mirror in his private chamber, without all his finery, did the raja agree.

Even the thought of that servant made his head pound.

One day, he called the servant aside and asked, "Did your mother ever work in this palace?"

This is the raja who is asking me a question. I'd better tell the truth, or risk having my head chopped off! thought the servant.

"Oh Raja, my mother comes from a town very far away. But my father worked in this palace, a long time ago!"   ❖

how betel leaf came to earth

"Do you know why, of all the leaves in this world, the betel leaf alone has that special, strong, pungent fragrance?" asked Thatha.

"What fragrance?" we asked.

Thatha pulled a leaf out of the compact bundle he kept by his side, closed his eyes, took a deep sniff, and with a secret smile on his lips, passed the leaf around.

At one sniff, I knew it. It was the same sweet, pungent, heady odour! I took another sniff to confirm. Oh yes, this was it!

216

I looked at the old man in amazement. How many times had I chewed on a betel leaf before! How did it escape me? Most importantly, how was it that this old man was in a position to remind me? As we gaped in awe, Thatha began his story.

Once upon a time, at Lord Indran's invitation, Arjunan came to stay as a guest of honour in Devalokam. That was during the time Arjunan had taken a vow of bhramachariyam. Indran had sent down several invitations to Earth before, but Arjunan had not made a visit until now.

Now in Devalokam, he had access to any pleasure imaginable by a mortal. Unfortunately, Arjunan could not have the pleasure of a woman because of his vow. Naturally, Indran felt bad that Arjunan could not enjoy what was there in abundance in his domain. After all, Arjunan's mother Kunti had been thinking of Indran when Arjunan was conceived, so Indran loved him like a son!

The four beautiful dancing apsaras of Devalokam—Ramba, Urvashi, Menaka and Thilothama—had become bored with entertaining only the aging devas with their flowing white beards. The presence of handsome young Arjunan sent a thrill through their bodies, unlike anything they'd experienced before.

Oh yes! Arjunan, before his brahmachariyam, had been available to any woman who desired him. As the saying goes, you could count even the number of grains of sand on the seashore, but not the number of women who willingly consented to Arjunan. (It wasn't only Arjunan. He and Krishnan both were like a couple of randy jack donkeys when it came to women.)

The four apsaras were bending backwards to attract his attention, but to no avail.

Oh fine! He's just not interested right now, thought three of the beauties, and decided to try later. But Urvashi—let's say she was made of a different material.

If a woman openly expresses her desire for a man, and the man still refuses—is there any sin worse than that? Finally, frustrated, she cursed him. "What are you, a eunuch?"

This curse, the effect of his sin of rejecting Urvashi, caught up to him much later in the *Mahabharatam* epic, when he had to spend one year of his exile as a eunuch.

"So, she cursed him there in Devalokam?" we asked Thatha.
"No no, she cursed him here on Earth."
"What? Why did she come to Earth?"
"She came chasing after him. He told her not to; but did she pay heed?
Anyway, now we come to the main story," chuckled Thatha.

Urvashi had the habit of chewing betel leaf; she loved it very much.
Now in those days, the betel leaf vine was not available on Earth; it
was only to be found in heaven. It was supposed to be chewed only by
the devas. It was Urvashi who brought the divine leaf down to Earth.
But even back then, it was not easy to bring plants from one world
into another.

When Urvashi heard that Arjunan was leaving Devalokam, she
quickly plucked a vine—not having time to pick only the leaves off—
and tucked the whole thing inside her.

"I'm sure you're aware what a big hassle one goes through at customs,
when one returns to one's own country from abroad. It was the same thing
for those leaving Devalokam to come down to Earth. Maybe the greater gods
could get around these rules, but they were strictly enforced for all the smaller
gods and demi-gods. And that's why Urvashi decided to hide the vine some-
where where it could never ever be checked," said Thatha.
"Chee! Thoo!" spat Kittan.
"What do you mean by all this 'chee' and 'thoo'?" Thatha snapped back.
"Remember this: tomorrow when you are married, that's probably where
you'll want your face buried, forever!"

Urvashi never managed to catch Arjunan's attention. Infuriated,
she pulled out the vine from inside her, threw it aside, flung her curse
at him and went back to Devalokam.

So that's the story of how the betel leaf travelled to Earth, where it
became the indicator of passion among men and women. The redder
one's tongue becomes when one chews it, the more passionate that
person is.   ❖

two-headed manian

Once upon a time there was a boy who had two of *those*. He had them since birth. It's very rare for a man to be born with two of *those*. But, just as there are five-headed serpents, once in a while there is a man like him.

Even more strangely, perhaps because he had two of *those*, he also had twice a normal boy's strength. His extra endowment was well-known; he had even earned himself a nickname—"Two-Headed" Manian.

Since everyone in the village teased him about it, one day he simply disappeared from the region. He left to a remote village and worked to earn a living.

Time passed. He grew up into a handsome, strapping young man.

Now he wanted a woman. Naturally!

He saved a bit of money and visited a prostitute.

When she saw what he had, she was surprised at first. But later, she would not let him leave. She kept him with her all night.

The next morning, when she went to bathe in the river, she told one of her friends about him. The friend also wanted to try him out, and insisted on coming back with the prostitute. The friend had her pleasure with him, and then she too shared the news with a few of *her* other friends.

And so, slowly, reports about Two-Headed Manian spread like fire among every interested woman. It finally drove our man quite crazy.

So he stopped going to work.

And why not? Don't our sportsmen generally get themselves employed in some government or corporate job?* It's not as if they actually work in the office, is it? They just spend their time playing the field.

By now the news of Two-Headed Manian had reached the rani's quarters in the palace. One of the rani's favorite maids had visited him, and had reported back to her.

---

* Until recently, the Indian government subsidized sports stars' relatively small salaries by hiring them to government posts. – P.K.C.

The rani yearned to see him too. She secretly sent word for him through the same maid.

He was shocked. *By god, this could land me in serious trouble,* he thought. "Listen woman," he told the maid. "I thought only you wanted me. Why did you have to go and gossip about this to the rani? How can I go there? One day they'll be grooming my head, the next day they'll be chopping it off. I will not come."

"You have nothing to worry about. The rani wants to meet you very badly. She will shower you with gold. You can live like a king there," said the maid. But Two-Headed Manian continued to refuse.

"Listen, this is the rani's order," said the maid finally. "If you don't come, there'll be a sword waiting for your head. If you do come, you'll have everything you could possibly want—the best food and luxury. All you have to do is be the stud. Come along!"

The same night, he was dressed in woman's garb and taken into the rani's quarters. The raja was not in town; he had gone on his annual hunt. Normally, he would rest in the forest for a few days before returning.

So, during that time, Two-Headed Manian had a good hunt himself inside the palace. If it were an ordinary affair, it would have stopped with the rani and the maid. But he was a miracle man, after all. The news slowly reached another rani in the harem. She wanted to see him too.

"He's my find, so I shall keep him," said the first rani. "If you want a man like this, go find him for yourself."

But that was easier said than done. So gradually, a war began between these two ranis.

The raja returned from the hunt, and came to know of Two-Headed Manian. He was furious.

"Motherfucker!" he ranted. "How dare he come right into my palace! Is it true that he has two?"

When it was confirmed that he did indeed have two, the raja decreed that Two-Headed Manian should be trampled to death by the court elephant.

The first rani heard about this decree, and arranged for Two-Headed Manian to escape.

He disappeared once again to yet another remote land. There, he was only able to earn a meager living. But he didn't dare go to another woman, for fear that he would be exposed.

The raja had sent his messenger-drummer to announce in all the fifty-six surrounding nations that anyone who could give information on a man with an "extra endowment" would be given fifteen thousand measures of gold.

Every cowherd, goatherd, merchant and farmer in those regions dropped their respective jobs and began searching for a man with two of *those*. After all, there were fifteen thousand measures of gold at stake.

Two-Headed Manian had to run to escape all these people, and finally he ended up spending his days in a forest. Months passed, and hair grew all over his body, thick and matted. So he went to a barber at the edge of the forest and told him, "Can you come into the forest and give me a shave this evening? I'll wait near the tree at the river. I shall give you one measure of gold."

At the river, Manian buried one of *those* in the ground and sat waiting for the barber.

The barber came, bringing with him a dish of water from the river. He sprinkled some on the ground and rubbed his hand hard on it, to better grip his blade.

Now Two-Headed Manian's one of *those*, buried there in the ground, had not felt the pressure of a hand in a long, long time. It leapt out of the ground and fell into the barber's hand, hard and hot.

"Hey, you're the one!" yelled the barber.

Manian took to his heels at once. The barber chased him calling out: "Listen man, I don't need fifteen thousand measures of gold. Give me the one measure you promised!"

Hearing the commotion, the other men bathing in the river also ran out and joined the chase, all of them yelling, "Is he the one? Aiyyo, there goes our fifteen thousand measures of gold! Catch him! Catch him!"

What happened next?

Two-Headed Manian fled to yet another remote region.

It is said that the raja is still hunting for him. (And the two ranis are looking for him as well.)

If you do find him, let us know. After all, there are fifteen thousand measures of gold at stake! ❖

two of these and four of those

Once we asked Thatha, "What is this law that says there should be only one woman for each man, and only one man for each woman?"

"It's only fair," replied Thatha. "If a man or a woman eats well at home, then he or she will never want to look for a meal outside. But it is a rare woman who can keep her man from straying. If a woman knows enough moves to keep things fresh, though, she can have her man following behind her crying 'meow, meow, meow!'" laughed Thatha, and with that he began his story.

Once upon a time there lived a prince who kept refusing to marry. At first, the raja and his minister were not worried. "It is only natural for a young man to refuse at first," they said. "Let him be; he will change his mind soon."

"Why is it that young girls and boys usually swear they'll never get married?" screechy-voiced Kittan asked Thatha.

"There are many reasons. But the most common one is fear. Before you learn to swim, you are scared of water, aren't you?"

They waited a few years, but the prince was still stubborn. The raja sent his minister over to the prince to find out why he was refusing to get married.

The minister was a very senior man, with plenty of real-world experience.

"Why are you refusing to marry, oh Prince?" he asked.

"I will not marry an ordinary woman."

"Then tell me what kind of a woman you want. I am sure we can find one from somewhere in the fifty-six neighbouring kingdoms."

"An ordinary woman has only one of *those*," said the prince. "I want to marry a woman who has two."

"What? You're kidding, right?" exclaimed the minister. "God has his reasons for giving us pairs of some things, and only one of others. You can go and look for a woman with two ears and two eyes, but how will you find a woman with two of *those*? Even *one* is capable of causing a man so much trouble. Why would anyone want two?"

The prince remained adamant. The minister went back and told the raja about the prince's condition. The raja found it all very amusing. *I know my son is very intelligent; he must have some reason for his demand. Why should I try to dissuade him?*

"Fine. Make arrangements to find such a woman," he ordered the minister.

"What do you mean, oh Raja? How will I find a woman with two of *those?*"

"Don't panic yet," laughed the raja. "Let us make sure that there is no such woman anywhere in the world first. Then we will decide what to do. Announce to the entire kingdom that the prince wants to marry a woman with two of *those.* Make sure you send word to all the neighbouring kingdoms as well."

The announcement was made.

Women from all over gathered in small groups on the riverbanks, or near the ponds, to giggle about the prince's wish. They tapped their fingers to their noses in wonder and puzzlement over this strange demand.

"Did you ever hear of such a thing?" asked one. "The youth of today!"

"What can you say," sighed another.

"Could there really be a woman somewhere in the world with two of *those?*" asked a naïve one. "Perhaps it's possible, just like there are a few people born with a sixth finger."

"Mmm, it might be nice to have two of *those,*" dreamt another.

This continued to be a hot topic of discussion for a long time.

Days passed with no news from anywhere. Then one day, a woman sent word to the palace, claiming to have two of *those.*

The senior minister went down to meet her.

"Woman, if you are playing a prank, please come clean. This is no ordinary matter, it's serious palace business. If you're lying, you stand to lose your head," he warned.

"It is my head; what do you care?" said the woman. "You asked for a woman with two of *those.* Here I am. Why waste time chitchatting?"

The minister saw that the woman was beautiful, quite sharp, and had a playful spirit. Thinking that she would be able to handle whatever sticky situation might arise, he arranged for the wedding.

On the nuptial bed, the prince was impatient.

"Show the second one! Show the second one! I cannot wait!"

"What's your hurry? It's not as if the well water will be swept away by a flood," said the new wife. "It is yours anyway. I will show you, on the condition that when you finish with this one, you must go on immediately to satisfy the second."

"Of course," he promised and proceeded into action.

After a very long time, the prince lay back exhausted. "Now, are you ready for the second one?"

When a man has filled his stomach on a spread so tasty, can you ask him to begin another feast at once?

"Oh no, please, woman! This one will do for me!"

When Thatha finished the tale, Kittan gave a nervous laugh, and looked at me for help.

"Nice," I said. "Do you know the one about the woman with four breasts?"

"No," said Thatha.

I began.

There was once a prince who demanded that he would only marry a woman with four breasts—two on her chest and two on her back.

"We cannot waste time with such useless searches," his parents told him. "You must look for her yourself."

The prince had a reason for his strange demand.

Early one morning, in his royal dream, he heard the jingling of bangles. He softly crept up to investigate the sound and saw a woman bathing, with her back towards him. On her back were two round, full breasts. As soon as he saw this, he woke up with a start. But isn't it said that an early-morning dream is bound to come true? He was convinced that such a woman really did exist.

And so he set off to search. He hunted at every stream, pond, and river.

One day, he was lying under a tree in the jungle, napping. He was imagining that he was asleep on his soft mattress in the palace, when he thought he heard the jingling of bangles.

He quickly opened his eyes. The sound continued. He crept towards it.

On the banks of a wild stream, he saw a woman bathing. The solitude had lent her confidence; she had stripped naked and was washing herself, sitting with her back towards him.

Sure enough, on her back were two round, full breasts. Not wanting to lose her, he sprang to her side at once.

They were married.

It was the nuptial night! The prince was in the bedroom, eagerly waiting for her. The moment she stepped into the room, he leapt up and hugged her tight. But except for her sharp shoulder blades, he could feel nothing on her back.

"What happened to them?" he demanded.

"You silly man, don't you know? Cows have their tails at the back, humans have their milk at the front," she said.

"What do you mean? I saw them myself!"

"Sure you saw them. They're here, on my chest. When I bathe, I throw them over my shoulders so I can scrub underneath!" she laughed. ❖

the death of the pillai

When we were young men, we used to spend hours sitting in the village mandap or on the riverbank, discussing sex with Thatha. I regret now that I didn't think of noting down those conversations; I can only remember a very few of the stories he told us.

One day, our friend Kittan asked Thatha in his screechy voice:

"What's the maximum age for a man to be able to have sex?"

Interested in the answer, I pricked up my ears.

"You know, in the villages they say that as long as a man has enough strength to carry a tiny box of rice husks, he can enjoy a woman."

Kittan and I looked at each other, expecting a good story.

Thatha was gazing at the ground, deep in thought. After a long pause, he said, "Age is not determined by the calendar. It's the body that dictates how old you are."

Once, in a tiny village in the Deep South, there lived a man, a Pillai by caste. The first thing I should tell you is that he looked like royalty. His thick moustache, broad physique, and dark brown skin made even men fall in love with him at first glance—a latter day King Arjunan!

"Have you ever heard the phrase, 'born from the chest'?" asked Thatha.
"No. How can anyone be born from the chest?" we asked.
"Of course, we are all born from our mother's vagina. But this phrase is used to describe someone special. This man was special like that; he must have had a lucky mole on his sugar lump*. It is believed that a man like that is conceived in the mouth, moves to the throat, and bursts out of the chest. And he was certainly an expert when it came to you-know-what."

The Pillai honed his naturally strong body by training in wrestling, boxing, and swordfighting. As you can imagine, he had no bad habits; he cared for his body as though it were a vessel made of glass. When he came riding through the streets of Thirunelvelli on his horse, people would push each other aside to get a glimpse of him.

Women were constantly chasing behind him. It was like the proverb says: "You can count the number of stars in the sky, but not the number of women who made love to Arjunan." Indeed, he was skilled in the art of love. The stories of his sexual prowess were shared amongst all the women—both those with first-hand experience and those that only dreamt of it. They flocked around him like flies on a jackfruit.

In his younger days, he became friends with a white man, and left to Colombo, where he worked as the manager of a tea estate. There were rumours that he had two white women and two Ceylonese concubines. Anyway, he returned with a huge fortune. Back home, he married three women and had six concubines, and had several relationships in the surrounding towns besides. As if all this activity was not enough, he even visited the mada veedhi**.

"Wouldn't so much activity ruin a man's health?" asked Kittan.

---

*   A common Tamil euphemism for the penis. – P.K.C.
** Usually the streets surrounding the temple, ghetto of devadasis or brahmins. – P.K.C.

"One would think! Nevertheless, for some strange reason, he remained healthy. Remember, Kittan, that in those days it wasn't so common for a man to fall ill because of too much sex. That was an illness imported by the whites."

"What's this story you're telling now?"

"Nothing new, my son. This is a known fact. The white man called that affliction syphilis, and we call it parangipunnu*. Anyway, back to our Pillai!"

The Pillai became friendly with a zamindar. He soon came to be the zamindar's minister and manager. The zamindar was useless below the waist, so he would let the Pillai graze around and watch the fun. Sometimes you can get full even just watching a feast!

When the zamindar died, the Pillai took over his entire household and estate. But no matter how much a man is blessed, he is cursed with the three insatiable desires: land, gold, and women. The human heart always thirsts for more.

After a long innings, finally, at the age of 97, he fell ill and was bedridden. A man's body is not cast in iron! Already there was a swarm of grandchildren and great-grandchildren in the huge mansion.

Days passed, but his life refused to leave his body.

The people thought that perhaps it was the want of land that kept him hanging on. So they fed him with a few grains of earth. But no, his life held firm.

Perhaps it was the want of gold, they thought, and mixed a few grains in his milk. But after drinking it, he was still there, breathing with laboured sighs.

After a while, it struck them. It must be the want of a woman that was keeping him lingering on in the material world!

It was easy enough to feed him earth or gold, thought the members of the household, amused. But how could they feed him a woman?

One of the grandchildren was cast in the same mould as the old man; he was even named after him. It was he who came up with an idea to finally help the old man rest in peace. When the family heard his plan, they snickered. "You're a real chip off the old block, aren't you?"

---

* Literally, "white man's sore". – P.K.C.

The story went like this: In his eightieth year, the old man had visited Kerala. When he returned, he brought along a Malayalee woman and set up a separate house for her. He used to visit her often—after all, there was no one who dared to question him. His wealth had been earned by his own sweat and toil, and no one wanted to risk being cut out of his will. The wives he had married were all long dead and gone. So were the concubines. Even at his age, he demanded three meals a day—for the stomach, and below the waist, as well! It was only after he became bedridden that all that had stopped.

The family paid the Malayalee woman a visit, and explained the old man's plight. She agreed to come over and help.

They bathed the old man and dressed him up in a silk dhoti and shirt. They bought the Malayalee woman a silk sari and dressed her up, too, like a new bride, and took her up to his room. The entire town had gathered to witness this ritual farewell.

The Malayalee woman went up to his bed and was shocked at his feeble state. She fed him a few drops of the milk that was on the table, then knelt near his bed. She whispered something in his ears. He seemed to stop his noisy rasping for a few seconds and actually listen.

She sent everyone out of the room and shut the door and windows.

The people outside were eager to know what was transpiring in the room. Well, we all know what happens on the first nuptial night; what would happen on the last night?

The door and windows were shut, but the skylight in the ceiling was still open. Some brought ladders, others brought chairs, which they placed on top of tables, and stools on top of that; and they all crowded around the skylight to peer in. They had to see what was going on, or else their heads would burst.

They could not hear what the Malayalee woman was saying. It seemed as if she was repeating her name over and over again, announcing that she was there. She was trying to excite him with her warm breath on his face. She kissed his cheeks, his ears and the throbbing vein in his throat. She rested her head on his chest—once the broadest in the town, but now like a skeleton's. She reached her hand into his stiff, new silk shirt and caressed his stomach. She loosened his dhoti and the people outside could see the gold araiyaan kairu tied around his waist.

The Malayalee woman pressed her face on his shrunken organ and kissed it hard. The eyes looking in through the skylight withdrew for a second, shocked, but soon curiosity drew them back.

The Pillai's gasps grew louder and longer, and now they were gasps of pleasure. At last, he gave one long, drawn-out sigh, and then all was silent. The Malayalee woman suddenly fell on his chest and began wailing. The people watching through the skylight did not understand at first, but slowly it dawned on them: the old man was finally resting in peace, thanks to the Malayalee woman.

"They could not understand the words the Malayalee woman was wailing, but then does one really need words to express true joy or sorrow?" asked Thatha. ❖

tamil family names and forms of address

Adey	Informal address to a man
Adiye	Informal address to a woman (especially one's wife)
Aithe	Paternal aunt or Mother-in-law
Aiya	Respectful address to a man (especially a feudal landlord)
Akka	Elder sister
Aley	Informal/disrespectful address to a man
Amma	Mother; sometimes used as a respectful address to a woman, or an invocation of the goddess
Anna	Elder brother
Anni	Elder brother's wife
Appa	Father
Athaan	Literally, male cross-cousin; a paternal aunt's or maternal uncle's son. This family member is considered an ideal husband for a girl in most Tamil communities, and so Athaan has come to be used as a general reference to the husband.
Ayah	Respectful address to an old woman
Da	Informal masculine address
Di	Informal feminine address
Dey	Masculine address, disrespectful or angry
Machchan	Brother-in-law; sometimes, husband
Maama	Maternal uncle, or father-in-law
Maappilai	Groom, or son-in-law
Marumagale	Daughter-in-law
Naina	Father, or any elder man (in Telugu communities)

Paatti	Grandmother, or any old woman
Thambi	Younger brother
Thangachi	Younger sister
Thatha	Grandfather, or any old man
Thayee	Respectful address to a woman, or an invocation of the goddess
Yejamaan	Master or boss

tamil months

Chiththirai	mid-April to mid-May
Vaikaasi	mid-May to mid-June
Aani	mid-June to mid-July
Aadi	mid-July to mid-August
Aavani	mid-August to mid-September
Purattaasi	mid-September to mid-October
Aippasi	mid-October to mid-November
Kaarthikai	mid-November to mid-December
Maargazhi	mid-December to mid-January
Thai	mid-January to mid-February
Maasi	mid-February to mid-March
Panguni	mid-March to mid-April

hindu deities and mythological figures

Aiyanaar	A village deity, commonly worshipped across Tamil Nadu and Northern Sri Lanka

Angaalamman	An avatar of the mother goddess
Arjunan	The third of the Pandava brothers in the *Mahabharatam*
Asthalakshmis	The eight avatars of Lakshmi, representing the different types of wealth (usually progeny, peace, courage, money, grain, livestock, knowledge, and victory)
Badrakali	Goddess destroyer of evil
Bheeman	The second of the Pandava brothers in the *Mahabharatam*
Bhumadevi	Earth goddess; mother of Sita
Brahma	God of creation and decider of human fate
Devalokam	Heavenly realm ruled by Lord Indran and populated by devas
Dhraupadi	Wife of the five Pandava brothers in the *Mahabharatam*
Dhuryodhanan	Eldest of the Kaurava brothers in the *Mahabharatam*
Govindha	One of the names of the god Vishnu
Iswaran	Another name for Shiva
Iswari	Another name for the goddess Parvathi
Maariyaatha	An avatar of the mother goddess
Meenakshi	The ruling goddess of the city of Madurai; an avatar of Parvathi
Mudevi	Goddess of bad luck
Nala	A forefather of Raman in the *Ramayanam*
Parvathi	Consort of Shiva; goddess of courage
Pillayar	A Tamil name for the god Ganesh
Raman	An avatar of Vishnu; hero of the *Ramayanam*
Ravanan	King of Elangai (now Sri Lanka) who abducts Sita in the *Ramayanam*

Shiva	Usually the god of destruction; in several stories here he has the role of both creator and provider
Sita	Wife of Raman, daughter of Bhumadevi
Sridevi	Goddess of good luck
Valmiki	The sage who compiled *Ramayanam*
Veeran Aiyanaar	Another name for Aiyanaar
Vijayan	Another name for Arjunan, the third of the Pandava brothers in the *Mahabharatam*
Yaman	God of death

other terms

adeyappa/ adi chake	Roughly, "Wow!"
aiyyo/aiyaiyyo/ aiyyoyo	An expression of surprise or dismay; "Oh no!"
appalam	Wafer snack
araiyaan kairu	A cord worn around the waist of an infant with a gold leaf pendant to hide the genitals; men continue to wear it throughout their lives
Avvaiyar woman	A mythical woman bard, who has skipped from childhood straight to old age in order to avoid sexual relationships, because she is devoted to the Tamil language
brahmachariyam	Period of vowed celibacy
crorepathi	Millionaire; literally, someone with at least one crore (1,00,00,000) rupees
harikatha	A form of musical storytelling in temple courtyards

karma yogi	Someone very devoted to his or her art
konakol	Spoken rhythmic syllables in Indian classical music
koothaadi	A street dancer/folk actor
mandap	Temple or town courtyard with a ceiling, held up by columns, but without walls
muththam	Inner courtyard in a traditional Tamil house
naamam	A Vaishnavite symbol, either V or U shaped, worn as a mark on the forehead
pallu	The part of the sari that covers a woman's chest
panchayat	Village governing body
pottu	A sacred mark on the centre of the forehead
shandy	Weekly market that draws goods and customers from several villages
shastri	An erudite Brahmin man
Thai Pongal	The first day of the month of Thai, celebrated as a harvest festival
thali	A gold chain or turmeric smeared cord; the tying of this around the woman's neck by the groom signifies the moment of marriage.
thinnai	A raised concrete structure attached to the outside of a village home
thombai	A cone-shaped structure made of hay and dung in which grains are stored
varnam	One of the five major caste groups
vibhuthi	Sacred ash
yaagam	Sacred fire ritual
yagna	Ritual in which the gods are propitiated by pouring oblations into a sacred fire
zamindar	feudal landlord

about the author

Ki. Rajanarayanan (b. 1922), popularly known as Ki. Ra., is a power-ful writer and teller of tales rooted in the soil of Tamil Nadu, and has been a recipient of the prestigious Kalaimamani and Sahitya Akademi awards. His 1958 short story *Mayamaan* is often seen as marking the beginning of the Golden Age of modern Tamil literature. Veering away from the European influences which characterized much of the fiction from the Tamil revivalist period, Ki. Ra. chose to relate tales in the spoken dialect of the land in which he was born.

He lives in Pondicherry with his wife, Ganavathiammal.

about the translator

Pritham K. Chakravarthy is a theatre artist, storyteller, activist, free-lance scholar, and translator based in Chennai. Her recent transla-tion projects include *The Blaft Anthology of Tamil Pulp Fiction* and *Zero Degree* by Charu Nivedita, also available from Blaft Publications.